A SMALL TOWN SOMEWHERE

A SMALL TOWN SOMEWHERE

A Logan's Creek Novel

Deborah Spencer Foliart

This is a work of fiction. Names, characters, places, and incidents either are the product of the author's imagination or are used fictitiously.

Any resemblance to actual persons, living or dead, events, or locales is entirely coincidental.

Copyright © 2024 by Deborah Spencer Foliart

All rights reserved. No part of this book may be reproduced or used in any manner without written permission of the copyright owner except for the use of quotations in a book review.

First paperback edition October 2024
Book design by Shanna Crow
Edited by Marla Cantrell
ISBN 979-8-2184-9651-7 (paperback)

Published by Chapters Publishing Company
www.deborahspencerfoliart.com

FOREWORD

Every writer knows that a title is important for their novel if he or she hopes to sell a copy and win a fan.

Debbie Foliart has been in the book business for over ten years. As the owner of a successful book store in a small town, she knew how mighty a good title could be.

With *A SMALL TOWN SOMEWHERE*, she reeled me in. Why? Because most of us are from small towns, and we naturally like to read about something that we know will spark a memory.

Abby Rose Carter left Logan's Creek, Arkansas, and landed in Chicago, working for a large advertising firm. By the age of thirty, she had a great job, a beautiful apartment, a 401K, and a handsome boyfriend. When a position in the firm opened up, she was passed over in favor of a man who was not as qualified as Abby. In a rash hurt-pride moment, she quit her job and moved home to Arkansas, leaving behind handsome and successful, Ian, who was also in the ad business.

Welcomed by her friends, who are known as the Leading Ladies, she was encouraged to get reacquainted with her high school love, Josh, who was running for mayor against the current and long-time mayor who is "crooked as a corkscrew." Abby and Josh formed a team to beat the mayor, and she managed his campaign. In addition to helping Josh, Abby had her own reasons for wanting to defeat the mayor.

On election night, at a town celebration to outdo any celebration I ever attended or heard of, I found out all the answers to the questions that I wondered about while reading the 200+ pages.

Even though I write about true crime, I found Deborah Foliart's novel a lovely diversion from murder and mayhem. And there's a racy love scene to boot.

— Anita Paddock, best-selling author of
Blind Rage, Closing Time,
Cold Blooded, The Killing Spree

September 2024

*"To my loving family
who have supported my dreams
always."*

Chapter One

Abby Carter wrestled out of her too-small Spanx. If she was going to throw away her ten-year career at Cromby, Pillar and Sax, she was at least going to be able to breathe while she did it. She'd even used the executive washroom to rip off the evil underwear. Technically, she was a senior account manager, not an executive, so she'd never been inside. Neither had any other woman at the prestigious marketing firm, she supposed. Abby looked around. Gilded mirrors filled one wall. The floor was Carrara marble. So were the walls. She might as well have been in Rome, given the two fluted columns that separated the gold-fitted sinks from an actual lounge area. The soap smelled like peppercorns and cedar. In a dish by the entrance were small bottles of cologne with a gold label that read *Shark*. No wonder all the executives smelled the same.

Until last night, she'd thought she had a shot at the Director of Digital Media position. Her interview had gone well, and she'd always done more than her job. She'd pulled in the chain restaurant, Wok and Roll, last month, and the win had been written up in *Business Insider*. What she hadn't been able to do was become a man. At this old-school agency, that's what she needed to advance.

Just last week, the CEO Dave Cromby, had asked Abby to make coffee for a planning meeting when he couldn't find his assistant. She hadn't said no, not really. But the coffee she brewed was so strong it could have eaten the polish off her carefully manicured nails. She pretended to drink it anyway. No one else took more than a sip.

Her friend, Cathy, one of the Leading Ladies from back home in Logan's Creek, would have asked, "Passive aggressive much?"

Abby hated when Cathy was right. Darn it, this job was changing her. And not for the better.

Last night, while Abby was working on a new campaign from her bed—it was nearly midnight—her computer pinged. An email had arrived. She read it twice before it sank in. "Join us," it read, "in welcoming John Willis as our new Director of Digital Media."

Dave Cromby was famous for scheduling emails in advance, but his timing was often suspect. Last year, she'd found out there were no Christmas bonuses on Thanksgiving morning, for example.

Abby hadn't slept since last night's email. Now, she splashed water on her face, chunked the hateful Spanx into the muted gold trash can, and grabbed a handful of Shark cologne on her way out the door.

Cromby was pacing inside Abby's glass-walled office when she made it to the twenty-third floor, mopping his bald head with an expensive looking silk pocket square. For a second, she could almost hear her mom back in Logan's Creek warning her about her temper. "Abby Rose," she'd say, "think about what you're doing. You can't unburn a bridge, and sometimes that bridge is the only way out."

Abby shook her head. Wasn't there always another bridge? In Logan's Creek, there were three bridges that connected the small town with the next city over.

Still, Abby took a deep breath. She owed her mom that much. She looked at her hands. They weren't shaking anymore. Over the last few hours, she'd gone through all the emotions. What she was left with was a calm and steely determination.

"Mr. Cromby," she said as she dropped her purse on her desk, her voice as light as a feather. She hadn't bothered to bring in her messenger bag.

"Abby," Mr. Cromby said as he nodded his egg-shaped head. He dropped into the sleek leather chair across from her desk, a look of relief crossing his face.

Abby picked up the Addy award she'd won for her campaign on

Chicago's Meals on Wheels and placed the statue in the gym bag she'd pulled from her bottom desk drawer.

Mr. Cromby's elbow was on the arm of his chair, and he leaned forward to rub his forehead. He opened his mouth and then closed it. Maybe Abby had confused him with her sweet voice.

"What do you need?" Abby asked, making sure she smiled. She swiveled her chair and faced her credenza, where at least a dozen framed photographs sat. She pulled a towel from her bag and started to wrap the largest photo.

"Now, Abby," Mr. Cromby said, his voice a reprimand.

"Silly photos," she said. Abby turned back. "Me with Mayor Johnson at that summit on truth in advertising." She lifted another. "Me and you at the company picnic." Abby squinted. "You asked me to check on your kids if I remember right. It was the year I started here. They were in the bounce house. The little one. Reagan? He'd thrown up. Now that was a fun day."

Mr. Cromby leveled his voice. The collar of his shirt looked too tight. "If you're mad about John Willis, just say so. No need for theatrics."

Abby leveled her eyebrows. "Mad?" she asked. "Me?" She opened another drawer, taking out a stack of thank-you cards she'd gotten from clients over the years. "Not at all. John is a much better pick." She paused. "Much better. For one thing, he doesn't have to work late like me. Must be a genius. Gets things done right the first time. Now that's a skill." She closed the drawer and tossed the cards in her bag. "He isn't afraid to ask for help. Another plus." You probably don't know this, but I came up with the slogan for his last campaign for that up-and-coming conglomerate of Southern lawyers. Yep, I sure did. They wanted something clever. Folksy. For clients who'd found themselves in 'uncomfortable' circumstances. So I came up with 'Arrested? Shut Yo Mouth. Call the Best Attorneys in the South!'" Not sure you noticed, but that slogan made it to *The Daily Show*. I can do clever."

Abby tapped her computer screen, and it came to life. She turned the screen toward Mr. Cromby. "Clicks for that ad are up 320 percent over last week. And that's just in Alabama."

Mr. Cromby rose. He was in his late fifties, but some days, like this one, he looked much older. "It's not like you to take credit for someone else's work," he said.

Abby stood as well. "Correction, Mr. Cromby. It's not like me to take credit for *my own* work."

Mr. Cromby pointed to Abby's gym bag, which was filling up with her personal things. "Now, Abby, you're not really thinking about quitting?" Mr. Cromby folded his arms.

Abby pretended to consider this. She bit her bottom lip. "I wouldn't quit, come to think of it. Not if I could figure out one thing."

Mr. Cromby let out his breath. "That's more like it. How can I help?"

Abby tossed her employee ID onto the glass desktop. She took out the company credit card that she'd put in her pocket this morning and placed it beside her ID. The employee photo was so old her auburn hair was still nearly to her waist. Her sky-blue eyes had faded to gray in the passing years. "Mr. Cromby," she said, turning the photo over. "If you could tell me how to overcome this one terrible flaw I have, then I'd stay."

Mr. Cromby's chest swelled. "Tell me what your problem is." He did love a damsel in distress.

"I'm a woman working for a company that's stuck in 1957. I really should be at home where I belong, don't you think? But darn it, I was raised by a mom and dad who told me I could do anything. Be anything. What they didn't tell me was that I'd have to do it twice as well and work three times as hard. And still, some Lazy Larry with half my talent would be promoted over me. Just because he's a man."

As Abby walked past Mr. Cromby, he reached out his hand and then seemed to think better of it. "I don't like what you're implying, Abby. Preferential treatment, my ass. I shouldn't say this, but one thing John has over you is that he'll take a lunch meeting, meet up for drinks, play a round of golf. You sit at that desk most days with your head down. I see your assistant handing you energy bars and espressos when you work through lunch. Marketing is about public relations as well as creativity. John works smart. You just work hard." When she was down the hall, she heard him say, "And you signed a non-compete. Don't you think I won't enforce it."

Abby certainly didn't have legal counsel, but she couldn't help saying it anyway. "My lawyer is already on it."

She bumped into John Willis at the elevator. He had the decency to look the other way, and then pretended to take a call. Then, he took a step away, hit a slick spot on the marble floor, and stumbled. Abby, true to form, grabbed his elbow and stopped his slide. All that training from her childhood, all those good manners. She couldn't get away from it. If John was embarrassed, he didn't show it. In fact, he glared at her as if she'd pushed him.

From a distance she could see her assistant, Joy Hackman, standing near the receptionist's desk, wearing a bright green dress. Joy loved color. Abby waved goodbye. She'd have to call her, give her the news. Of course, the way office gossip traveled, Joy probably already knew.

After that, Abby had no idea what to do.

Chapter Two

Abby sat on a wooden bench in the pocket park near the offices of Cromby, Pillar and Sax, her olive-green gym bag sat beside her. Summer in Chicago was steamy, and when Abby would arrive home at night, she'd often have to step right into the shower. The city had a way of getting beneath your clothes. Even those awful Spanx. She thought about home. About the swimming holes and the water misters that lined Main Street. When it was summer in Logan's Creek, people knew what to do to stay cool. She missed Logan's Creek.

Abby rubbed her temples. She felt the way she did after a night spent drinking in her early twenties. All the bluster of the night before reduced to a monster headache and nausea. All the memories of what she'd said causing her face to burn. Abby looked around.

Was it too late to beg for her job back? She shook her head. No, no going back. She'd meant what she said. Enough was enough. But who could she tell? Who would understand?

Abby pulled her phone from her purse. She had the Leading Ladies set up in a group chat. The Leading Ladies were her friends from Logan's Creek, her ride-or-die, her North Star.

She typed quickly, refusing to censor herself:

A quick heads-up. I did it. I quit my job this morning. Just walked in and quit! I'm sitting on a park bench, wondering what's next. Having a little buyer's remorse. This is what I wanted, right?

Cathy was the first to write back:
> *Yes! It's exactly what you've wanted! Get your hiney back to Logan's Creek and I'll plan a party!*

Janie was next:
> *What did that SOB do to you this time? I swear, if I ever come across your Mr. Cromby, I'll not be responsible for the outcome! I'd snatch him bald, but, well, you know.*

A laughing emoji followed.

Amy sent a link to the country song, "Take This Job and Shove It." It was like Amy to sidestep the actual question. She needed to have all the information before she commented.

Lisa wrote:
> *YOLO, Abby! And what you've been doing in Chicago is NOT living! I agree with Cathy. COME HOME!*

Amanda, Logan's Creek's prosecuting attorney, responded last:
> *You may have a legal case. Mr. Cromby has been horrible to you for years! I can't practice in Illinois, but I know a few good attorneys in Chicago. I'm so mad I could spit!*

Abby felt her body relax. Those were her girls. If she'd gone in and smashed the office up, they'd still be on her side. She shielded her eyes and looked up. The sun was blazing.

Her phone buzzed. A notice from her calendar: *Ian arrives home at noon.*

Ian.

Her boyfriend.

The man she didn't tell before deciding to blow her world apart.

Cromby, Pillar and Sax was one of Ian's top clients. It was how they'd met, how they'd become a couple. He was one of the top photographers in Chicago and had a shelf of awards to prove it.

Abby leaned her head back and closed her eyes, remembering their last day together, working on the campaign for a new Illinois company Prairie State Libations. When the shoot was over, they'd tried the corn whiskey. She'd always been a lightweight drinker, and the alcohol hit her hard.

Ian laughed before he'd kissed her. "You're a cheap date," he joked, and Abby sagged against him. He bent down, his mouth to her ear, and brushed her auburn hair away from her delicate neck. "You make me happy, Abby." She'd shivered at the sound of his low voice. "I want more than this," he said, cupping her backside with his hand.

Instead of saying anything back, she'd pulled his face to hers and kissed him. Every cell of her body craved every cell of his.

Now, she could almost feel Ian beside her. His wavy brown hair hanging to his shoulders. His jeans slung low on his hips. Without a shirt, she could see his six-pack. With his shirt on, she couldn't resist squeezing his upper arms, the muscles hard beneath her small hands.

Ian hiked. He worked out. He had cans of protein powder sitting on his kitchen counter. He could lift Abby as well as she could lift her purse. He could make her heart beat so fast she thought she might pass out. Not to mention he looked like Liam Hemsworth, if Liam were better looking.

Abby shook her head, clearing her thoughts. If anyone could read her mind, she thought. Taking a deep breath, she stood and hailed a cab. She'd have to rush home and get her car if she was going to surprise Ian at the airport. The drive would give her time to think of something to say.

O'Hare International covers 7,627 acres and served 54 million passengers in a recent year. Ian was a platinum member of American Airlines and the equivalent at United. Abby had loved that about Ian when they'd first started dating. He would fly away for a shoot, then come back with souvenirs from places she'd never been, like Marrakesh or Tokyo.

Lately, she wasn't so sure. Deep down, Abby was a small-town girl. "A small town somewhere" was how Ian had described where she was from the first month they'd been dating. He'd forgotten the particulars. It couldn't be helped. They'd learned so much about each other that didn't translate to words: small crevices and secret places, the teasing brush of eyelashes on bare skin.

When she'd elbowed him over the comment, he'd turned red. "It's Logan's Creek," she'd told his group of friends. "In Arkansas. Not just a small town somewhere, but the best town anywhere."

It had become a joke between them.

Ian, like most of the people she'd met in Chicago, wasn't born there. His dream was to own a house in Hyde Park, where Frank Lloyd Wright had made his mark, and a cabin in Colorado, where he'd been born. She and Ian couldn't seem to live without one another, but they had never talked about living together.

Now, she sat in the waiting area, watching the passengers from Ian's plane walk by. She spotted him from far away. He was a head taller than most men in the airport, and he moved with determination. She stood as he came closer, ran her fingers through her hair, put on a new coat of lip gloss.

It was then that she saw the woman beside him. She was taller than Abby. Tall enough to be a model. Pretty enough, too. She wore dark sunglasses, and a Hermes scarf. She had her long fingers cupped around Ian's shoulder while they walked. She leaned in to say something to him just as they passed by. Ian hadn't even glanced Abby's way.

Abby plopped down onto the plastic chair. All her strength had drained away in the time it took to see Ian with someone else. She exhaled. They could be working together. She tried to believe it. Or, more likely, they could have fallen in love in the two weeks he'd been away. It had only taken Abby a day to love Ian. He was that special. Abby pressed the heels of her hands to her eyes. She would not cry.

That was when her plan formed. She'd go home, not to her apartment, but home to Logan's Creek. Ian and her old job be damned. If Ian wanted to know what had happened to her, he had her number. Abby laughed a mirthless laugh. He had her number, all right. It looked like she'd been what her mom would call a dad-gum fool.

Abby's head pounded. Her mom. Oh my gosh, her dad. She'd have to tell them she'd quit. She couldn't imagine they'd be happy.

Chapter Three

Abby took a ragged breath. She'd taken a chance by not calling her parents, but quitting was something she needed to talk about in person. The Leading Ladies promised to keep quiet, no easy feat, and no one else in town knew she was in Logan's Creek. When Abby opened the gate to her parents' yard, she saw that her mom's irises, coneflowers, and roses were blooming. On the porch, baskets overflowed with red, yellow, and purple petunias. Six wooden rockers sat behind the flowers, all in a row. Nearby, the old wooden table that often held Mason jars of sweet tea stood empty.

Abby felt her shoulders tighten. On the drive home, she'd had time to catastrophize leaving the firm. How would she find another marketing job that paid as well? She wasn't cut out to do anything else. She'd scrutinized every billboard on the roadways, edited every misplaced apostrophe, and made the time pass by thinking up clever jingles. Even when she stopped at a chicken place, she'd nearly asked for the manager. The special was called "Fowl Dinner." How off-putting was that? To be fair, the truckers at the next table didn't seem to mind; they'd all ordered it.

Now, she had to tell her parents she'd left—no, quit—her job. She was a good marketer, but even Abby didn't know how to spin this.

Quit was a word her parents hated. She and her younger brother Dan grew up knowing that once they began something, they followed through. Always.

Memories of this lesson came flooding back. Hate the violin

two weeks in? Tough luck. Decide you're going to build your own playhouse? You might want to pick up a how-to book at the library first, because once the first board went up, you were going to finish it.

And then there was baseball. She'd wanted so badly to play when she was in sixth grade, but there were no girls' teams anywhere close. She begged her parents to join the boys' team. Her mom was against it, but her dad said yes, on one condition. If she started the season, she would play to the bitter end.

Abby rubbed her knee, feeling the jagged scar she got that summer. She thought about what she learned. Perseverance, maybe. But more than that, she made some lifelong male friends. Guys that still slapped her on the back when they saw her. Good friends and a bad scar. The yin and yang of baseball.

Abby stood taller. She wasn't a quitter. She was a woman who happened to have quit her job. Explaining the difference was the key to making her family understand.

She walked through the front door just as her mom Gabrielle (Gabby for short) came down the stairs with her arms outstretched. "Abby," she said, "you didn't tell us you were coming home!"

Gabby was a petite woman, three inches shorter than Abby. Her highlighted blond and silver hair fell to her shoulders, and she smelled like Chanel No. 5. She always took Abby's breath away when they'd been apart too long. Gabby was a beauty, though Abby doubted she knew it.

Abby dropped the overnight bag she'd been carrying. "Hey, mom! I know. I just needed some home time."

Gabby held Abby at arm's length. Abby felt like she was being X-rayed. "What's going on, honey?" her mom asked.

Wanting to postpone the inevitable, she said, "I was homesick, Mom. Is there anything going on tonight? Maybe we can get Dan to come over for dinner. I'd love to see everyone."

Gabby walked the few steps from the foyer to the living room. She motioned Abby to follow. Gabby sat in her leather reading chair, and Abby took the couch. "Nothing's wrong, is it, baby?" Gabby asked.

Abby thought about all the ways she could answer that question. So much was wrong. The job she quit, for one thing, but she'd tell them soon enough. Then there was Ian.

"Not a thing, Mom." Abby looked at her smart watch. "Mind if I call Dan now? See if he can come over tonight?

Gabby rose from her chair. "You call Dan and I'll call your dad," she said, as she headed for the kitchen. Their yellow rotary telephone hung on the wall by the double oven, one of the last landlines Abby knew of. Abby heard her mom dial the first number, the sound like a playing card tied to a bicycle wheel.

Jim Carter, Abby's dad, was the person she least wanted to disappoint. Abby was suddenly afraid he'd ask to talk to her. "Let me get my things up to my room and I'll call Dan from there," Abby called to her mom.

Abby hustled upstairs to her old bedroom. Tomorrow, the moving truck would be here with her things. Her dad would say she'd gotten herself into a real pickle. That is, if her dad was still talking to her after he found out.

The room was decorated in yellows. Her stuffed animals still lived in the middle of her bed, atop the sunshiny, puffy comforter her grandmother had given her for her sixteenth birthday. All of her posters were still on the wall. Most were images of rock bands that looked like they'd just been given terrible news. Her desk held the prom picture of Abby and her high school beau, Josh Moore. Her dress? Yellow, of course.

Prom. Now, that was a night. Josh at his finest. Abby dressed like a Disney princess. She hadn't thought of it in years.

She dropped her suitcase on the bench at the foot of the bed, shuffled her clothes into her dresser drawers and took a deep breath.

Back in the kitchen, she hunted for snacks, her mom nowhere in sight. Did her mom still buy Fruit Roll-Ups? Abby hoped so. As she stepped inside the pantry, the front door opened. She could hear the baritone sounds of her dad and brother.

"Where's my Abby?" her dad asked.

"My guess is the kitchen," her brother Dan said and laughed.

Her mother answered from somewhere deep in the house. "I can hear her in the kitchen, Dan. Messing up my pantry if I had to guess."

Abby straightened the pantry shelf she'd rifled through and headed for the living room. There, the family took the seats they'd always taken, as if they'd been assigned. Abby hugged Dan, who was so much like her: blue eyes, auburn hair. But he'd grown into a mountain, and she felt safe in his arms. She hugged her dad, noticing how gray he'd gotten. He adjusted his tortoiseshell glasses as he held her, and she wondered if he was wiping his eyes. His emotions ran deep where his family was concerned.

When she pulled back from him, he waved his hand to include the rest of the family, "Is there something we all need to talk about?"

When she hesitated, Dan said, "Maybe I should go."

Abby found her voice. Might as well rip off the Band-Aid. "The truth is that I left my job in Chicago." She bit her lip to keep from crying.

"But you were doing so well," her mom said.

"I sure clocked a lot of hours, Mom. I worked my ass off at Cromby, Pillar and Sax."

"Abby!" her mom said, scowling. Ass was not a Carter-approved word.

Abby felt her temper rise. She needed her family to have her back. "It's true, and Mr. Cromby couldn't have cared less. I was up for a promotion-Director of Digital Media. They gave the job to a man *because* he was a man, not because he was qualified. So, I quit. I got tired of fighting it."

Jim wore a short-sleeved plaid shirt that snapped down the front. He sat forward, elbows on his knees, his hands steepled. "Abby, you know how we feel about quitting. And what about your bills, your car payment, living expenses?" He got up and paced through the room with his hands on his hips. She knew this stance well.

Abby felt about six years old, but she was a grown-ass woman, for goodness' sake. She wondered what her quick-witted friend Cathy would say, and she tried to channel her. "Let's think about this. If I never quit my job, I'd live the rest of my life in Chicago. I could be fired, and believe you me, it's possible that I would have been one day. But I couldn't quit. I could win a billion dollars. Still couldn't quit. So, no matter what, I'd stay there. You and mom would get older, and you'd need help. I'd say, 'Sorry, Dad, no can do. I've got this dang job in Chicago.'"

Jim didn't take sass. He pointed. "Now, missy," he said, but then he grinned. "Couldn't even come home to your dear old, decrepit parents," he said, putting his hands over his heart.

"Not even then," Abby said and smiled back. She snuck a look at Dan. He was grinning.

Gabby finally chimed in. "I hope you can stay awhile, sweetie. Take a much-needed break."

"You wouldn't mind having me around?"

"We'd love it," Gabby said.

"I might outstay my welcome."

Jim said, "Not possible."

Dan picked up the conversation. "Are you moving home, Sis?"

"I'd like to," Abby said. She was looking at her feet.

Gabby clapped her hands. "Our girl's coming home! You don't know how much I hoped this day would come!"

Jim rolled his eyes as if to say Gabby was such a softie.

Dan put his feet on the coffee table, and Gabby tried to swipe them off. "What?" Dan said. "If Sis can be a quitter, I should be able to put my feet on the coffee table. Let's throw all the rules out the window." He turned and winked at Abby.

"Dan!" Gabby said. Jim raised his hands in defeat, and suddenly they were their best selves again.

Abby asked if anyone wanted a drink. While she took orders, she said. "Um, one more thing. The moving truck's coming in the morning. I thought I could use the barn to store a few things."

Jim laughed. "You're serious, then. Well, good for you. I have some extra space. Store what you need." He jingled the coins in his pants pocket. "And if you can't find a job, I'm still looking for a salesperson down at the car lot."

Abby's eyes sparkled. "Now, Dad," she said. "I couldn't possibly. You'd make me promise never to quit, and as I've proven today, it's something I occasionally do."

Jim pulled his best sad face. "You kids are a mess," he said. "Both of you." But Abby could see a smile playing in his eyes.

Chapter Four

Abby's five-year-old nephew Timothy and three-year-old niece Kennedy nearly knocked her to the ground. They'd barreled through the back door, dragging their mom, Emily, with them.

"Hold on, kids!" Emily said. "You'll hurt Aunt Abby." She mouthed the word *sorry* to Abby.

Emily was nearly as tall as Dan. She wore her thick blond hair in a claw-shaped clip. Her dark eyes, on such a fair face, were always a surprise, like two pieces of coal sitting in the snow.

Abby recovered, pulling Timothy and Kennedy close. "How are my little rabbits?" she asked, and Timothy laughed. "We're not rabbits, silly. We're your family."

Kennedy had her head buried in Abby's flowered piazza pants. "I'm a bunny," she said, her voice muffled and then started hopping down the hallway toward the living room.

"They're growing like weeds, Emily. I wish you'd make them stop."

Emily took Abby's arm as they walked to the dining room. The whole house smelled of the yeast rolls Gabby was famous for, and Abby breathed deep.

The dining table was made of walnut and had been in the family as long as anyone could remember. Abby and Emily unfolded the linen tablecloth and spread it carefully across the surface. Gabby wouldn't let Abby carry one thing to the table or help in the kitchen. Instead, Abby watched as all her favorite things appeared: meatloaf, corn on the cob, mashed potatoes. Dan, sitting next to Abby whispered in her ear. "A little bird told me we're having peach cobbler with vanilla ice cream for dessert."

After the kids' plates were filled, Abby shared her news with Emily. "What now?" Emily asked.

Abby felt as if a spotlight was trained on her. She refolded the napkin in her lap. "That's the million-dollar question."

"Not too many people hiring," Emily said.

Abby squirmed before saying, "I'm thinking about working for myself. I've had enough of 'the man.'"

Emily flashed her enviable smile. "I hear you, girlfriend." And Dan answered, "Hey, you two, we're not all bad."

Emily took a tiny bite of potatoes. "I'll tell you what we should be talking about. That new blog."

Before Abby could ask, Dan said, "L.C. Confidential. L.C. for Logan's Creek, get it?"

"What in the world is confidential in this town?" Abby asked. "When Cathy got engaged to Peter, she was the last to know. For heaven's sake, the staff at the Tuscan Table knew. They'd seen the ring. Cathy was the only one caught off guard."

Gabby put down her fork. "I remember that." To Jim, she said, "You remember, honey. Abby's friend, Lisa, told us after church one Sunday. Swore us to secrecy."

Jim, who'd taken a bite of his yeast roll, nodded.

"Seems there's a lot that we don't know about the goings-on in this town," Emily said. "And this anonymous blogger is putting it out there in a kind of folksy, aw-shucks way. Some of it is hilarious. But I tell you, the blogger is on to something. She—I mean if it is a she—is even going after the Teflon Thornton."

"The mayor?" Abby asked.

"The one and only," Emily said.

Jim, whose motto had always been not to say anything unless it was nice, said, "About dang time."

All this was news to Abby. Max Thornton had been a fixture in town since Abby had been in diapers. He drove his cream-colored

1985 Mark VII Lincoln Sport Coupe around town with a personalized license plate that read TOP DOG. If the weather was right, he'd have the windows down. He'd wave at you with his index finger and nod his head. Kind of a Logan's Creek blessing. Abby thought of him as a town legend, or at least a town symbol.

Dan said, "Thornton's Teflon may be wearing off. I heard your old Loverboy, Josh Moore, is throwing his hat in the ring. Wants to be mayor himself."

"I'd do just about anything to see Thornton defeated," Emily said. "I heard him at Walmart one day. There was a new checker, and she wanted to see Thornton's I.D. He threw a fit, said, 'Don't you know who I am?' The girl was in tears."

Abby's phone buzzed, and she looked at the screen. Ian was calling again. She put her phone face down on the table and picked up her corn on the cob. Ian could wait. And why did she feel her face flush at the sound of Josh's name?

In her room that night she treated her phone like it was the one thing in the house she wasn't allowed to touch. Which meant, of course, that she picked it up every ten seconds. Did she expect Ian to keep calling? She'd ignored his dozens of texts. She hadn't listened to one of his messages. The thought of him with that woman made her see red.

If it was still light outside, Abby would have gone running. But the moon was hidden by clouds tonight. Seemed like her whole world was covered in clouds. Abby picked up the phone one more time before calling it a night. No more messages from Ian. Her heart felt as empty as a ghost town.

The following Sunday, when Abby was still in her bedclothes, she decided enough was enough. It was seven hours later in the Alps where Ian had flown for the cover shoot for *Powder* magazine. She had his schedule on her calendar, three months out. She couldn't seem to delete any of it. Anyway, by now, he'd been up for hours.

When he answered the phone, he said, "This is Ian."

Abby's stomach was in knots. She almost hung up when she heard his voice.

Since she'd called him from her parents' landline—there was an extension in her room, a white phone shaped like a daisy—the number must have been unrecognizable to him. She'd left her mobile on the dresser, forgetting to charge it overnight, so it was her only option. "It's Abby," she said, sounding a little too casual for the situation.

Knowing Ian as she did, she could almost see him running his hand through his wavy hair, his shoulders tense. "Where are you, Abby? I called you as soon as I was back in Chicago. You never answered. I had to hear that you'd resigned from the firm from that asshole, John Willis." He took a breath. "I was sideswiped, Abby, and I felt like a fool that I didn't know. So I called your assistant Joy, and she said you'd given her your new address as Logan's Creek, Arkansas. Are you really in Logan's Creek?"

Neither of them spoke for a second. "You left just like that." His voice rose. "Like it was nothing! You didn't even call me. What were you thinking?"

Abby sat down heavily on her bed, Ian's self-righteousness making her blood boil.

Before she could say anything, Ian asked, "What was so hard? What was so devastating that you couldn't say goodbye? I get that Cromby is an ass. I knew you were at your wit's end. But I could have been here for you, Abby. You could've come to me. I would've helped you."

"Cromby gave the promotion I deserved to that sniveling backstabber, John Willis." Abby punched her pillow. "Did John happen to tell you that when you talked to him?" She waited a beat. "No? I didn't think so. He's a little afraid of you. Another perk of being a tall, strong man." Abby squeezed her eyes shut. "Anyway, Ian, it might have been a little crowded. Me, you, and whoever your new girlfriend is."

Abby heard Ian blow out his breath. "What in the hell are you talking about?"

She tried to keep her voice steady. "I was at the airport," she said.

"What airport?"

"O'Hare."

"You flew home?"

The words caught in Abby's throat. "No, when you came in from London. I was there to surprise you."

"This isn't making sense. You came to the airport? But you didn't find me?"

"Oh, I found you all right. Trouble was, there was a tall, lanky woman hanging on to you. She looked like she might fall if she let go."

The image came full-screen and in technicolor. Abby felt like she was going to be sick.

"Esme," Ian said.

"Who the hell is Esme? Tell me. I can take it."

"Google her."

"What?"

"Google Esme."

"Now you're telling me what to do."

Abby could hear Ian trying to keep his voice steady. "Fine," he said. "I'll tell you. Esme—one word, like Beyonce or Prince—is a model from South Africa. We met on a shoot for Clinique a few years ago. She was in the airport in London waiting on the same flight as me." Ian paused. "I can't believe I'm having to say this to you. I thought you knew me better. But since you need to hear this, here goes. Esme was crying in the lounge. I was having a drink. I asked her what was wrong. Her father had just died. Her father, who lived in *Chicago*. I sat with her. We had a stiff drink. I told her I'd get her home safe and sound. I didn't want her to be alone."

Abby felt about an inch high. "Oh," was all she managed to say.

The line went silent for a second. "Abby, I could say all of this has been a misunderstanding, and it has. But it also shows that we're not in the same place. You doubt me. You make major life decisions without telling me. Hell, you move away from me like I'm a bill collector you're trying to outrun."

Abby thought about her temper. When she got mad, she was mad all over. And when she was mad, she did rash things. This couldn't be all her fault, though. Ian had given her mixed signals. Ian was the king of casual dating, "No labels." How many times had he said that to her? And Abby hadn't wanted to get married, not exactly. Somedays she didn't even feel like an adult. "Ian," she said, and then nothing. What was there to say?

Abby knew what was coming. Ian was going to say he needed time, the adult version of breaking up. Before he could do it, Abby said, "Apparently, we both need a little time." Abby felt needles in the back of her throat. "Let's take a break, see how things feel in a month. That will give me time to sort some things out. It will give you time to, I don't know, do whatever it is you need to do."

Abby wanted Ian to protest. To say he couldn't live without her. "Fine," he said instead, ending the call just seconds before Abby started to cry.

QUESTION: What's Love(y) Got to Do With It?

Who else has a coupon for a free cone at the Milk Maid, courtesy of Lovey Willmocker's Used Car Emporium, on Day Lily Drive? Raise your hands! There's a whole bunch of you, from the looks of it. And all it took was a test drive in a "pre-owned and slightly driven" vehicle. Well, enjoy your treat. Preferably while riding in a car you bought elsewhere, if Mrs. Jesse Willet, of Logan's Creek, is to be believed.

As she tells it, on a pretty May day, she test drove a 2010 Ford Focus that Lovey Willmocker had on the lot.

Mrs. Willett fell in love. It looked as if the car had barely been driven, plus, it had that new car smell—like new baby dolls. And it was burgundy. So pretty!

Mrs. Willett bought it on the spot—she had just gotten her tax return money from the IRS. All was well, until two weeks later. "The car was offensive!" Mrs. Willett told L.C. Confidential. Every time Mrs. Willett put on the left turn signal, the Focus made a sound like passing gas.

"I couldn't believe it!" Mrs. Willett said. "I took it straightaway to Lovey, and demanded my money back. But Lovey wasn't having it. She swore she couldn't hear a thing, but then she's deaf as a doorknob, isn't she?"

After the encounter, Mrs. Willett felt she had no other recourse, so she painted the car with a big lemon on the side and drove it around Lovey Willmocker's Used Car Emporium every day for a week. "I honked a lot," Mrs. Willett admitted. "I wanted everybody to know that Lovey was selling lemons."

The police finally asked Mrs. Willett to stop. "They said I was disturbing the peace, so you know what I did? I sat there with my left blinker engaged. That caused quite a stink," Mrs. Willett said, laughing at her own joke.

Mrs. Willett has been forced to drive the Focus only where she can turn right. "It's enough to make your head spin," she said, "but as a lady, I can't abide folks thinking that awful sound is coming from me."

L.C. Confidential contacted Lovey Willmocker, repeatedly. To date, she has not returned our messages. The Logan's Creek Police did say they responded to a call from Lovey Willmocker concerning a disturbance at the lot. But as no report was written up, they were unable to comment further.

At L.C. Confidential, we make it our business to stand up for the underdog. We can't always make change, but we can be a warning to others. If you have stories that just don't smell right, reach out. You can email us through our "Contact Us" link at the top of the page.

Chapter Five

Abby felt her toe catch the exposed tree root of Mrs. Norma Spencer's maple tree. She tried to right herself, but like everything else lately, it hadn't worked, and Abby went down. Hard. Mrs. Spencer lived two blocks off Main Street in a white house with a red roof and blue shutters. The mailbox near the sidewalk was covered by a blue clematis that looked like tiny saucers from Abby's current vantage point.

"Damn it," she said and then looked around to see if Mrs. Spencer might have heard her. Mrs. Spencer had been her Brownie leader when Abby was in third grade. No need to disappoint her now with her foul language. Abby sighed. No one inside the house seemed to have noticed a young woman sprawled on the ground, examining her right knee. Her leggings were torn there, and blood was trickling onto the black fabric. Abby checked her ankles. All good. Her elbows and hands were fine too, although her palms stung. She pulled herself up and tested her knee. She could walk well enough. A Band-Aid would fix her knee. She decided to go on.

This was the first time since she'd been home that she'd ventured out on foot. The previous three days she'd spent either in her bed or on the couch, but there was only so much reality TV she could take. When her hair had gotten tangled and her t-shirt stained, her mom said. "Up you go, Abby Rose. To the shower." She yanked the throw off Abby's lap. "I'm not kidding, young lady. To the shower, then fix your hair. No more of this wallowing." Her mom stood with her feet apart, her hands on her hips. "Carters," she said, "do not wallow."

So, today, Abby wasn't wallowing. She was limping if she was being honest. But her hair was shiny. She had sunscreen on. Even a bra. Well, a sports bra, but still. Improvements.

Two doors down, there was a white colonial. Black shutters. Black iron fence. A gold plaque, shaped like an eagle, hung above the front door. When Abby was nine or ten, her mom had explained the eagles that appeared around town. "When a customer pays off their house loan, Neighbors Bank sends them an eagle to hang. It's shorthand for 'I did it!' For financial freedom, and folks love that."

Josh's parents lived in the white colonial. Good for them, Abby thought. Debt free. And then she remembered her first visit there. She'd still worn braces. Her hair, stylish now if she used enough hair products, was a bird's nest. She'd spilled a Coke in the living room. The one room with white carpet.

And they'd loved her anyway.

Determined, Abby moved on. The streets in this part of town were cobblestone. Ferns hung from porches whose ceilings were painted Robin's egg blue. Miss Nestor lived one street over. She taught art at the high school. Her house and post-stamp yard were filled with metal sculptures. Her door was painted purple. The door jamb was sunshine yellow. Abby smiled thinking about it.

Her knee felt as if it was disappointed in her, and every few steps it would stiffen up. "Join the crowd," Abby muttered. She was thinking about Ian of course. That's what she'd heard in his voice. Disappointment. Abby pulled her lips into a tight line. Disappointment didn't compare to the feeling of being betrayed. And that's what she'd thought Ian had done. Truth be told, she still wondered. For instance, if an average woman, one who didn't look like she'd been sent down from above to show other women what to strive for, had been crying, what would he have done?

But Abby knew. Ian would have done the same thing. Abby felt her cheeks flush. Sometimes he was so darn complicated.

Abby looked up. She'd made it to Main Street where a string

of Victorian-era buildings had been refurbished. There was an apothecary on the next corner, with a turret as an entrance. Really, it was just a drug store, but Mr. Mason, who owned it, had the windows painted with the words "Mason's Apothecary Shoppe," and the town went along with it, although she'd once heard Mrs. Spencer say the druggist was putting on airs.

The bell above the door rang as Abby entered. When Mr. Mason saw her limping, he said. "Sit down this minute, young lady." He pointed to the old church pew that sat along one wall. "What's happened here?"

Kindness had always been Abby's weakness. "I fell," she said, her voice shaky. And Mr. Mason said, "Now don't you worry, we'll fix you up in no time."

He returned with gauze and antiseptic that smelled the way the school bathrooms used to after the custodians had done their work. It stung when he dabbed away at Abby's knee. "Looks like you already have a scar here," Mr. Mason said. Abby sighed. "That's from playing baseball, like, a hundred years ago."

Mr. Mason smiled. "I remember now. You're Abby Carter. Toughest kid on that team. I was the sponsor, remember?" Mr. Mason pulled off his disposable gloves. "Haven't seen you in a month of Sundays. You're in Chicago now, right? Are you here visiting your folks?"

In Chicago, Abby could go six months without running into someone she knew, let alone someone who knew her as a child. And Mr. Mason was right, she was tough. It was about time she acted like it. "I'm home for good, Mr. Mason. Chicago wasn't everything it was cracked up to be."

Just then, pain zapped her knee. It was a good reason for the tears in her eyes. Otherwise, she couldn't have explained them.

Abby looked at herself in the full-length mirror. Sleek blue dress, a half dozen silver bracelets on her wrist, strappy heels. She still had a bandage on her knee, but she'd fixed that by wearing a dress that hit mid-calf. She had to be at her best. When the Leading Ladies got together, it was dress-up night. No jeans. No sweatshirts. No sneakers.

Abby turned, looking at herself from every angle. She looked fine, maybe even better than fine, but tonight she wasn't feeling it. In Chicago, her life had been filled with clients who needed her to be at her most creative. With Mr. Cromby, who sucked all the air from a room just by being in it. And with Ian, who could make her forget about all of it just by touching the base of her throat.

Maybe there was a reason people said you couldn't go home again. Abby put on her best perfume, touching it to her wrists. It smelled of sandalwood and violets. She shook her head. When her mom was right, she was right. Abby had become a wallower. She grabbed her gauzy wrap and headed for her car.

The Tuscan Table closed to the public at 8:00 p.m., and it was 8:30 p.m. when everyone arrived, meeting at the front door like a troop of flamingos, which Abby happened to know were called a flamboyance. The word made her smile.

Once they'd scooted inside, giggling for no good reason, her friends spread out, and Abby took a closer look. They were dressed to the nines: green silk, black leather, a few sequins. Suddenly, they were all around her, talking over one another. It sounded like a bee swarm. And then Cathy appeared from the kitchen, a starched white apron covering her slinky pink dress. "Ladies," she said, clapping her hands. "Let Abby catch her breath."

The chatter stopped. "Poker Face" by Lady Gaga was playing on the sound system. Candles flickered on the tables.

Cathy pulled out a chair. "Abby, you sit in the middle of this long table since you're tonight's main attraction."

Abby sat in the plush chair. "I'm so glad to see you all." She then set a bag with three bottles of wine on the table. Cathy grabbed them and sent them to be opened right away. A skeleton crew had stayed to serve the group.

They all began to pick chairs around the six-top table as Cathy asked one of the servers to bring them wine glasses and appetizers.

"Is everyone drinking wine?" Cathy asked. "Abby brought our favorite, merlot."

Amy, just over five feet tall and wearing a zebra print wrap dress, said, "Bring on the wine. It's been a long week already!" It was only Tuesday.

Amy made soap and lotions and sold them from her shop, Treasures Abound, which was only a block away. She was the youngest of the group, and was married to her high school sweetheart, Casey, who was a fireman. They had three children. Stairsteps. Adorable.

Cathy patted Amanda's back, who was sitting beside Amy. "Hey, Ms. Prosecuting Attorney, are you allowed to have some wine with us?"

Amanda flipped her long black hair over her shoulder. "I don't see why not," she said. Amanda was the smart one, always at the top of their class. In college, she'd graduated summa cum laude at Florida International University. And now she the town's prosecuting attorney.

Cathy poured the wine. When the glasses were full, she proposed a toast. "I'd like to toast the eternal friendship of the Leading Ladies." She raised her glass. "Accepting our failures, which lead us to our continued success." She tipped her glass forward. "Together forever."

When the moment passed, Lisa blew her curly red bangs out of her eyes. "I need a haircut," she said, and laughed. Lisa Miller's hair fit her: unmanageable and unpredictable, and absolutely wonderful. She had been the class clown, which some mistook as a sign that she lacked intelligence, but Lisa was crazy-smart. Now, she spent her time developing the properties she and her husband, Don Barham, bought. Like Logan's Creekfront Village, and several of the buildings downtown that might have fallen into mortal disrepair without them.

"First, I want you to know how happy we are that you're back," Lisa said. The others nodded. "Second, didn't you leave some arm candy behind in Chicago? You know, that hunk of a photographer?" She laughed. "How's that developing now that you're here?"

Janie, who was sitting next to Lisa, covered her mouth for a second. "I get it! Photographer. Developing." As she tugged her dark hair into a rope, she said to Abby, "Time to spill, Miss Chill."

Abby felt as raw as her knee. How was she going to explain this?

Instead, she said, "Is anybody else hungry? I'm starving."

In a New York minute, everyone had grabbed a breaded mozzarella stick. They were cutting them into little ladylike pieces, and for a minute all you could hear was the sound of cutlery hitting china. That and, in the background, Mariah Carey singing "We Belong Together."

Amy, who hadn't said anything yet, looked at Abby. She put down her fork and asked, "So, what's the plan, now that you're here?" Amy was the practical one. She rarely got emotional.

Abby had read a recent article about why couples fight. A woman, for example, might want to tell her husband about her rotten day at work. All she wants is for him to say, "That sorry S.O.B. I get why you're mad." But the man isn't having the same conversation. He's trying to fix things, so he says, "Why don't you go to HR, see if they can sort this out?" And suddenly, she's livid. He's being practical. She's being emotional. They aren't even on the same floor of the same building.

That's what Abby felt like now. She'd appreciate it if Amy said she hated Mr. Cromby for not giving Abby the promotion she deserved. She had to know how that felt. They all did. Hadn't all the Leading Ladies been at the mercy of a bad boss at one time or another? Hadn't they all cried in a bathroom stall at work, then fixed their mascara and gotten on with it?

Abby caught Amanda staring at her, and then she saw Amanda whisper something to Cathy, who said, "Want us to go key Cromby's car? Want us to toilet paper his yard, 'cause we'll do it!"

Abby felt a cinder block fall from her chest. "I'll give you directions," she said. She looked at her glass. It was empty.

"That's our girl," Cathy said.

Abby was only partially kidding.

And then Cathy said, "That's a big reason I work for myself, Abby. Nobody telling me what to do but me." She tipped her glass. "Well, the bank has plenty to say. They hold the loan on this place. But still."

The Leading Ladies laughed. When dinner was served, Abby found herself behind a giant plate of Chicken Parmigiana. After a few bites, she said, "I'm thirty years old. Unemployed. Living with my parents.

How did this happen to me?" She picked up a breadstick.

"Like I said, Abby," Cathy answered, "I work for myself so I can't get fired. I can lose my job only if the restaurant fails, and I have a lot of control over that. Have you thought about starting your own advertising agency?"

Abby gripped the napkin in her lap. "I have," she said. "But I signed a non-compete, meaning I can't work in advertising for a year from the date I quit." Abby heard Janie groan.

Amanda spoke up. "That non-compete is nonsense. Why, in California they're not even enforceable. I'd feel fine if you started an agency tomorrow, but I know how you are, Abby. Dot the I's and cross the T's. But I'm telling you, don't give Cromby any more power over your life."

Abby didn't particularly like being told what to do. It must have shown, because Amy changed the subject. "I've got something I've been meaning to ask you all. Have you seen the blog, L.C. Confidential? Somebody is putting out all the dirt on Logan's Creek."

"Who could it be?" Lisa asked.

Amanda said, "Whoever it is, it's causing a stir in the community."

"The blogger was badgering Josh Moore the other day about a speeding ticket he got seven years ago. Seven years ago! He didn't even respond. He needs someone monitoring his social media or he's never going to be mayor," Lisa said.

Amanda leaned toward Abby. "Abby, that's it!" she said. "Be Josh's campaign manager. He needs you. You need the money. And you'd be a campaign manager, not a marketing manager. I'm sure the non-compete only covers roles in advertising."

"I don't know," Abby said. "There was a lot of bad blood when we broke up."

Cathy waved her hand. "Water under the bridge." Lisa added, "We were children."

Even if that were true, their relationship had been Abby's first taste of adulthood. What they felt and how they expressed it went beyond their years. Even now, she thought about how tender he'd been. How devoted he'd been, at least until the end. Working with him would only add another high-wire act to the circus that was her life.

"Worth a shot, Abby," Amy said, and Janie added, "I think it's brilliant!"

Amanda drummed her fingers on the table, a sure sign she was on a roll. "Speaking of which, we never did talk about your good-looking photographer. What's up?"

Amanda was like a dog with a bone, once she got started on something. "Ian is fine." She folded her arms. "I think."

"What do you mean, 'you think'?"

Abby felt tension in her neck. "We're taking a little time."

Abby swore Amanda was taking notes on one of the cocktail napkins. "Like a break? Isn't a break shorthand for a breakup?"

Cathy had had the exact amount of wine to loosen her tongue. "Come on, Amanda. You know Abby. She loves 'em and leaves 'em. Ever since Josh, well, you know."

Abby looked at Cathy, who now had her hand over her mouth and seemed horrified.

"Just so everyone knows, I did not walk out on Ian," Abby said. "I hit my breaking point with Cromby while Ian was on a plane with no phone service. He'd been gone for two weeks." Abby pinched the bridge of her nose. "He's gone a lot. I couldn't work for Mr. Cromby one more day. To be honest, I didn't even factor Ian in, and that worries me. We're in this kind of middling place." Abby sniffed. "No labels, you know?"

The room grew quiet. The sound system had switched to instrumental music, like background in a sad movie. "It's hard out there." Concealer was covering the dark circles under Abby's eyes. When she took it off later, she'd look like an older version of herself.

The Leading Ladies reached out their hands and put them on top of Abby's, like a sports team before a game. "We'll get through this, Abby, I promise you," Cathy said. "We're getting you a job, girlfriend," Amanda added. "We might even fix your love life." For a moment it felt as if they were at a therapy session, and then Amy said, "Boys are so freaking dumb."

Abby smiled. "They really, really are."

Chapter Six

The tonic that was the Leading Ladies had done its job. Abby was feeling more like the tough girl on the baseball team than the overwhelmed thirty-year-old who was without a job, and quite possibly without a boyfriend. She could hear birdsong from her open bedroom window. Her knee was healing nicely. As a Carter, rarely a quitter or a wallower, she knew what she had to do. She was going for a run, albeit a gentle one. As she moved into reverse lunges to warm up, she felt that old surge of adrenaline. Running gave her the time to think without distractions. It cleared her mind of all that useless junk and worry.

As she ran past her parents' drive, she noticed a pair of orange monarch butterflies on the baby's breath bush near the old well. By the time she reached the dirt road leading to town, her mind had become a blank page. On it, she was breaking down her life into manageable tasks:

One: Get a job, any job.
Two: OR, ask to work with Josh on his campaign.
Three: Sell her apartment in Chicago.
Four: Find a permanent place to live.
Five: Figure out her love life.

Abby doubled over after her five-mile run, her hands gripping her waist, and gulped air. Once she'd gotten started, she'd not been able to go gently. She checked her knee. The bandage was still white, so she'd not done any more damage. She chugged water from her water bottle and wiped her brow. After she'd caught her breath, she headed to the bookstore/coffee shop, called Chapters, to get a latte. She deserved a treat.

Abby had cooled down enough to slip her light jacket over her snug Spandex running top. When she approached the stoplight that moved traffic across Main Street, she pulled lip gloss from her pocket and swiped it on. Up ahead, she saw the Tuscan Table. She knew Cathy would be in there working herself to a frazzle, but smiling while she did it. Maybe Abby would have her own business soon enough.

While crossing the street to Chapters, she heard someone call her name. She looked around and saw several people, but no one she knew. She heard her name for a second time. The voice was coming from behind her on the sidewalk. It was none other than Josh Moore.

Abby jostled the keys inside her jacket pocket. "Well if it isn't the next mayor of Logan's Creek." Abby said, her voice light.

Josh shielded his eyes against the sun and walked toward her. Abby's breath caught. At six-foot five inches, he towered above her; he nearly blocked out the sun. He'd been too thin in high school, but now he was perfect, his shoulders wide and the muscles beneath his dress shirt impressive. He scanned her body, and it was as if each place he surveyed warmed under his gaze. When he smiled, she saw the dimples that had first attracted her to him. When he dropped his hand, she saw the depth of his nearly-black eyes. "Abby Rose Carter. What in the world have you been up to?"

Maybe it was the endorphins from her recent run, or maybe it was having a conversation with a man who, unlike Ian, wasn't disappointed in her. Whatever the case, Abby felt her face flush. "The clothes are a hint, Josh. I've been running. And now I'm going to treat myself to coffee at Chapters." Abby wiped her brow dramatically. "It was a latte night followed by a brutally early morning. I earned it."

Josh laughed at her awful joke. "Let's get coffee together," he said when the laughter ended. "I can tell you all about the mayor's race, and you can catch me up on life in the city."

Josh looked as if he had recently shaved, and he smelled the way Abby remembered: like the inside of an Abercrombie and Fitch. All that talk about bad blood between them seemed impossible now. Josh stood with his hands in his pants pockets, rocking on his heels. Easy as a Sunday morning. His shoes were the kind of leather that had to be polished regularly, and Josh's were nearly sparkling. He had an American flag pin on his lapel. He looked like someone you'd trust with a bank deposit or a well-kept secret.

"Sure." Abby scuffed the sidewalk with the toe of her Nike. "Why not?"

Josh and Abby chatted about the weather as they ordered their lattes and walked out front to grab a table overlooking downtown. After sitting, they both grew quiet.

Main Street had flourished since she'd moved to Chicago. And Lisa's Creekfront Village sat just beyond downtown, creating much more foot traffic than Abby remembered.

On this day, red geraniums and white petunias were bright in the redbrick planters at the corner of each block. The storefronts of the Victorian buildings were already bustling with shoppers, mostly tourists who had disembarked from the weekly passenger train from a city seventy miles north. Chalkboards stood in front of many of the shops, the specials of the day written in bright colors. The Whistle Stop Café even had the rusted door from an old farm truck at its entrance, with the words *Kiss My Grits* painted on it.

Abby broke the silence. "So mayor, huh?" she said.

"Does that surprise you?"

Abby looked at Josh's hands. His square nails were pristine, and she wondered if he'd been to a nail salon. "Not that you're running. I've known you wanted to be mayor since middle school. It's more why are you running now? You're pretty young for a mayor."

Josh turned the cardboard sleeve that shielded his latte, his brow furrowed. The Chapters' staff wrote famous quotes on each of them. His read: *A woman is like a tea bag: you can't tell how strong she is until you put her in hot water. —Eleanor Roosevelt.*

Josh shifted in his seat. "Not that young," he said. He looked around, as if seeing if anybody was listening. "It's just that..." He hesitated. "It's just that the time has come, you know?"

Abby didn't know but she shook her head anyway.

Josh lowered his voice. "Plus, the town could be run better. There are things..." he said, and then seemed to decide against going further. "Anyway, a few of the younger business owners approached me at the end of last year. Wanted to see what my plans were. At the time, being the City Attorney and establishing my private practice were my only goals—I'm only needed at the City three days a week—so I told them I wasn't ready. But then something happened that made me reconsider."

Abby slipped on the sunglasses she kept in her jacket pocket. The sun was glinting off the windows at Chapters, throwing a glare across their table. "What happened?"

Josh seemed to consider his next words. Then, he shook his head. "Let's talk about you for a change. How's life treating you?"

There was part of Abby that wanted to tell Josh everything. He'd been the one beside her when her grandfather learned he had dementia. She'd stood beside him when his sister married a man everyone in town knew would break her heart. She'd been there when that same sister moved to London, breaking the family's heart. They'd talked like two people confessing as the plane went down more times than she could count. Abby blew out her breath, deciding to use restraint. "Let's just say working for 'the Man' turned out to be a deal-breaker for me."

Josh scooted back, putting his ankle across his opposite knee. "You aren't at the ad agency anymore?"

Abby laughed a bitter laugh. "Not at the agency. Not in Chicago. I've come back home, Josh."

Was it her imagination, or did Josh suddenly relax? "Well, it's their loss, Abby."

The feeling of failure, of quitting, hit Abby again. She tore little pieces off her napkin. Josh looked toward the street, but said to her, "What are you going to do now?"

She waited a moment, pushed the torn napkin around on the table as she thought about how to answer him. "I'd like to start my own agency, but I signed a non-compete that's in place for a year. I'll need to find something else for a while."

Abby could see Josh's wheels turning. "I could look at the non-compete. Those are usually bullshit."

"Amanda's already looked, and she said the same thing. But Josh, I'm uneasy about it. I've worked too hard to build my reputation. If I took on clients and then had to step back because of the non-compete, it could stop me in my tracks." Abby looked at her smartwatch. It showed her heart rate increasing. She covered the watch with her sleeve. "I do have an idea, though. Actually, the Leading Ladies came up with it."

Josh looked at Abby as if she was contemplating something criminal. "Do you need to hand me a dollar? Secure me as your attorney before you speak?" He shook his head. "The Leading Ladies aren't known for following the rules."

Abby laughed. "They did offer to key my old boss's car."

"Abby."

Abby touched Josh's arm. The contact felt electric. "I didn't agree to it," she said, "and that has nothing to do with their advice."

Josh's dimples showed. "Let me have it."

"I'm going to be your campaign manager."

Josh leaned forward. He smelled like heaven. "I'm intrigued," he said.

Abby felt butterflies. Surely, it was because she was nervous. "It would work like this. I'd be your campaign manager. I'd handle everything to do with your image, and I'd make sure every voter in

Logan's Creek knows who you are and what you stand for. I've been tracking what your current advertising firm is doing, which, let's be honest, isn't much. You have no social media pages, no ads on the local radio stations, no print or TV ads. I haven't seen one yard sign.

"And there's a blogger in town. Did you know that? L.C. Confidential. The blogger targeted you about an old speeding ticket. Seven years ago. You never responded. What if the blogger decides to call you crooked or immoral or backed by a cult out of Missouri?"

Josh grinned at Abby. "A cult out of Missouri?"

"You know what I mean. Your agency, whoever they are, isn't serving you well."

"The Gordon Agency out of Little Rock. There wasn't anyone local who would work with me because of the hold Mayor Thornton has." Josh rubbed his chin. "Thornton is like a tree with invasive roots. His tentacles reach way too far."

Abby felt her confidence soaring. "I know social media, advertising, and communications. I've planned events for as many as a thousand people. Plus, I know this town. The Gordon Agency definitely does not."

"It's August already," Josh said. "Don't you think it's too late to make that kind of change?"

"We have until the polls close on November 5, Josh. I'd say that's plenty of time."

Josh reached across the table and took her hand, then dropped it just as quickly. "Sorry," he said, "old habits and all." He cleared his throat. "It's just that I'm surprised you'd do that for me. I was afraid our past might keep us from ever being close again."

Abby felt her heart soften. "Josh, you know things about me no one else knows. I figure it's the same for you. Before I left Chicago, I probably felt the same way about us. But here I am, looking for a chance to start over. And there you are looking for a chance to make Logan's Creek better. I'd say it's worth two old friends putting their heads together to make that happen."

Abby held out her hand to shake. When Josh took it, he said, "What do we do now?"

"Fire the Gordon Agency," Abby said. "Look up L.C. Confidential. We need to figure out if there's a way to use this blogger to our advantage. And tonight, go home and scrub your social media. When folks look you up, and they will, I want them to know only three things about Josh Moore. He loves Jesus, his mama, and Logan's Creek. Take down any posts that mention alcohol, clubs, or travel outside of the state. You are a hometown boy, Josh. Our job is to make you look as close to perfect as possible."

Josh saluted like Abby was a drill sergeant. "Now get going," Abby said, "you have a latte to do."

Whats (Really) *Going On?*

QUESTION: Who's on the City Council?

I'm guessing here, but I'd say MOST of YOU couldn't pick our council members out of a LINEUP! If you're ONE of those people, you need to find out, NOW! For years, Logan's Creek has been asleep at the wheel, and we've been electing the same old kinds of people to run our fair city. Oh, we have a lot of nice things like the new splash pad for KIDS, and the senior center for SENIORS. But every time the City Council is asked to set aside money for something teens and young(ish) adults could get behind—like an ice-skating rink or a fitness center with a POOL—it's voted down.

Like my dear grandmama said when my friends and I jumped on her divan until the springs broke that time, "I can't have nothing nice."

How many times has this THEORETICAL fitness CENTER come up? SIT DOWN FOR THIS ONE. Eight times in the past TWO years.

Why don't you know about it? The council meetings are OPEN TO THE PUBLIC. The Logan's Creek Courier reports on it—LOOK IT UP! But where do they put the story? On the page behind the obituaries, which is in the SPORTS section, if you can believe it. And on the front page will be a story about the biggest pumpkin grown in the county or an exposé on the Ladies Auxiliary of the Devoted Vines. Seems they used a MIX for their annual cookie sale, and certain people were in TEARS about it.

Want to do something for the MAJORITY of the people in Logan's Creek? Show up for THIS Thursday's City Council meeting, which starts at SIX O'CLOCK (or when the mayor can be bothered to show up. He's notorious for being late.) It's at the SENIOR CENTER, of course—in my opinion, the nicest building in town. Get INVOLVED. TAKE names! FIND out who your representatives ARE. In OTHER words, be a GOOD citizen.

When they open the mic for public comment, your first question should be, "Why do you hate the young people of Logan's Creek?" When they say they don't, just ask them, "Then WHAT have you EVER done for us?" If we citizens don't ACT, we'll NEVER get ANYTHING changed!

In other news, Lovey Willmocker has settled things with Mrs. Jessie

Willett, who had bought a 2010 Ford Focus with an unusual problem! (See earlier post.) Both parties are happy with the settlement, and that folks, is what we call the POWER of the press.

Check back next week, Logan's Creek, when I'll be talking about the MAYOR'S RACE! I will say, I heard from mayoral candidate Josh Moore, who's running against Mayor Thornton. City Attorney Moore HAD PLENTY to say about his SPEEDING ticket, which I reported on not long ago. Keep checking in, FOLKS! I'll let him have HIS SAY in MY next blog post. VROOM, VROOM!

Chapter Seven

The City Council meeting was set to begin at six, but Abby had shown up early. She needed to see Mayor Thornton in action, and she needed to see how Josh interacted with him. Plus, she figured the blogger would be around somewhere, and maybe, just maybe, Abby could figure out who the blogger was.

She smoothed the fabric of her linen blazer while she waited outside the Senior Center for the others. The last time she'd worn the blazer was with Ian. Linen blazer, white t-shirt, ripped jeans, pearls. They were on a photo shoot at an animal shelter on the outskirts of Chicago. She and Ian were part of a group of creatives who volunteered their time for charities with non-existent budgets, and that day, they were doing glamour shots of the dogs and cats that needed a home. Ian had laughed when Abby took off her double strand of pearls and wrapped them around a yellow cat's neck. The cat already had the look of royalty about her. The pearls were the icing on the cake. Now, Abby sighed. If she'd known she was moving back to Logan's Creek, she would have taken the cat with her.

Josh interrupted her thoughts. "I knew you'd be early." He took off his sunglasses and Abby noticed the way his perfectly arched eyebrows framed his face. He really could have been a model. "Carters are always on time," he said, doing a lousy impersonation of Abby's dad.

Abby raised her hands. "'Carters never quit,'" she said, making her voice deep. Her dad had a string of these mandates for the family.

"Nobody like him," Josh said. "I still visit your folks, you know. Not like a stalker or anything, but I stop by, bring your dad that molasses he likes from Sage Farm. Take your mom a bottle of Chanel No. 5 at Christmas."

"I guess Carters can keep secrets, too," she said, mildly annoyed. "They never mentioned any of this to me."

"Another reason to stay here," Josh said. The sun at six o'clock in the evening was slanting low and beams of light had turned Josh's black hair nearly midnight blue. "You won't get left out of all the excitement that is Logan's Creek."

Abby leaned against the brick wall, the heat of the day radiating from it. "How boring are these meetings?" she said, changing the subject.

Josh stepped beside her and leaned against the wall. Looking straight ahead, he said, "Remember Civics class? Mr. Ralston?" Mr. Ralston had spoken in a monotone, a slow, drawn-out monotone. "That was a carnival compared to these council meetings." He pushed himself off the wall. "See you inside, Abby," he said, and Abby remembered watching him walk away, all those years ago, when Abby had wanted to set sail and Josh had wanted nothing but Logan's Creek.

Her phone buzzed. The Leading Ladies had just parked. Well, the Leading Ladies who were available: Lisa, Amy, and Janie. They were here to support Abby, and to help her catch the blogger if they could.

Once they'd found their seats, the women looked around. Lisa had a legal pad, and she was drawing a floor plan of the room. Lisa always did more than was needed. Amy had her own notebook, this one decorated with bits of lace and stickers in the shapes of flowers. Janie sat with her hands in her lap, her eyes roaming the room. Abby felt confident they'd be able to sniff out the L.C. Confidential blogger.

Once the Pledge of Allegiance was recited, and Reverend Powell, with the Presbyterian church, said the prayer, the meeting got underway. Old Mr. Abernathy had filed a complaint about the crosswalk downtown. Seems he couldn't cross the street before the Do Not Walk sign came back on. When he was finished, an agitated woman took the spot at the podium. "I've been reading this mess on L.C. Confidential." She was maybe fifty-five or sixty, wearing bright pink Crocs with olive green knee socks that had Big Foot marching across them. "And I agree with most of what the blog says. Things are going on in this town that would raise the eyebrows on a sailor."

Mayor Thornton interrupted. "My good woman. L.C. Confidential is nothing but a gossip rag." He waved his arm. "Is there any point to this?"

The woman grabbed the edge of the podium. She raised her chin. "This isn't about you, Mayor, although it's common knowledge that you're a bald-faced liar."

The audience erupted, and Councilman Jeffries yelled, "That's enough!"

The woman waited out the crowd. "Well, he is," she said, her voice defiant. "But this is about our good City Attorney, Josh Moore."

Abby pivoted in Josh's direction. He was sitting on the front row adjusting his tie, an attempt, it seemed to Abby, to look unconcerned.

The woman scanned the crowd. "Does anybody else wonder why our City Attorney is allowed to sell his services to other city councils in this county?"

"No?" she said. "For instance, why does Logan's Creek, the county seat, pay him a full-time wage while he's working against us, for all we know."

She held up a printout with rows of green and red numbers. "See for yourself. Thirty-six months ago, Lone Elm paid Josh Moore $550 for legal counsel. That was the month they closed on the old Walmart where the fitness center is today. As L.C. Confidential pointed out, we should have gotten that center. We should be swimming in our own indoor pool. But no, if we're lucky we get to sit on the edges of the splash pad with umpteen children whooping and hollering and causing a commotion. We might get damp, but we sure as heck aren't swimming. Anyway, I digress." She pointed to the spreadsheet. "Lookie here, Lone Elm paid him again the month the fitness center opened. And once more since then."

The woman scratched her head—her gray roots were showing.

"I remembered seeing Mr. Moore's picture in the paper when I was having my hair done that one time, down at Lula Beth's." At the mention of Lula Beth's, Janie nudged Abby. Lula Beth had given Janie the worst haircut of her life, right before their senior prom. But then, who could pull off a mullet?

The woman continued. "He was at the grand opening of the Lone Elm Fitness Center," She pointed at Josh, whose mouth was slightly agape. "It seemed odd at the time. Why was he there? Now, I get it. We didn't get a fitness center because Mr. Moore was helping Lone Elm get theirs. He didn't have time to help us."

Abby looked at the exit. Someone in a hoodie and jeans was zipping out the side exit. Could that have been the blogger? Abby had been too caught up in the discussion to notice much more than an outline. Slim, tall, quick.

Mayor Thornton stood. He looked like someone who might play an older gangster in a movie: hair slicked back, gray pin striped suit. Instead of an American flag pin on his lapel, he wore a red rose, plucked from someone's garden. He wore no tie, and his crisp white shirt was unbuttoned at the neck. Even though he wasn't moving, the word that came to mind was *swagger*. "That is quite an accusation, ma'am," he said, his hands on the table in fists.

"Are you condoning your attorney doing the bidding for another town?" the woman said. "Is that even legal?"

"If the City Attorney is doing anything nefarious, make no mistake, I'll handle it." With that, the council meeting stopped, and the council went into executive session, behind closed doors, which meant no outsiders allowed, not even the press.

Abby sat on the edge of her seat. This had to be a mistake.

That's when she caught Josh's eye. She stood and held two fingers in the air. It was their sign from high school. It meant *I'm going to rescue you*. They'd used it when one of them was cornered by a major flirt. Which happened a lot. They even used it when Abby was low on gas. Josh, sitting beside her in her Ford Mustang convertible, would look at the gauge, raise two fingers, and they'd pull into the nearest station.

He'd touch the back of her head and say, "I got you, Abby," then jump out to fill her tank.

Abby pointed to the lobby and Josh nodded. As she scooted by her Leading Ladies, they wanted to know where she was going. "Josh," was all she said.

Once in the lobby, the two pushed past the front door. Outside, a train chugged by on the nearby tracks, and an owl hooted in the distance. Farther away, a car was blasting its radio, the thump of the music pulsing in Abby's body.

"Joshua Moore, what in the world was that about?" Abby asked as they walked down the steps and headed for the gazebo that stood near the oak tree behind the building.

Josh pressed his lips together, before saying, "It's nothing, Abby. Not really. Lone Elm's attorney had resigned and moved off. They needed a lawyer to handle some mundane language in a noise ordinance. Mayor Thornton signed off on it, although he seems to have forgotten that now. The other two times, they were in the same circumstance. I charged the bare minimum, and I did it as one town helping another. And nothing had anything to do with the business in Logan's Creek, most certainly not anything to do with a fitness center."

They were sitting on the bench inside the gazebo, their knees touching. "When you say the mayor signed off, do you mean there's a paper trail?"

"Nothing formal like a signature. He told me that Lone Elm needed some help until they secured an attorney for the city. As the biggest city in the county, it was 'our duty' to lend a hand. His words."

"What about the next two times?"

Josh closed his eyes, a line of concentration forming on his forehead. "The next time, there were some zoning documents that needed to be reviewed and signed off on. Lone Elm's mayor asked if I could help."

"What did you do then?"

"I went through the procedures, filed the paperwork, and moved on. I remember asking Thornton for permission, just like the first time. Mayor Thornton was late for a meeting. I remember him saying,

'Josh, would you quit acting like a new hire? I trust you, boy. Do what you have to do, but quit nagging me about it.'"

"Then what the heck was all that about in there?" Abby asked, pointing to the senior center.

Josh laughed a humorless laugh. "That was a man running for office."

"Who's the woman who brought this up?"

"That's Cynthia Burke. Last year, the City fined her $500 for not keeping her property up. She had piles of pallets all across her unmown yard. Said she was going to build a doghouse with them, but they'd been there for at least two years." Josh rubbed his temples. "Plus, I might have dated her niece a few years ago." Josh grimaced. "It didn't end well."

Abby patted Josh's knee. "Uh oh," she said and grinned. "Affairs of the heart meets affairs of the city."

Josh pouted and still his dimples showed. "It's not funny," he said, and when Abby looked closer, she could see the hurt in his eyes. "Of course not, but it's not that serious either. Mayor Thornton needs to be reminded of your conversations and clear your name. Surely, he wouldn't lie."

Josh took Abby's hand, and the heat from his skin melted something inside her. "Abby," he said, his voice almost a whisper. "Did you not hear me? The mayor has the race to consider. I'm running against him, and he doesn't like it one bit. If he sacrifices me to clear his precious name, he'll get a bonus prize. He'll be a shoo-in for re-election."

"I won't let him," Abby said, and a thousand memories flooded back. There was a half-moon scar on his right shoulder. When he'd carried his backpack in high school, he'd used only one strap, so the bag dangled by his side. He'd bought her Dr Pepper from the vending machine on the mornings she'd drug herself to school, too tired from studying to fully wake up. One night, with the stars woven above them, he'd cupped her face in his hands and said her name like a question. "Abby?" She'd kissed him instead of answering, but the answer was yes.

Abby shook her head to clear it. She was being drawn into the eye of a hurricane, she knew that for sure, but wasn't the eye the one place that was calm and steady?

This feeling was something not even the Leading Ladies talked about. What to do when desire threatened to override common sense. Maybe they didn't struggle. The ones who were married had a man at their fingertips, after all, like a love-on-demand service. But Abby was a woman in her prime, and she was alone. What if, for once, she allowed her body to take the lead, all consequences be damned? Here with Josh, with Ian all but throwing her to the curb, she was tempted more than ever.

One small move and she was in Josh's strong arms. She could feel his breath on her neck. He felt both familiar and foreign, old and new. When his lips found hers, everything else fell away. The gazebo might as well have been a hotel room, with everything Abby was feeling. But if it had been, she'd be in a heck of a lot more trouble. Abby pulled away when Josh's hands began to roam. She straightened her clothes.

Just then, the bell sounded for the council to reconvene, Abby and Josh were still breathing heavily when they headed for the senior center.

Mayor Thornton said the executive session had been about an employee issue, which let him off the hook for further public comment. When the meeting adjourned, Cynthia Burke huffed out. Abby, hair disheveled, blazer rumpled, watched from her seat as Josh, tie crooked and his once-crisp shirt wrinkled, headed for the mayor, but Thornton raised his hand and sidestepped him.

Abby touched her cheek. She could feel the damage Josh's stubble had caused. Heat rose to her face and rushed to her belly, just as Lisa, Janie, and Amy pulled her aside. "What the actual heck just happened?" Lisa asked, and Abby knew she wasn't talking about the meeting.

Whats (Really) *Going On?*

QUESTION: Which City Does Our City Attorney Work For?

Joshua Moore, Esquire, Logan's Creek City Attorney and candidate for mayor, MAY be a fine-looking man. Okay, a GORGEOUS MAN. If you think gorgeous means looking like you're a Roman god carved from a slab of MARBLE. Wait, what was my point? Ah, yes, Josh Moore, City Attorney, got called out in last night's CITY COUNCIL MEETING for some allegedly/reportedly/possibly NEFARIOUS dealings. (Using my "ly" words to cover my tail with this one!) And no, this had NOTHING to do with the SPEEDING ticket I uncovered.

During the PUBLIC COMMENTS segment of the meeting (my favorite part!), Ms. Cynthia Burke said she'd been READING L.C. CONFIDENTIAL. Not only reading but taking ACTION. Which meant she'd done her OWN INVESTIGATION into what I'm now calling #FITNESSGATE.

Turns out, Cynthia found RECORDS that showed #lawhunk Josh Moore has been WORKING for OUR COMPETING TOWN, Lone Elm, during that city's successful attempt to get a FITNESS CENTER (which Logan's Creek, doggone it, doesn't have.) WHERE IS OUR FITNESS CENTER?

Anyway, Cynthia SHOOK up the entire meeting, and the council IMMEDIATELY went into EXECUTIVE session, which means EVERYTHING they said was in PRIVATE, and we, the GOOD citizens of Logan's Creek, will NEVER know what kind of wheeling and dealing went on out of our EARSHOT.

In the end, MAYOR Thornton told the audience it was a PERSONNEL issue and promised to look into Josh Moore's PRESUMED double-dipping and POSSIBLE double-crossing of the town he's SUPPOSED to serve.

Eek! It's getting REAL all up in here, y'all. Raise your hand if you want to attend the NEXT city council meeting to see what happens to Josh. Tell you what, if he gets FIRED and needs a little lovingkindness, my door is WIDE open!

Oh yes, I also have his statement about his old speeding ticket. Seems as if he was rushing home to check on his sick mama. OH. MY. WORD. Could you LOVE that any more?

In other news, I've been informed that I'm not ALLOWED to publish the contact information, i.e. home addresses, et al, for THE council members. I took THEM down, y'all. But I still stand by the fact that they live in absolute DOLL HOUSES compared to my HUMBLE abode.

Also, sorry I got everyone to go to the city council meeting to oppose Gus Abernathy's plea for longer TIME in the crosswalk at Cherry and Main. That measure was DEAD IN THE WATER the minute it was pointed out that City Ordinance No. 5-1997 requires that Logan's Creek accommodate ALL REASONABLE requests for time extensions on city crosswalks. (I still THINK we need to define "reasonable"!)

As my grandmama always said, though, pick your battles. So I've given up on THIS one. I've decided to take up crochet and ONLY work while I'm sitting at city stop lights. I should have an AFGHAN in no time. And NO, Gus Abernathy, you CAN'T have it.

Finally, good news for me and @littlemama123. The OFFENDING, potentially pornographic hedges on the COURTHOUSE lawn will be allowed to grow out in a more natural form. Soon, they'll LOOK like what they are—modest shrubs—and not CERTAIN male body parts that God gave us the GOOD sense to cover.

I know, I know. No update on the mayoral race between MAYOR Thornton and CITY ATTORNEY Josh Moore, which I promise you I WILL do, and it WILL be worth the wait. I'll just leave you with THIS. While Cynthia Burke was taking down Josh Moore, she ALSO called Mayor Thornton a bald-faced LIAR. What exactly does she KNOW? Cynthia, reach out! I'd LOVE to hear your story. Okay, y'all, that's it for now. Talk to YOU soon!

Chapter Eight

"Sometimes you need to leave and never look back." That was the last thing Josh had said to her last night, his voice raspy. They'd been discussing failed strategies of other candidates, but somehow it felt like he was telling her something else. Also, Ian was now ghosting her.

Work and love were a heady combination—she knew that from her time with Ian—but it was also dangerous. So far, she and Josh had only talked on the phone.

Mayor Thornton had yet to speak to Josh about the council meeting. The way Josh put it, he was being treated like a relative you knew was being cut from the will, but you still had to get through the funeral with him. Courteous and formal, but absolutely no warmth. Neither Abby nor Josh had mentioned what had happened in the gazebo.

Still, the sentence was ringing in her ears when Amanda messaged her this morning:

> *You're meeting the Realtor at the cabin by the creek at ten this morning. No excuses! Enough time with Mr. and Mrs. Carter, Abby. I swear, living at home is making you regress. Did I really see you in your Logan's Creek Cougar letter jacket the other day? LOL. Next thing you know, you'll be wearing a high ponytail and binge-watching New Girl. Go look at the cabin! It's a steal.*

Abby texted back:
> *Yes, Kween!*

She figured using the vernacular from the 2010s would only solidify what Amanda had been thinking, but so what? Maybe she was reliving a little bit of her high school days. It wasn't like she planned to stay there. She was a campaign manager, for goodness' sake. Okay, so the campaign was for her high school boyfriend, but still. She was doing the best she could.

Abby sipped her coffee at the kitchen island. Both her parents had gone to work, and the place was hers. She looked at the clock on the microwave. She had two hours until she needed to be at the cabin. She thought about calling Cathy. If she was going to drop that much cash while she was still in career limbo, she needed another opinion. Then she realized it was a busy day at the restaurant (it was ten-dollar lunch day) and thought better of it. Lisa would have been the obvious choice, but she was out of town.

Abby hurried to the den, where her laptop sat on the oak desk. She had time to look over the media buys for Josh's campaign. When she'd nearly finished the budget for radio ads, her phone rang. Abby sighed as she picked up the phone. And then she looked. The name on the screen read *Ian*.

Ian's voice was smooth, and Abby closed her eyes at the sound of it. "How are you?" he asked, and she felt the question pinging through her body. How did he do that?

"I've been better," Abby said, feeling the familiar sting in her throat. She realized she was angry. Or maybe she was feeling guilty. She had kissed Josh, after all.

Silence. And then Ian said, "That makes two of us." Abby was ready for a fight, but then Ian said, "Listen, Abby, I didn't call to argue." He took a breath she could hear.

"If I recall," Abby said as her temper flared, "you didn't fight me when we agreed to a break. Now, we're two weeks in and you're calling me. Why, Ian?"

She didn't know how she did it. Abby was both thrilled Ian had finally called, and furious that he'd done so. A therapist would have a field day with her.

"All I did was agree to it; it was your idea." Another pause. "Things were so good between us in Chicago. I should have told you how much you mean…" Ian stopped. Was he going to say the L word? "I know I was part of the problem." Abby could hear him swallow.

"*Part* of the problem?" Abby repeated. "I'd say it's a lot more than that. I'll admit I left abruptly. So, bad on me, Ian. But I did try to tell you how unhappy I'd become. You spent so much time away that when we were together, all I wanted to do was be with you. Make the rest of the world go away. You knew some of what was going on at the firm, but not nearly everything."

Abby could hear Ian sigh. "We did that, didn't we? Made the world go away."

Was he sweet-talking her? Incredible! Abby felt her anger rise higher. "So, what? You think you can make one phone call, and all this will be behind us?"

Abby could hear Ian turning down the television. News was playing, and Abby had heard the word *hostages*. "Not Esme again," Ian said.

Abby paced. "If I never hear her name again, it won't be soon enough."

"Look, Abby, I thought we could have an honest conversation. I miss you. On shoots especially."

Abby loved being on shoots with Ian. The attention he gave his subjects was volcanic. As he moved with his camera, she imagined what he saw. So much more than anyone else, she supposed. When he tilted a model's head this way, or adjusted a nearby light, she could almost interpret what he was thinking. She knew what that kind of attention felt like. When they were alone, his eyes trained on her, his hands following the map of her body, she felt exceptional.

She wanted him back, she did, but she also wanted more. Hadn't her dad chosen her mom the first time he'd seen her? Hadn't he stayed by her side every day since?

"We *are* having an honest conversation," she said. "A not-so-very-pleasant honest conversation. I did what I did, and I'm sorry it hurt you. But what about you? A real man might have jumped on a plane and followed me to Logan's Creek. Taken me in his arms. Told me everything was going to be okay. But you? You dropped out at the first sign of trouble."

The line was so quiet, that Abby wondered if he'd put down the phone. And then he said, "I never in a million years thought you wanted a man like that. Since the day I met you, you've been adamant about having your freedom. Your independence. Your space. The woman I thought you were would have hated a man showing up in her hometown like some stalker."

Abby remembered the way Ian looked after they'd spent the night together. Ian, without a shirt, whipping up omelets, and biscuits, because Abby had grown up on biscuits. The tattoo of an Argus 75 camera on his left bicep. His wavy dark hair falling to his shoulders.

It would be easy for Abby to say I'm sorry, to say she still wasn't the kind of woman who wanted to be chased, that she'd made a huge mistake. But Ian was right. They'd been lovers with separate lives. Was that enough? Abby didn't know anymore.

Abby let the hammer down. "I'm selling my apartment in Chicago," she said.

"Well," Ian said, and then nothing else.

"Well," Abby repeated. They'd been as close as air and smoke, and she could feel him still.

Finally, he said, "I won't call again. Not until the month is up. Per your instructions," he said, the sarcasm heavy in his voice. "But we owe it to ourselves to figure this out. I care enough about you to want you to be happy, with or without me. That's how I know this is real. You rammed a dagger in my heart, and all I could say was, 'Don't worry about me, folks. Make sure Abby is okay. Make sure my girl is fine.'"

After the line went dead, Abby felt the kind of jittery energy that comes with great emotion. She almost felt euphoric, but that wasn't quite it. It was the other side of euphoria. She was like a woman who'd planned her own doom and was thrilled because she was still around to witness it happen. What did that say about the kind of person she was?

Abby pushed away thoughts of Ian when she pulled up to Josh's office to drop off proofs for the yard signs she planned to plant all over town. She wanted to get the proofs to him before she met with the Realtor. She needed to see him, to prove that the kisses they'd shared were from the emotion of the moment and nothing else.

Josh rose from his antique desk, the legs carved with images of pineapples and tropical birds. She'd have to get the story behind it one day. "What a nice surprise," he said. When he stood, she was caught off guard by his physical presence. He held so much power in that frame.

Focus, Abby thought. And then she said, "I messaged L.C. Confidential to thank them for clearing up your speeding ticket controversy. But that still leaves the Lone Elm allegations."

Josh motioned for Abby to sit. "Listen," he said. "I've been thinking. Let's give it a little time. I've done nothing wrong. I was a little thrown at the meeting, but I'm better now."

Abby wondered if "thrown" meant he regretted what had happened between them. He probably did. "Look," she said, ready to tackle what had happened between them.

Josh said, "Let's not rehash last night. It was a moment. I get it. But if we dissect it, it will turn into a diagnosis. A slip back into the past. I'd like to keep last night exactly as it was."

"We can't—," Abby said, and Josh interrupted. "I know. I know."

Abby pulled the proofs from her portfolio. "Right," she said. "Here are several options for your yard signs. I like the blue ones with the white font. 'Do Moore for Logan's Creek. Vote Josh!'" Abby said, like a cheerleader. She reached for another and blushed. "On a whim I had this one made. 'I Want Moore.' There's one for families and businesses that reads 'We Want Moore.'"

Josh laughed, and the laughter reached his dark eyes. "Catchy," he said. Then she said, "And we haven't even discussed my swimsuit idea."

There was that spark again.

Josh had a squishy stress ball on his desk, about the size of a golf ball. He tossed to her. She caught it, while he said, "Do not objectify me, Ms. Carter." And then he grinned. "Nah. Objectify me all you want."

The air felt alive, and finally, Abby looked at the floor. Josh said, "Stay for coffee." And Abby answered, "I wish I could. I'm meeting my Realtor in a bit."

"You don't say."

"I'm looking at a cabin on Logan's Creek. You know the one. Green metal roof, next to the swimming spot we used to go to in high school."

Those dimples again, and then Josh said, "How could I forget? Remember when we used to go down there and..."

Abby threw the ball back at him. "Josh!" she said, and it was enough to make him stop.

"Hey, want some company? Or is your family going with you?"

"They don't even know I'm looking. According to Amanda, I'm reverting to my teenage years by living with my parents. She set up the showing. Doesn't want me to get stuck."

"Well then." Josh said. "But just so you know, if you do return to your teenage self, let me know. You were fire!"

"Oh, stop it," Abby said and grinned. Those days weren't the worst in her life. Not by a long shot.

Josh had been fiddling with the radio as they drove. Right now, "Uptown Funk" by Bruno Mars was playing. "You used to love this song," Josh said, and Abby said, "I still do."

The gravel path to the cabin had a few weeds growing in it, but that was to be expected. There was a wooden fence with a wide gate that was open. On either side was a pine log that reached high, holding a shorter log between them. A welcome sign hung by one corner in the very center. Beyond that, there was a cabin that made Abby want to start a new Pinterest board called "Heaven on Earth."

Dawn Collins, the Realtor representing the owner, met them at the front of the cabin and introduced herself. Abby couldn't tell how old she was, maybe fifty? Dawn wore beige pantyhose, something Abby hadn't seen in a while, and her pale hair was piled on top of her head in a tumble of curls. The hot pink blazer she wore had the cuffs turned up, showing a polka-dot lining. The turned-up cuffs said a lot to Abby, but mostly that Dawn was wider than she was tall.

After introductions, Dawn said, "It's lovely, isn't it? And quite the bargain." Not waiting for an answer, she tapped the code in the lockbox and opened the pebbled glass door. "Take your time," she said. "I know couples need privacy when making a big decision like this." Abby started to protest, but then Josh said, "With instincts like that, Ms. Collins, I'll bet you're making a fortune." You could almost see Dawn collapse at the attention.

Dawn touched Josh's sleeve and said, conspiratorially. "Mr. Johnson just wants out of it. He bought the cabin thinking he would be living here half of the year, but his wife hated it." She rubbed Josh's arm. "Can you imagine? She was a city girl." Dawn scrunched her nose as if something smelled off when she said the words *city girl*. "The missus wasn't having any of this country cabin business, poor thing." She waved her arm. "Take all the time you need."

The cabin sat about fifty yards from the water. Logan's Creek was an anomaly; it was bigger than any creek Abby had seen, and it was a tributary for the Arkansas River. Here, though, the water resembled a small lake. Abby couldn't wait to see the sun set. She had a thing for sunsets.

As they entered the front door, Abby saw rafters made of northern white cedar.

The two-bedroom, two-bath structure had light pine floors and large, west-facing windows that let in lots of afternoon light. The cabin had normal signs of wear and tear—there was a missing cabinet pull in the kitchen, and a water stain on the floor near the back door—but nothing that couldn't be fixed.

What she loved the most was the back deck that overlooked the creek. There was a small two-person hot tub right outside the French doors, directly off the living space.

Oaks and elms grew near a patch of pine trees. A small boat dock sat on the opposite shore. It had just the right amount of privacy.

A heron swooped across the creek, visible from the wide windows. Farther away, a boat's motor hummed. Josh put his hand on Abby's shoulder. She could feel the energy pulsing from his body to hers. "Let's check out the other rooms," he said.

They walked upstairs and into one of the two bedrooms. Abby rested her hand on the iron bedstead. "I wonder if the beds stay with the sale?" she asked, and suddenly *bed* sounded like a word from an R-rated movie. Josh sat down on the floral bedcover, and the springs squeaked. The two of them alone in a bedroom felt far too intimate, maybe even dangerous. Abby rushed to the window and pulled aside the sheer curtains. She looked through the glass as if she was trying to see something a far distance away.

Abby could see Josh reflected in the window. He was leaning on his elbow. He had his legs bent at the knees, his polished shoes hanging off the bed. "Sometimes furnishings are negotiated with the sale, depending on the situation." He grinned, and the corners of his eyes crinkled. He patted the mattress. "Nice bed, though," as if tempting her to sit next to him. Abby folded her arms and turned to him. "I'm more interested in the view," she said.

Josh sat up, and in that bedroom voice of his, said, "The view is astonishing."

Dawn met them on the front porch.

"A great little place, isn't it?" she asked. "Won't be on the market long." She tapped a glittery ink pen on the cover of her rose-colored notebook.

"I really don't understand Mr. Johnson. I'd have kept the cabin and gotten rid of the missus," Dawn cackled, amused by her own joke. "But then I wouldn't be making a nice commission, would I?"

Although Dawn was talking to Josh, Abby spoke up, "I know I'm supposed to play hard to get, but Dawn, I love this place." Abby handed her a slip of paper with her email address. "Could you email me the particulars?"

Josh looked at her sideways. "When you know, you know," she said. And just like that, she felt like her old self again. Decisive, unafraid.

Dawn tugged the sleeve of her pink blazer, her impressive bosom challenging the pearl buttons of her blouse. "I certainly can, Ms. Carter." She'd probably realized she would be dealing with Abby alone. It likely disappointed her.

It was nearly three o'clock when Abby dropped Josh off downtown. The sidewalks were busy with shoppers. A few people on the courthouse lawn, at the end of Main Street, were eating ice cream by the fountain.

"Thanks for your help today," Abby said, careful to keep her hand on the gear shift.

Josh turned toward her, put his hand on the top of her headrest. "The cabin suits you, Abby," he said. "I'm glad you're home."

Coming from a Leading Lady, those comments would have been welcome. But Abby felt Josh was saying so much more.

Whats (Really) **L.C.** *Going On?*

TOPIC: They call her the streak.

While most of us are tied up in knots over this year's political season, not everything that happens in Logan's Creek is about the danged election.

Take for instance, yesterday. I was MINDING my own business, doing some face yoga, (You're never too YOUNG to start worrying about wrinkles.) when I heard my handy-dandy police scanner blaring.

A patrol car was called to Willow Street, near the high school, by a caller who claimed a NAKED woman was sprinting down the sidewalk. When they arrived, a Mrs. Evelyn (LAST NAME OMITTED FOR PRIVACY) was indeed in a full trot, with not one piece of clothing on.

What happened is this. Mrs. Evelyn had been using her outside shower, after GARDENING, and she'd stripped down to her birthday suit, like you do, when she noticed a big, brown snake hanging from the shower spout.

Mrs. Evelyn told police, "I was so scared, I just took off. Didn't even grab my towel. Now, half the town has saw more than my husband has in more than fifteen years." (I heard this on the SCANNER.)

Well, one of the officers took off his OFFICIAL shirt and threw it across Mrs. Evelyn, at about the time the three o'clock bell rang. The high school students were spared a lesson in anatomy they certainly weren't ready for.

I kept listening, wondering if the poor Mrs. Evelyn was going to be charged with indecent exposure, but I'm HAPPY to report that didn't happen.

Calling back to the station, one of the officers said, and I quote. "Nah, we're not taking her in; it was an HONEST mistake. If I had a medal, I'd give it to her. Fastest sixty-year-old woman I ever saw."

Police took Mrs. Evelyn home, got rid of the snake, and waited for her to dress so they could get their uniform back.

My grandmama, rest her soul, loved Ray Stephens. He had a song in the

1970s about the phenomenon of public nudity. Back then it was called streaking; the NUDE and PROUD would run across a football field, the stage at the Oscars, or most anywhere a crowd gathered. After Mrs. Evelyn was home safe, I looked up the song on YouTube. I'd send it to Mrs. Evelyn if I wasn't afraid she'd take offense. I think she'd get a kick out of Ethel, one of the song's main characters, that is, if she could ease up on herself the least little bit.

Chapter Nine

Two weeks had gone by and still Abby was waiting to hear if Josh was in trouble with the City. In the meantime, Abby had staged a photo shoot around town, showing Josh at all the places he loved. One photo was by the trophy case at Logan's Creek High School. In the background, an entire shelf held Josh's old football trophies.

In another photo, he was helping Mr. Abernathy cross the street. Potential voters, or at least potential female voters were eating it up. Abby knew, because now *Josh for Mayor* had a Facebook page, Instagram, X, and TikTok. His followers were mostly female.

The Logan's Creek Courier had run a story on Josh. The local radio station contacted Abby to see if she wanted to buy spots. Even the state paper, the Arkansas Caller, featured Josh in an article titled: Moore Ideas Influence Mayor's Race.

Josh had made appearances at the Blackberry Festival, the Vintage Car Rally, and the Stuff the Bus event in front of Walmart. He'd helped load school supplies for kids who needed them onto the yellow bus. A slew of young moms had shown up to help him. Abby had never seen so much eyelash batting and hair flipping in her life.

Abby had seen the Leading Ladies a few more times, but she'd only told Amanda she was attracted to Josh. Amanda was single, for one thing. For another, she didn't pull punches. She had said, "Take it easy, kiddo. Losing a job is a big life event, even if you orchestrated it. Slow down. And don't forget, we had to bring you back to life after your breakup with him. Plus, what about Ian?"

What about Ian? Abby wondered. She hated it when Amanda was right.

―――♦―――

At home, Abby was being pampered by her parents. Her clothes turned up laundered and folded on her bed, which she hated to admit she loved. Her mom bought Fruit Roll-Ups and an espresso machine just for Abby. But other things were happening too, and these caused her chest to clench. For instance, her dad had borrowed her AirPods and lost them. And once, while she was on the phone, her mom said, "Isn't it about time for bed, sweetheart?" The time was nine o'clock.

It was going to be hard to tell her parents she was moving out; they'd done so much for her. She and the Leading Ladies had recently gone back to the cabin for a thorough going-over. How the word hadn't spread to her parents, she'd never know. Then, Dawn the Realtor had taken her low-bid offer to the Johnsons, who'd immediately accepted it.

Sure, it was a rash decision for a barely employed woman. But she had years to recoup the money she'd taken from her 401k, and she could pay the insurance and taxes she'd owe from the sale of her apartment, and make a rather significant down payment. That was the real news. A recent graduate of The University of Chicago, who'd lived in a studio apartment one floor up from Abby, was looking to buy. Well, her parents wanted to buy, but the new grad would be living there. In the rush to leave Chicago, it had slipped Abby's mind. When she'd contacted the tenant, they'd made a quick deal.

The same day, Abby had heard from her former assistant Joy. It seemed that John Willis had tanked his newest dog food campaign, and Mr. Cromby was livid. As Joy described it, the head of Bow Wow Chow Chow had come to the office for the final reveal. John, who'd never had a pet in his life, and didn't have Abby to save him, depended on his creativity alone. His tagline was, "Buy Bow Wow Chow Chow; It's Now or Never. Your Four-Legged Friend Won't Live Fur-ever."

Melancholy music played as a senior collie walked into the sunset. Or as Joy said, limped into the sunset.

Maybe Cromby was missing Abby about now. The thought made her smile. Now, on to the next step. She had to tell her parents she was moving.

It was after dinner on a Tuesday night when Abby found her parents sitting on the patio drinking their after-dinner coffee and having dessert. Tonight, it was cherry cobbler. As Abby stood in the doorway, listening, Abby caught her mom say, "As naked as a jaybird." Just then, her dad laughed. "You're greening me, Gabby," he said. "Come on."

They still seemed so young. Her mother loved to dance. Her father loved the outdoors and old cars. He still talked about the times he'd taken Mom on dates in the cars he'd fixed up to sell, showing her off to the town. Abby could close her eyes and see her mom now. Red lipstick. High heels. Abby's dad with his dress shirt on, smelling of after shave.

This must be what it's like to have someone to share your whole life with, Abby thought. She smiled as she watched them sitting side by side, holding hands. When her parents noticed her, they unclasped their hands and waved her in. "Sit," her dad said, and pointed to the wicker settee across from them. There was a handmade coffee table separating them. Jim had built the wooden frame, and Gabby had covered the top with pieces of broken crockery she'd collected over the years. The table looked like a happy accident—a pink flower here from a cracked teapot, an orange fish there from a platter Abby had dropped when she was eight.

"How's the campaign going?" Gabby asked.

Before Abby could reply, Jim said, "I hate to say it, but Thornton is going to be hard to beat. He's been in politics his whole life." Jim stretched out, putting his hands behind his head. He crossed his legs at the ankles. "He was the dog catcher right out of college."

Gabby slapped his arm. "Max Thornton was not the dog catcher. He was animal control. He wrangled that copperhead out of Mama's garden for her, remember?" Jim shook his head yes, and Gabby continued, "He's right, though, honey. Thornton has a whole lot of name recognition. I hope you and Josh don't get disappointed."

"Maybe I should quit," Abby joked, and Jim said, "Oh, you."

Abby put on her best adult face. "There's something I wanted to talk to you about. I should have already, but I hadn't had the guts to."

"What is it?" Gabby asked.

"I sold my apartment in Chicago. It closes next Wednesday, and I have to be there to sign the papers."

"Why, Abby, that's good news," Gabby said.

"The other thing is, I'm buying a cabin on Logan's Creek. The one with the green roof that we used to float by when we'd take our innertubes."

Gabby frowned. "Oh, honey, don't you think you're moving rather quickly?"

"You know you can stay here as long as you want. I understand you need your space but—" Jim said.

"That's it, dad. I do need my space. I'm a thirty-year-old woman, and I'm starting to plan my whole day around what mom's cooking for dinner. If you two tucked me in bed tonight and read me a story, I wouldn't resist. I have to start adulting.

Gabby said, "It's just that we've missed most of your adult life. You were out of Logan's Creek like a flash when you were barely eighteen. We like having you home."

Abby felt, what? Maybe a little shame? She had left as soon as she could. The world was too enticing. Logan's Creek was too small. And it had hurt her parents. "You know you mean everything to me," Abby said, her voice an apology.

"Oh, sweetie," Gabby said, and for a second Abby thought they both might cry.

Jim, who was always quick with a diversion, but seldom great at its execution, said, "Save your drama for your grandmama, little lady.

Now give us a hug."

Abby felt like going to her bedroom, getting on Instagram, and posting a story. "I can do hard things," she'd say in the video. "I can do all the hard things."

Maybe she was dramatic.

The following Wednesday, Abby looked around her Chicago apartment one last time. There were grooves in the carpet where her couch had been. There was a circle of nail holes, hidden by the beige carpet, where Ian had hammered a Christmas tree stand into the floor, when the fir tree kept falling over. As she checked the closets, she remembered moving in, the rush of buying a place. She'd been young, but she knew property values would skyrocket one day. She'd stayed long enough to see that happen.

In an hour or so, none of it would be hers.

Mostly, it was Ian she felt here, or the ghost of him. She could see him standing by the large windows that overlooked the Chicago River as it worked its way through downtown.

They had made love on a quilt thrown over this carpet more times than she could count, a blanket of stars right outside. The moon had been like a giant's lamp, illuminating them both. These windows had witnessed it all.

Their month long break was up now. Actually, it had ended yesterday. Neither of them had called.

Signing the apartment over wasn't as hard as she'd expected. It was done in a sterile office at a nondescript table, so it had the feeling of signing a tax form. The neutral atmosphere made the transaction so much easier. And the money helped her afford the cabin. She could even redecorate if she wanted.

Once the signing was done, she went to the Hilton and thought about what to do next. She didn't want to leave town with unfinished business. Selling the apartment made her realize that. And since keying Cromby's car wasn't on the agenda (well, it was still *penciled* in), she knew her only other option was to see Ian.

Ian picked up before the phone even buzzed. "Abby," he said. "Abby."

She made sure her voice was even. "It's been more than a month," she said. "You haven't called."

"I didn't know what to say. All I wanted to say was come home. But home isn't Chicago anymore, is it?"

Abby paced. "I did it, Ian. I sold my apartment. Just now, thirty minutes ago." She hesitated. "I'm in Chicago, Ian. I'm here."

"I would congratulate you, Abby, but my heart's not in it."

"Do better than that," Abby said. "Take me to dinner."

"Dinner?" Ian asked. In the seconds it took him to respond, he seemed to give in to something. "Sure," he said. "At our usual place? Seven o'clock. We'll beat the crowd."

"I'll see you there," she said. It felt as if she were mapping out a new continent. She wasn't about to turn back now.

Two hours later she was waiting at a table at Luigi's on Tenth and Cleveland Street. Luigi's was the first place he'd taken her to dinner. They'd shared a bottle of merlot that night. Later, they'd told each other their life stories.

Ian was walking toward her now. Abby didn't know how he did it. Ian was three inches shorter than Josh, but he seemed to take up more space. She felt that familiar buzzing in her body, like she'd been awakened even though she hadn't realized she'd been asleep.

Dressing for tonight had been difficult. She didn't know what message she wanted to send. It felt like the end of something. She remembered a line from a book where the main character said that the only gift she ever wanted was to be forewarned of an ending. If she knew, she'd dress the part. She'd wear the gold jewelry. She'd paint on a pouty lip. A woman should be able to leave a lasting impression at the end of a relationship. So, Abby had rummaged through her luggage until she'd found what Ian liked. Her oldest jeans, worn soft as a baby blanket. Black leather booties with spiked heels. A halter top, in emerald, covered by a cropped white jacket.

Ian looked as if he might faint when he saw her. It could have been her eyes. She had eyeliner wings that extended a little too far past the corner of her eyes. Her eyeshadow was the color of storm clouds. And there was a lot of it.

"Hi," she said, reaching out her hand.

Ian took it. He was wearing a Henley shirt. Hiking boots. Jeans without an impressive label. A rough metal cross on a leather chain hung around his neck. Abby's eyes were as blue as the sky, but Ian's were the blue-gray of a troubled sea.

His hand felt like a magnet.

"You look..." He ran his hand over his shoulder-length hair. She could smell the shampoo he used, something with sandalwood. "Took me a few to find a spot to park."

"No worries," Abby said. Her voice was soft and low. "I've been sitting here remembering how many dinners we've had in this place. All good, no?"

Ian sat. "Yes," he said. "Good."

When the server arrived, Ian waved her away. "A few minutes, please," he said. Again, he raked his fingers through his hair. "Let me start by..."

But Abby cut him off. "I have an idea," she said. "No *I'm sorry*. No apologies. I don't know what tomorrow holds any more than you do." She rubbed his foot with hers. "All I have to offer is tonight.

"What do you say?" she asked. Abby leaned forward, her elbows on the table. A red candle covered in black webbing flickered between them.

"Let me get the car," Ian said as he stood. He left a fifty-dollar bill on the table. Abby took a sip of her water, dropped her linen napkin on the table and followed him.

Abby shivered as Ian worked the lock on his apartment. He pocketed the key and led her by the hand into his living room. It had been months since she'd been in his apartment, but it looked much like it always had. She took a breath. The place smelled like Ian. He had that outdoorsman, cedary, woodsy smell.

Abby slipped off her jacket while Ian went to the kitchen to fix them a drink. A series of his photos from Cambodia lined one wall. On another, a mural of the remains of Tintern Abbey in Wales took up most of the space, a clear sky showing where the roof should have been. He fiddled with his phone until David Gray began to sing from the speakers mounted near the ceiling. "Babylon" was playing, and Abby felt the music in her bones.

Ian wasn't a clean freak, but he was neat enough. His couch and chairs seemed super-sized, as if he'd gone to the drive-thru window of a furniture store and decided to upsize the whole room.

He handed Abby a mimosa, her favorite cocktail. "For my girl," he said, his eyes a tempest. He'd always kept champagne for her in his refrigerator, and orange juice. She was shocked he still did. Abby felt liquid heat rush through her veins. It would have happened with or without the alcohol. He was drinking bourbon—he always drank bourbon. They both seemed nervous.

Was Abby his girl? She wondered. It barely seemed to matter now, with him so close she could see his pulse thrumming in his neck. "So," Abby said after she took another sip.

"So," Ian repeated.

Abby had taken a poetry class in college. The professor had said there was as much being said in the spaces of a stanza as in the words themselves. The quiet spaces, the silences. Ian was that poem come to life. He craved her, she knew it. Abby's heart pounded.

Without a word, Ian closed the distance between them, his hand caressing her cheek. He took his glass and set it down on the nearby table. He took her champagne flute and did the same.

Abby leaned into his touch, her eyes fluttering closed as she felt the warmth of his hands against her skin. He touched the spot where her heart beat, and seemed to marvel. "Abby," he said, his voice a plea.

Ian pulled her into his arms. Abby melted against him. At that moment, the rest of the world seemed far away, leaving only the two of them here. And the fire that was between them.

His mouth was hard on hers. His fingers tangled in her hair. Her silky top left her shoulders exposed, and she groaned when Ian's teeth grazed her skin.

There was love and there was desire, and then there was this. It was primal. Necessary. If someone had come to the door, they both would have yelled for them to leave, manners be damned. What was happening felt like a spell, like something otherworldly. If they'd taken flight, she wouldn't have batted an eye. Weren't they flying already?

Abby gripped Ian's hair with her fists. They tumbled onto the big couch. "Not here," he said, tugging her up again.

Without another word, he led her to his tidy bed, his hand holding hers. It almost seemed innocent. Then, he lifted her onto the bed. He was looming over her, his hair hanging around his face. She said, "This is probably a mistake." Her hands were cupping his face. Her breathing was rapid.

"It's a terrible mistake," Ian said. He kissed her neck, her eyelids, the fine bones of her wrists, the corners of her mouth.

Abby called his name. It was all she could think to do. "Ian." Two syllables that contained the entire universe. "Ian."

He answered with his body. They were past language now. Words wouldn't make sense.

Chapter Ten

Abby and Ian had always gravitated to their side of the bed, but last night, Abby had slept with her head on Ian's chest, her arm thrown across him. Now, Ian raised up on his elbow and smiled down at her. The morning sun came in through the window, and a swatch of light illuminated them. Abby tugged the white sheet higher just as Ian reached to tug it down.

Her phone began to buzz, threatening to bring Abby back to the real world. She kissed Ian. Then kissed him harder, willing the phone to stop. He climbed over her, and tossed her phone from the nightstand to the floor, where it landed on last night's discarded clothes. For as long as they could, they ignored the buzzing, and then her ringtone started, which was Miley Cyrus singing "Flowers." Ian grinned down at her when he heard the tune about a woman sending herself flowers, taking care of her own needs. "You really think you're better alone than with me?" he asked, referencing the song. He was teasing her, touching her, knowing at that moment at least, he was in charge. When Ian raised her arms above her head and held both her wrists with one of his hands, she said "maybe," knowing it was the one word that would make him keep doing what he'd been doing.

Ian climbed out of bed to shower, and Abby pulled the comforter around her. She'd been in a fog since the night before. It was as if time didn't matter, rules didn't matter, only she and Ian mattered. She would have stayed there, too, if that damn phone had only stopped.

"Somebody's really trying to find you, Abby Girl," Ian said once he was in the adjoining bathroom.

Abby walked to the pile of clothes, and retrieved her phone and Ian's shirt. She slipped on the Henley, watching it fall to her knees, and crawled back in bed. Forty-two missed messages. Abby sighed. She waited for the shower to start, to open the messages. As she read "WHERE RU? and CALL ME! and several versions of PICK UP THE PHONE, her heart sank, and she felt her cheeks flame. All the messages were from Josh. She remembered the feel of his arms around her, the stubble on his cheeks, his mouth on hers. She trembled at the thought of what might have happened between them.

Abby sat up straighter. The facts were this: she and Ian had been on a break. Might still be on a break for all she knew. Nothing had happened, when you got right down to it. Abby was done judging herself.

She'd deal with whatever was going on with Josh, but first, she needed coffee. As she poured two cups from the coffee maker that looked as complicated as a time machine, Ian came into the kitchen, his hair wet. He came up behind her and kissed her on her neck.

He smelled of Dior Sauvage, his favorite scent. She'd bought him a bottle last Christmas. It had staying power, just like him. She almost said as much, but then he was at the fridge, leaning in. They'd been so good together and now, well...

"Would you like a yogurt or some berries?" Ian asked. She was grateful he wasn't going to discuss last night—or this morning—with her. He turned back to her. "Or I could make an omelet and biscuits before I head out."

"I've got to head home. I've done what I came to do."

Ian raised an eyebrow. "Have you now?" He was teasing her.

"You know what I mean."

"What if I'm not done?" he said, something like a dare in his voice. It took one step to reach her, and another to lift her onto the granite countertop.

Memories came flooding back. The meals they'd cooked together. The ones he'd cooked for her while she was working on a project. The movies they'd watched while piled on his sofa. The time she'd introduced him to Jason Isbell's music, and they'd danced for hours. "Ian," she said, when he kissed his way down her neck to her shoulder.

And then her damn phone rang again.

"You should get it," Ian said, pulling away. Abby didn't want to talk to Josh in front of Ian.

"No," Abby said, lifting her chin, and with that word the fog that had made everything a fairy tale lifted.

Ian folded his arms across his chest. He was shirtless, and his muscles flexed when he did it. "Why not?" he asked.

Abby hesitated, but finally said, "Fine," and slid off the counter. Once in the bedroom, she picked up the phone. "This is Abby."

Josh explained the crisis. Someone identified only as a *concerned citizen* had distributed political flyers titled Moore Trouble than a Bag of Snakes. The one-pager asked questions. Was Josh a crook, a conman, a dirty lawyer, a no-good politician, and the worst of all, not a Razorback fan?

Abby sat on the bed and rubbed her forehead. "Josh," she said, "I'll make a plan. I'm in Chicago right now, but I'll head home. Do not talk to the press without me. Do not issue a statement without me. We'll figure this out."

When Abby went back to the kitchen, Ian was wiping down the counters. "Everything okay?" he asked. "It's not your parents, is it?"

Ian looked so wholesome standing there, a sponge in his hands.

"That was Josh," Abby said.

"Josh, as in Josh, your first true love?" Ian's voice had a sharp edge.

"It's not like that," Abby said. "He's running for mayor. I'm running his campaign."

Ian tossed the sponge in the sink. "That's news to me," he said.

Abby walked to the bedroom and dressed, then returned. She picked up her purse from the leather chair that sat nearby. "It wouldn't have been if you'd bothered to ask." The temperature in the room had dropped, and Abby shivered. "I'm going home. I've got some things to attend to."

Ian narrowed his eyes. "I can see that you do."

Abby faced him. "Not that I owe you an explanation, but here it is anyway. I needed a job. Josh needed a campaign manager that understood him. I have a non-compete, so no ad work." Abby closed her eyes and shook her head. "Which is pretty stupid since I'm in Logan's Creek." She paused. "In Arkansas. By the way, is Cromby still a client of yours?"

When Ian was upset, he tapped his foot. Right now, he was a woodpecker. "Don't turn this around on me," he said.

"Of course not. Why should you give up a client just because they did me wrong?" She laughed a hollow laugh.

Before he could answer, Abby turned on her heels and marched out of the apartment.

As soon as Abby got in the Uber she'd called, she messaged the Leading Ladies. She wasn't ready to talk about Ian, but Josh was another subject.

Abby:
> *Sold my apartment. Heading home. What's going on with the flyers?*

Cathy:
> *OMG, Abby! The flyers. One was on my car windshield when I was leaving the restaurant this morning. I'll bet that old battle ax Thornton is behind it.*

Janie:
> *I saw one on the desk of the bank president when I was in there. I told him he should throw it away because it was crap.*

Amanda:
> *I'd bet money that Thornton's behind this. He plays dirty.*

Abby:

And not one of you told me?

Abby could see dots appear on her phone screen. Apparently, each of them had called and texted multiple times. Before they could ask what was up, Abby typed:

Had phone issues. Sorry.

After Abby checked out of her hotel, she called Josh but got his voicemail. "Call me when you get my message. We need to talk more about damage control."

It was after midnight when Abby arrived home, so she was careful not to wake her parents. On the drive, Josh had called back. They'd meet in a few hours to sort out this mess. Abby had just grabbed a bottle of water from the fridge when she noticed the flyer on the counter.

Of course, by then she'd seen a screenshot, but that didn't do it justice. It was red and white with bold blue lettering. It looked like something you'd see on a community board when people were angry about something and wanted to lash out.

The body of the flyer read:

Do you want a crook, a conman, a dirty politician, a no-good lawyer, a man who DOES NOT support the Razorbacks as your mayor?
Vote AGAINST Josh Moore.

A: Does our City Attorney line his pockets with gold from Lone Elm?
There are receipts you need to see.

B: Is he responsible for Logan's Creek not getting its own fitness center and pool? **Sure looks like it!**

C: Is Moore just another lowdown political hack? **Hmm!**

D: Have you ever heard him Call the Hogs?
Me either. Woo Pig Sooie! Razorbacks!

Paid for by a concerned citizen. (This paper is recycled. The ink is soy based.)

Abby couldn't believe what she was reading. These allegations could derail the momentum she'd created. She chugged the entire bottle of water before going upstairs to bed.

She woke when her mom shook her shoulders. "Abby, dear, your alarm is going off." Before Gabby left, she added, "At least wear a little lipstick, honey. You look a bit dreadful this morning." She paused. "No offense."

Abby was too tired to respond. When her mom shook her fifteen minutes later, Abby shot out of bed. She threw on jeans, a clean t-shirt, her running shoes, and a ball cap. Her lipstick was called Black Honey. Not her normal attire for an appointment with a client, but today it would have to do.

"We have a lot to fix here," Abby said as she walked up to Josh's table at Chapters. She was carrying her favorite latte, the steam curling above it.

Josh was dressed nearly identically to her. If Gabby were here, she'd tell him to go splash water on his face. He looked as bad as Abby felt. After Abby sat, Josh lowered his voice, "Makes me want to punch that S.O.B. in the face. I know he's behind this."

Abby started to pat his hand but thought better of it. "You can't go punching the mayor. We have to offset the damage, not cause more. First, we'll issue a statement. I'll write it this afternoon. Then, we'll make a video of you calling the Hogs."

Josh groaned. "You're not serious."

"As serious as a third overtime," Abby said and finally smiled.

Josh grinned. "Back in the day, fans used to sing that old Mac Davis song, 'It's Hard to Be Humble.' Do I need to do that too?"

"I don't think anybody's going to believe you're humble," Abby said, and suddenly the flyer didn't seem like the monster under the bed.

"That's it?" Josh asked, and Abby said, "Not quite. We're going to throw a party."

"Why?"

"Everyone loves a party."

Josh tapped his fingers on the table. He looked Abby in the eye. "We sure loved parties back then."

Abby knew the party he was thinking about. It had been summer. Someone had spiked the punch. When either of them told the story, they ended it with these lines. "Some guy with a raccoon on his shoulder broke it up. We never did know who he was."

Abby rolled her eyes. "We need to get you in front of voters. Let them know you have a plan. So, let's have Cathy host a party at the Tuscan Table to show you off. Glad hand. Kiss a few babies. My ex-boss gave me a nugget of advice when I left. He said I worked hard but didn't entertain clients enough. You're hiding your light under a bushel right now. I'll make you shine.

"Thornton couldn't compete with you in the courtroom, but he does know how to drive that Lincoln like he's leading a parade. Waves with his index finger like he's saluting. Nods. Gets noticed. Give 'em something better, Josh. Give Logan's Creek a genuine connection."

"You think that will work?" Josh asked.

"I do."

"What now?" Josh asked.

"I'm going to see Cathy to compare calendars." Abby poked Josh in the chest. "You stay available. Also, have your assistant contact all the printers in the community to see who printed that mess of a flyer. We've got to find out."

"It has Thornton written all over it," Josh said. "But how is Lacey supposed to get them to tell her who placed the order?"

Abby put her phone away. "You're the attorney, Josh. Figure it out."

Josh side-eyed Abby. He probably wasn't used to so much pushback. "Yes, ma'am," he said.

On her way across Main Street, Abby noticed Ms. Vivian motioning to her from the library door, her black hair bright in the sun.

"Ms. Vivian, are you all right?" she asked when she reached the older woman.

"Oh, of course, young lady. I just thought I'd say hello and see how you're doing since moving back. News gets around, you know."

"I'm well," Abby said. "Thank you for asking."

"I understand you're working with Mr. Josh Moore on his mayoral campaign. How do you think things are going?"

Abby wasn't sure how much to say. Ms. Vivian knew most of the town gossip and might have information Abby needed. "It's been a little rocky, to tell the truth. Why do you ask?"

"No reason. Except..." Ms. Vivian furrowed her brow. "Mayor Thornton's family has been around forever. And like Bermuda grass, the Thorntons are both invasive and aggressive." She rocked on her heels.

Abby stepped closer. "Should I be worried, Ms. Vivian?"

Ms. Vivian looked both ways. She hesitated before saying. "I'm probably being silly, young lady. It comes from having a good imagination."

Just then, someone called Ms. Vivian back inside. When the wind caught her skirt, Abby could see she was wearing knee-high stockings. The sight made her feel tender toward the town librarian.

Still, she wondered exactly what Ms. Vivian knew.

Chapter Eleven

When Abby walked into the Tuscan Table, Cathy was giving last-minute instructions to her servers who'd formed a circle around their boss. It was almost time for the lunch crowd to arrive. Cathy wasn't much different now than when she'd been captain of their high school cheerleading squad. Abby could almost hear her now, clapping her hands and yelling, "Let's get it together, girls!" Abby closed her eyes, remembering. Green and white pom-poms. The smell of popcorn coming from the concession stand. Abby's green and white polyester cheerleading outfit: a short, box-pleated skirt. A polyester sleeveless top. Green Nikes. She'd thought life couldn't get much better. She'd probably been right.

Now, Cathy clapped her hands at her new team. "Let's go!" she said, and the group dispersed, leaving Abby in full view for the first time since she'd come into the restaurant. "I didn't realize you were here." Cathy said. "I was just getting things in order."

"No worries. I'll wait."

"I'm ready. Want an iced tea?"

Abby nodded yes as she walked to what had become their regular table.

"So, what's up? You sounded desperate on the phone." Cathy looked Abby up and down, and Abby tugged the bill of her ball cap lower. "You don't look so good."

"Long night," Abby said, "which is another story altogether. But, yes, I am a little desperate," Abby said, while rummaging through her bag for the party notes she'd written earlier. "The campaign needs help." She shook her head. "With these stupid flyers all over town..."

Just then, a server dropped off an assortment of tiny sandwiches and their drinks. While Abby declined the food, Cathy grabbed the tuna salad. "No rest for the weary," she said as she woofed down the sandwich. When she was finished, she dabbed the corners of her mouth with a cloth napkin. "What do you need from me?"

"I need an over-the-top party for Josh. And I need it to be here. With your food. Your staff. We'll pay your going rate, of course."

The thing Abby had on her side was that Cathy couldn't say no to her. Still, Cathy seemed hesitant. "Girlfriend," she said, "do you know how booked we are? I'll need some advance notice before I can shut down for a night. And it couldn't be a weekend, or Friday night. I'd lose too much money."

Abby waited. In a few seconds, there it was. Cathy's widest smile. "Of course I'll do it."

After they made preliminary plans, the tray of sandwiches was nearly gone. Abby had eaten two. She'd run off the calories later. Maybe drive to the cabin and jog along the creek. Cathy brushed crumbs from the tablecloth into a napkin, and Abby knew it was time to leave. "One last thing," Abby said. "I need another favor."

"You're all out for the day, girl." Cathy joked and then asked, "What is it?"

"I closed on the cabin at the lake."

"Oh my gosh, Abby!"

"I'm moving this weekend. I'd rather Mom and Dad not help. They're not old-old, but still. They've already done so much for me."

Cathy raised her palm to Abby. "Stop right there. The Leading Ladies will do it. How's Saturday morning at eight?" She was typing something into the phone she'd pulled from her apron pocket. "Now get out of here before I put you to work."

As Cathy walked through the swinging doors to the kitchen, she said, "Make sure you have some wine ready for after the move. The Leading Ladies don't work for free."

Once Abby had finished writing Josh's statement concerning the flyer, she emailed it to him to review. It was five o'clock by then. Abby stretched and yawned. Downstairs, her mom was listening to the oldies radio station. The Beatles were singing "Here Comes the Sun."

Abby's phone chimed. She'd set an alarm to remind her to run, but she ached from the long ride home, and her head hurt from worrying about the campaign. She felt an edginess in her heart but was unwilling to investigate. She'd likely find Ian there, and then what would she do?

Instead, she closed her laptop and went downstairs. Gabby was standing at the kitchen sink, a vegetable peeler in one hand, a potato in the other. She was looking out the window above the sink. Abby could tell by the slope of her shoulders that she was sad.

"Mom," she said, and Gabby turned around.

"Come give me a hug," Gabby answered, emptying her hands. When they embraced, Gabby smelled of carrots and garlic and chopped onion.

"You're making roast beef," Abby said.

"My mama's recipe." Gabby wiped her eyes. "She was independent like you. Married late. She might not have married at all if she hadn't wanted us kids so badly."

Abby took a seat on one of the bar stools and raised an eyebrow. "Mom?" she said for the second time.

Gabby waved her hand across the space. "I'm just missing you in advance, is all. This was everything I ever wanted. Jim. You and Dan. A family around the dinner table." She sniffled. "It goes too fast, darling. You'll see that one day."

"How did you know Dad was the one?"

Gabby pushed her fallen sleeve back up to her elbow. "He didn't give up on me."

Abby was asking her to explain when her dad walked through the door.

Moving day had arrived. Abby adjusted the blue bandana that was covering her curls. It was after seven in the morning, and as Abby straightened her bedspread, she remembered the conversation she'd had with Cathy last night. Cathy had ticked off the numbers on her fingers. "Two trucks. Four Leading Ladies at your service. Eight o'clock sharp." Cathy tapped Abby's arm for emphasis. "Your job? Be ready."

Now, Abby placed the last throw pillow on her bed. With that group, she knew they meant it. You could leave a man waiting all you wanted. Days, if you so desired. But never each other.

By seven o'clock, she was ready. Abby poured a coffee to-go and snuck out the kitchen door, heading for the barn, where her stuff was stored. No need to wake her parents. Just then, two pickup trucks barreled up the long drive, honking their horns. Abby rolled her eyes but ran toward them laughing, anyway. The Leading Ladies were not known for their subtlety.

Cathy, her hair in two pigtails, jumped out of one of the trucks, waving. "Ready to head to your new home?" Without waiting for an answer, she said, "Let's get this stuff loaded, buttercup!" The others were right behind her. Lisa, of course, had turquoise running shoes on that matched her yoga pants, that matched her hoop earrings.

The cabin was as lovely as Abby remembered. It took a few minutes for her friends to get to work; they were too busy roaming the house, looking at the water, and commenting on the rock fireplace. But by noon, everything had been unloaded and was inside. Some boxes were halfway unpacked, some empty and ready to be thrown away. Abby decided it was time to take a break. The day before, she'd bought cheese and crackers, along with lunchmeat, and three kinds of chips. She'd added a couple of bottles of their favorite wine for the occasion. It wouldn't be a housewarming without a toast to her new home. Abby found her wine glasses, already put away in an upper cabinet, and rinsed them out.

The day was clouding up, rain on its way. Too cool for a September day in Arkansas. She had stopped long enough to start the first fire in her fireplace. By two in the afternoon, she might need the air conditioning, but hadn't living with Arkansas's fickle weather always been that way?

Janie flopped down on a skirted armchair near the fireplace. "I could stay here forever." She was wearing green khaki overalls with a Nickelback t-shirt underneath. Janie took a lot of flak for liking Nickelback, but she had since they'd been teenagers, and she wasn't changing her mind now.

Amanda, her dark hair gathered in a messy bun, laughed. "If only finding the right man was so easy."

Janie had finally gotten to the point, two years out, where she could take jokes about her very public divorce. Still, she threw a pillow and hit Amanda on the head. Amanda plopped down in the armchair while the others found a place on the sofa.

Abby arrived, a dish towel in her hands. "Did I tell you the previous owners left most of the furniture?"

Lisa covered her mouth with a perfectly manicured hand. "What a steal," she said and then giggled. Lisa swept her red hair away from her eyes. "It's not cheap, Abby, that's for sure. Well-built, good material." She pointed to Amanda's chair. "But I knew you didn't pick out that Early American chair. It has actual horses and carriages on it."

Abby was about to be offended, but then she sat on the arm of the sofa—her mid-century custom sofa in turquoise velvet from a designer in Chicago—and said, "I know, right? My apartment in the city was perfection." She swung her foot back and forth. "For a while, my life was too."

Cathy said, "No sir, missy, no gloom today. I love that chair, and I think it works with the sofa." She tilted her head, looking at the black horses prancing across the burnt orange fabric. I mean, it's a little Hallooweenie, but hey, who doesn't love Halloween?"

They were all laughing by then, when Lisa said, "I'll give you the name of my guy. He's a furniture wizard. He'll redo that chair so well you'll think it's time traveling from straight-up 1957."

At the kitchen bar that separated the two rooms, Cathy poured the merlot. When everyone had a glass, Abby said, "To the Leading Ladies."

Amanda's sneakers slapped across the pine floor. "No, no. Let me toast. This is about more than the Leading Ladies. This is about you, Abby, our brave girl. You were the wanderer, but now you're home. We've wanted you back for so many years, but we've enjoyed watching you make it in Chicago. You had a part of all of us with you." She raised her glass. "And don't think for a New York minute that we're ever letting you go back. Welcome home, Abby."

Abby wiped her eyes while her best friends in the world went to town on the snacks. It had been a morning. But she was finally home.

As they talked, Janie stepped away. When she came back, she was holding a framed photo of Abby that had been mistakenly packed away with the dishes. In it, Abby lay on her back on white bedsheets, her auburn girls fanning across her pillow. A snow-white coverlet was tucked under Abby's arms, and her eyes smoldered. Janie said, "Girl, no one in Logan's Creek has a photo like this. Why, I couldn't take communion if I had a picture like this in my house."

Lisa wolf-whistled. "Dish, Abby."

Abby could feel her cheeks burn. That photo could have been from her recent trip to Chicago, and no one in the room knew but her. Of course, it wasn't. Ian had taken that picture at least a year ago. He'd said, "I've photographed a lot of beautiful women in my time, but no one comes close to you." She'd laughed, but then she realized he meant it. In the photo, she was looking at him like she was seeing water after a long journey in the desert.

Grabbing the photo, Abby said, "Give me that. I forgot how nosy you all could be. This, my friends, is called art."

Cathy moved close and whispered in Abby's ear. "If a man could make me look at him like that, no way would I leave him behind."

"Stop," Abby whispered back, but Cathy wasn't wrong.

Changing the subject, Abby said, "Has anyone figured out who's behind L.C. Confidential?"

Amanda grabbed the tray of cheese and crackers Abby had put out earlier. "Only that we believe it's a woman. Or a gay man. The way they wrote about Josh's good looks. Whew."

Lisa held a chip to her mouth. "Woman. Definitely a woman," and the others nodded in agreement.

Amy sat on the sofa, curling her legs beneath her. "She acts cute, but then she'll throw out an accusation that'll make your teeth hurt. I said to Casey last night, 'You know, honey, she's like that comedian Will Rogers, back in the 1930s. Funny as heck, but smart as a whip. Will Rogers knew his politics. Told it exactly how it was.' Plus, I agree that we've had the same kind of elected officials forever. It's time for new blood. We absolutely need to get Josh elected."

Abby smiled at Amy. In one of the unpacked boxes, there was a framed cross-stitch she'd found at an antique shop when she was in college. It was one of Will Rogers' quotes, stitched in black, surrounded by purple flowers: "Live in such a way that you would not be ashamed to sell your parrot to the town gossip." She'd have to muzzle any parrot that knew her now.

Janie, always full of trivia, said, "Will Rogers married a girl from Rogers, Arkansas. He was known as Oklahoma's Son."

Abby cleared her throat. "We're getting off track, ladies. Back to L.C. Confidential. I'm hoping they'll run Josh's statement about that awful flyer. Of course, we'll pay to run it in the newspaper too. I want to address the flyers, but I don't want to give whoever wrote it more attention. It's a fine line."

Janie said, "It's less than two months until the November election. It can't be easy to do all this damage control *and* get out Josh's message."

Abby adjusted her bandana. "Nothing with a campaign is easy. Cathy and I have a plan, though, that I hope includes all of you."

Lisa laughed. "As long as we don't have to haul things."

Cathy spoke up. "Nah. All you have to do is come to the Tuscan Table for a party."

The Leading Ladies twittered. Nothing could get them going like a party.

"Actually, it's a bash for Josh," Abby said. "Two weeks from Thursday. Heavy hors d'oeuvres, a dessert station, a signature cocktail, a few charcuterie boards. Josh will speak briefly, and we'll have live music. We may need a little help."

Lisa said, "What if Mayor Thornton shows up?" And Cathy laughed, "We'll slap a *Josh Moore for Mayor* sticker on his back."

Amy grimaced. "Mayor Thornton is a dirty double-crosser. He still owes my granddaddy for a chainsaw he didn't pay for back in the 1980s. Plus, my daddy calls him Mirror because whenever you tell him about a problem, all he ever says is 'I'll look into it.'" She folded her arms. "And that's the beginning and end of what he'll do."

The friends roared with laughter. Janie said to Amy, "Didn't your daddy call that crooked mechanic down at Fix and Go, Taillight?" Without a beat, Amy said, "He did. Because he wasn't bright enough to be a headlight."

Amanda wiped her eyes. "Don't be mean," she said, and then she broke out laughing again.

Abby officially switched to water at that point. Trying to get her friends to focus, she said to Amanda, "You know the law. If Thornton has been up to no good, he'll be found out, right?"

Amanda said in her best Prosecuting Attorney voice, "You'd be surprised at what happens that nobody finds out about. Some of the things aren't necessarily against the law, just not ethical. Like a certain friend of the mayor, who's sold land for every public-school building in Logan's Creek, going back decades." Amanda huffed. "Does no one else have viable land to sell? That's an example of one of our very real gray areas."

The Ladies were stifling laughter now, their mouths drawn in tight lines. Daytime drinking could do that. And then Cathy, holding her wineglass up for a refill, said, "Taillight," and they nearly fell off their seats.

Chapter Twelve

Abby woke to the sound of birdsong. Outside, the world was waking up, and leaves rustled in the breeze. Abby's heart swelled; the cabin already felt like home.

She stretched her limbs, reaching out to touch the worn patchwork quilt that lay at the foot of her bed. It had been given to her by her paternal grandmother, Grace Carter. The morning sun painted golden streaks across the room. Light bounced off every surface. If she looked at her reflection in the windows, she believed she'd see a halo around her head.

Abby was going to love it here.

She sat up, pulled on yesterday's socks that were beside her bed, straightened her extra-large t-shirt that hung from her shoulder, and headed to the kitchen. By the front door was a picnic basket with a ribbon on the handle. The Leading Ladies must have left it there on the way out. Inside was a bag of gourmet coffee, a bottle of vanilla flavoring, a jar of strawberry jam, homemade biscuits, and two boxes of Fruit Roll-Ups. They did know her well.

Outside, after coffee, Logan's Creek and the deck waited. Today she would take time. The creek's surface was like a mirror reflecting the sky. She'd sit on the porch, savoring the warmth, and watch the ripples kiss the land. The air smelled like sour-apple chewing gum, a scent she associated with every summer she'd spent in this town.

She looked at her hot tub. When Josh and Ian came to her mind, Abby said aloud, "No boys allowed. Not today." She spotted a mourning dove, its gray feathers and beige belly soft in the light. The bird's pointed tail looked like the blades of closed scissors. When it started its call, Abby felt she was witnessing something eternal. She lifted her cup to the dove, then dipped her head in salute.

It took Abby two trips to Cougar Grocery to get everything she needed. The second trip was to collect all the things she'd forgotten the first time, plus a giant bag of bird seed and three feeders. Her mom and dad had called. Dan and Emily had left a fall wreath on the front porch, with a card signed by the kids. The Leading Ladies had texted, and Josh had sent no fewer than a dozen messages. Most of them had to do with the campaign, but there were also hints that he'd like to come over. Late Sunday night, she'd almost asked him to, even though she knew better. There was something between them she couldn't identify. It wasn't what she had with Ian. Or, maybe, she should say what she'd had with him, since it was likely over. But it was something. Lust, maybe.

The truth was, she didn't need a man; she'd proven that by leaving Chicago and starting over. But she sure did want one from time to time. She wasn't certain what was happening to her, but it seemed she was becoming a new version of herself, or maybe she was getting to know the old version. There'd been no time to sit and think in Chicago.

Abby shook her head, doing her best to clear it. In front of her was her planner with her bullet-pointed to-do list. On the top of the page, MONDAY was written in all caps. She'd officially begun a new work week. She'd start by calling Josh, even though it was a few minutes before eight in the morning.

When he picked up, she put her phone on speaker. "I'm sorry to call so early, but I wanted to ask if Lacey had been able to find out who's behind those flyers." Her voice sounded like it was trying to outrun something.

"And good morning to you, too, Miss Carter," Josh teased. "Fine weather we're having."

Abby had opened the front windows, and the breeze lifted the kitchen curtains. "It is a fine day," she said, slowing her breathing.

"Enjoying the cabin?"

Abby sighed. "Immensely."

"Good. Now, about the flyers. Lacey called all four of our local printers. Each of them denied printing it. Any ideas?"

Abby thought carefully. "They could have gone to Lone Elm or ordered them online." Abby tapped her pen on the kitchen table where she'd been working. "Who else in town could have a good-sized printer?"

"Let me close the door for a second," Josh said. When he came back to the phone, he said, "That's hard to say, Abby. The City Offices, of course. The bank. Insurance companies. But listen, I'm not so sure this flyer is such a bad thing. I've gotten three donations since it came out, and Ed, over at the Logan's Creek Courier, said he had a good mind to endorse me. It seems that many of the citizens of Logan's Creek have made up their minds that the mayor is behind this, and they're mad as hornets."

Abby wasn't sure what Josh was saying. Did he not want to find out? If it wasn't Thornton, he could lose some of his new momentum. Then he said, "All I'm saying is if we do find out, I'd like to have a conversation about what to do next."

Abby thought about what Amanda had said about the gray area in local politics. Not exactly illegal, but shady nonetheless. She wondered if Josh had been affected by that influence. A knot formed in her stomach.

When she didn't immediately reply, Josh said, "You still there?" His voice was softer. She imagined him frowning, a line forming between his eyes.

"Still here," Abby said. "Now, about the guest list for the party. How's that coming?"

If Josh caught on that she hadn't answered his question, he didn't say. "I put Mom on it. After Lacey called the printers, I realized what a mistake I'd made. Lacey gets paid from the City's coffers, so she has no business working on the campaign." Abby could hear a car honking, then the squeal of brakes. Traffic must be picking up along Main Street. "I want to do everything right, Abby."

That was the Josh she knew. Maybe she'd misjudged him.

It took two days for Mrs. Moore to get the guest list back to Josh. Now, Abby was running to Printer's Alley to ask if they could do a rush job. The girl behind the counter didn't look older than fourteen, but she made up for it by wearing elastic-waist slacks and a top with sequined cats on the front, her out-of-fashion glasses tethered by a gold chain. She looked like someone who read instruction books, who filed warranties for small appliances. When Abby asked for a quick turnaround, the girl pointed to a stack of orders. "You should have planned better," she said. "All these are ahead of you. Plus, Carl called in sick." She shrugged. "Sciatica." And then she popped her chewing gum.

Abby shut her eyes. Radical acceptance, she said to herself. Radical acceptance. She got back in her car and messaged the group to ask for suggestions. The Leading Ladies all said the same thing: the library had the best printer in town.

Abby watched Ms. Vivian speaking to a boy about six years of age. She was leaning forward, her hands on her knees. "*Pete the Cat* is one of my favorites, too," she said, and the boy skipped away.

When Ms. Vivian stood up, Abby said. "Good morning."

"Well, good morning, Abby," Ms. Vivian said and tucked a stray curl back into the tight bun on top of her head. Just as she'd always done, the librarian wore an A-line skirt, starched white blouse, and a soft sweater thrown over her shoulders. What made her look eclectic were the neon-green high-top basketball shoes she'd taken to wearing on the days she read to the children's group. When Ms. Vivian shook Abby's hand, Abby smelled her familiar smell: lavender and Shower to Shower body powder.

"I'm in a mess," Abby blurted out. "I have invitations to print for Josh's party at The Tuscan Table. Printer's Alley couldn't do it. The Leading Ladies sent me here.

"Now, I know this is political, so if you can't help, I understand. Either way, Ms. Vivian, I'll hope you'll come to the party."

For all the years Abby had known her, Ms. Vivian's sweater had never fallen off her shoulders. Now, Abby could see the gold, rhinestone sweater clip, shaped like a poodle, that held the garment in place. "We serve all the citizens here, dear. And I'll only be letting you into the copy room. I'll have no idea what's being printed. We believe patrons deserve a dose of privacy added to a smidgen of trust."

Abby reached into her bag and pulled out the linen stock she'd brought with her. "Will this work?" she asked. "I'm not sure an Ink Jet printer will do the job. The ink might run."

Ms. Vivian's fingers fluttered at her neck. "It absolutely would," she said, "but lucky for you, we have a nearly new laser printer, compliments of the Jaycees."

As soon as Ms. Vivian said *laser printer*, Abby saw the light bulb go off. Whoever printed those awful flyers, likely did it here.

"I'll bet you do a lot of printing," Abby said. "At a nickel a copy, you offer a great bargain."

Ms. Vivian folded her arms. "We do a fair amount."

"Have you seen that terrible flyer going around town? The one about Josh?"

Ms. Vivian seemed cautious. "I have."

"We're trying to find out where it was printed."

"I have no idea," Ms. Vivian said, "and even if I did, I wouldn't tell you. Any more than I'd tell you which books Pastor Altus checked out, or which movies one of your Leading Ladies borrowed. As I said, we honor privacy here."

Abby had done it now. "No, no, Ms. Vivian. I wasn't trying to... Well, maybe I was, but I'm sorry."

"Libraries are sacred spaces, Abby."

"Of course, of course."

To get off this terrible track, Abby asked, "How's your family, Ms. Vivian?"

Ms. Vivian waited a second. "My niece, Folly, came to stay with me last year. Rather flighty girl, full of ideas. But precious to me. I'm surprised you've not met her. She sees a great deal of your sister-in-law Emily."

With that, Ms. Vivian led Abby to the print room to be alone with her thoughts.

Whats (Really) Going On?

QUESTION: Is he crooked as a bag of snakes?

City ATTORNEY (eye candy) Josh Moore is not only under investigation for his alleged role in #FITNESSGATE (see previous blog posts), but NOW a quote/unquote CONCERNED citizen has ANONYMOUSLY sent out flyers calling our youngest MAYORAL candidate as crooked AS a bag of snakes.

To SET the record straight, the FLYERS were NOT sent out by yours truly. I CONSIDER myself a Gonzo JOURNALIST (look it up!), and TELL it like it is, but with a little flair. AKA you can TRUST me. And if IT WAS me, why wouldn't I put it out on L.C. Confidential? I'd SURELY get a bump in TRAFFIC. Not that I NEED it. Numbers are UP thanks to each and EVERY one of you! Yay!

The author of the flyer hedged their BETS by ASKING questions about Josh Moore instead of TELLING us he WAS an unfit candidate. NASTY little trick, IMHO.

So today, 2 THINGS. FIRST, Let it BE known that THIS is a public invite for Mayor Thornton to send L.C. Confidential a statement concerning the CITY'S progress in INVESTIGATING his opponent, Josh MOORE. We have a RIGHT to know! (Just EMAIL me from my page, Mayor! Use the CONTACT ME tab.) Also, if YOU OR YOUR MINIONS are behind the offending FLYER, you got some explaining to DO.

SECOND, I HAVE a STATEMENT from City Attorney Josh Moore, who DIDN'T have to be shown how to use EMAIL. To see the OFFENDING FLYER, click on the PHOTO tab.

To the Good Citizens of Logan's Creek

From Josh Moore, Candidate for Mayor of Logan's Creek

There are pitfalls to running for office. I knew that when I entered the mayoral race against my opponent, Mayor Thornton. Since that time, I've gotten to speak to so many of my neighbors, and I've learned how desperately you want change.

But change does not come without disruption. For me, it's meant long nights, overscheduled weekends, and listening to opinions that don't always align with mine. All of this is fine. What's not fine are the actions of an "anonymous concerned citizen" who has attacked my character, my reason for running for mayor, and even questioned my love of the Razorbacks. #WPS

I had hoped that ignoring the flyer that many of you have received would make it fade like yesterday's news. Sadly, that's not been the case. I can assure you that whoever is behind this is an unhappy person, perhaps even a disturbed one. Furthermore, I feel sorry for anyone who relies on lies and misinformation to influence an election. We should be better than that, and that's not how I was raised. It's likely you weren't either.

On a positive note, the flyer has caused the citizens of Logan's Creek to talk even more about the campaign. I've taken dozens of calls and emails from you, answered your questions, and chatted with you when I saw you in town. You are riled up about this election! And you are not hiding your convictions behind a piece of copy paper.

Thank you for your support. Pray for the person behind these unfounded attacks, and ask yourself what Moore you want for Logan's Creek. When we win in November, we'll call the Hogs together! And yes, as a matter of fact, I do own a Hog hat. And snout. ~Josh Moore

That's ALL, folks. Stay tuned to L.C. Confidential. This is turning out to be the ELECTION of the century!

Chapter Thirteen

Abby felt the butterflies that always accompanied her before a party. She'd been careful not to add a dress code to the party invitations. Many would come outfitted in all their bling. Others would show up in their Sunday best, and still others in overalls and Carhart shirts. Those overalls could fool you. More than likely, they'd be the ones with the real money. Josh needed them all, the haves and the have-nots, the younger crowd in ironic t-shirts (One Wild and Crazy Episcopalian) and army boots. The thirty-somethings in designer brands from the big outlet stores in Branson. Those in office attire, just leaving their desk jobs.

Abby would be on the clock, so she chose her outfit carefully. A little black dress, silver earrings, and silver bangle bracelets with moonstones. Silver slingback heels. She cocked her head in the mirror. She'd wear her hair half-up, tethered with a silver clip, and let the rest of it curl its way across her shoulders.

She arrived well in advance of the others to help Cathy with the last-minute details, but she wasn't needed. The Tuscan Table was perfect. There was even a bandstand with a podium, where Josh would speak, after the country band had warmed up the crowd. At the front doors were two giant posters of Josh. In one, he was five or six, sitting on his dad's shoulders at a Razorback football game. Little Josh had a red hog painted on his face. The other poster showed Josh in his Logan's Creek Cougar football jersey, his helmet in his hand, his hair slick with sweat. His fist was in the air, and he looked like the winner he was. If Abby wasn't careful, she would remember that very night. The two of them at the Pizza Parlor after the game. The two of them in Josh's car after. She shook her head to dislodge the memory.

Abby's phone was in her evening bag. She took it out to get a few photos. "Cathy, this place looks amazing! I can't thank you enough."

"Sure you can. Just make sure our guy wins." Cathy winked. "Plus, be sure he pays his invoice on time." Cathy gave Abby the once-over. "You make that dress look like a million bucks."

By 6:50 p.m., cars were pulling up to the front of the restaurant for valet parking, which Abby felt added another special touch. For the first thirty minutes, Josh stood at the door, welcoming his guests.

Abby watched him. He was polite, smiling, calling many of the guests by name. A few of the women leaned in for a hug. A few others slipped him cards. Abby was hoping they were donations, but from the looks of things, they might just have been their phone numbers.

She couldn't blame them. Josh wore a dark gray suit that hugged his body. His starched white shirt was fitted, showing off his trim waist. Even his royal blue tie looked sexy. As she was thinking this, a woman maybe ten years older than Abby was wrapping Josh's tie around her fingers as if she was reeling in the catch of a lifetime.

Abby stepped in. "Hey there, cowboy," she said to Josh. "There are some folks over here who want to meet you."

The woman, wearing a sequined dress, turned on her heel and headed for the bar.

"Close one," Abby said, and Josh grinned at her. Maybe he liked Abby serving as chaperone.

Abby took him straight to Leading Lady Lisa, a woman she knew would behave. "Hi, Josh," Lisa said, holding out her expertly manicured hand. "I can't believe so many people showed up tonight." Lisa dropped Josh's hand and smoothed the skirt of her pink Grace Karin wrap dress. She sparkled when Josh took a glass of white wine from the nearest waitperson and devilishly handed it to her.

"I've already had one," Lisa said. And Josh laughed. "I've had exactly zero. If I can't enjoy the bar, at least I can watch you."

Something about Josh's good humor made Abby quiver. "Later," he said to Abby, "when this party's over, we'll have a drink together. It'll be worth the wait."

Abby turned to Lisa. "Where's Don?" Don was Lisa's husband. Lisa examined her nails. "Home, I guess."

Lisa drained her glass. Abby took Lisa by the arm and pulled her aside. "Honey," Abby said. "Tell me what's wrong."

Lisa shook her head. "You're working."

"It's fine. Josh can handle it. I need to know that you're okay."

Lisa's eyes were shiny with un-spilled tears. She pulled back her shoulders and waved Abby off. "Go mingle," she said. "It's nothing, really. Nothing that has to be fixed tonight." And with that, Lisa walked away.

The air smelled like pinot noir and Italian bread. The band was playing the Logan's Creek High School fight song, and a few former cheerleaders were doing an impromptu routine. The moneyed men in overalls were at the donation table, a good sign, Abby thought.

For a minute, Abby stepped away from Josh. She looked around. She couldn't tell how many people were there, but there was spillover on the patio. She stopped by the bar for a glass of wine, figuring she'd only drink half. The crowd had heated up the room, and as she shimmied through the mob, she felt perspiration on the back of her neck.

After the band played "Friends in Low Places," Abby signaled them to stop. She stepped onto the bandstand and took the podium. "I'm here tonight to introduce you to one of Logan's Creek's finest sons, Josh Moore. He loves this town like he loves his own family. And he's ready to take our town to new heights. Let's hear it for Logan's Creek's next mayor."

Josh was beside her, the heat of him like a fire beside her. He placed his hand on her lower back, and gave her waist a squeeze. It was all she could do not to lean into him.

To the crowd, Josh said, "I'm proud to be a citizen of Logan's Creek. When I went to college in Mississippi, I never once thought of not returning to Logan's Creek. I'd gotten so much from this town: an education, a religious upbringing, a love of the land. I started my law practice here and eventually became the City Attorney. But there's so much more I can do." Josh looked across the crowd. So much we can do together."

"We need more for Logan's Creek. More of the good things that have been going to other cities. More of the tax dollars that filter out of here and into nearby cities. More infrastructure improvements. More downtown development, more walkability. More focus on tourism, because this is the prettiest town in Arkansas. We need more of MOORE!"

The crowd cheered. An older man pumped his fist, while his wife clapped her hands; she wore rings on every finger. Abby's parents were near the front of the crowd, standing near Dan and Emily. Abby could see them beaming.

At the end of the speech, Josh motioned to the two sides of the podium. Cheerleaders from the high school came out of the wings and made a formation. Clapping to the beat of the band, they chanted, "We need Moore."

Abby was smiling so big her face hurt. She noticed another glass of wine in her hand. How had that gotten there? She hadn't eaten since breakfast, and she felt a bit tipsy. She locked her knees, making sure she wasn't swaying.

The next surprise was for Josh. Jasmine Cooper, one of the girls from the high school theater group, walked onto the bandstand and was handed a microphone. She said, "This is called, 'Dreams Take Flight.'" Abby had written the song on one of the many nights she'd had trouble sleeping.

In the heart of our city, where dreams take flight,
  We stand united, ready to ignite.
  With passion and purpose, we'll soar to new heights,
  'Cause we need more of MOORE, day and night.
More compassion, more progress, more unity,
  Let's build a brighter future, can't you see?
  From the streets to the shore, we'll strive for more,
  'Cause we need more of MOORE!
From the hills to the bay, our voices rise,
  A chorus of hope under sun-kissed skies.
  With courage and vision, we'll reach for the prize,
  'Cause we need more of MOORE, no compromise!
Bridges over troubled waters, hearts intertwined,
  Inclusion, justice—our shared design.
  Let's write a legacy that stands the test of time,
  'Cause we need more of MOORE, in every rhyme!
More compassion, more progress, more unity,
  Let's build a brighter future, can't you see?
  From the streets to the shore, we'll strive for more,
  'Cause we need more of MOORE!
So rally the neighborhoods, spread the word wide,
  With courage and purpose, let our spirits collide.
  Together we'll rise, with hope as our guide,
  'Cause we need more of MOORE, side by side!

Jasmine had a Broadway quality that ignited the crowd. The song sounded a little like "Part of Your World" from *The Little Mermaid*. When Jasmine took a bow, the crowd roared.

The night was winding down. Abby watched as Josh hugged his parents, then made his way to her. "Abby, that song." He waved his hand across the room. "The whole night. Magic. If I didn't think you'd hit me, I'd kiss you."

Abby frowned. "That's what you pay me for." She stepped forward and nearly fell into his arms. "It's my job. Don't say things like that. It cheapens what I do."

Josh had taken her by the shoulders, steadying her. "I didn't mean it like that."

Abby's bracelets jingled on her arm as she held Josh by the collar, and whispered, "And I'm certainly not cheap." She desperately needed to get something to eat.

Abby heard raised voices coming from the front of the restaurant. Josh took her hand and led her toward the noise. At the entry was a uniformed police officer. Cathy stood holding a dish towel in her hand.

This was a moment when Abby should have shined, but her thoughts were as muddy as the Arkansas River.

"What is going on?" Josh asked.

Cathy was talking with her hands. "Harassment, pure and simple." She pointed at the officer. "John here says I've broken the City's fire code, meeting code, and some other code I'd have to look up."

Officer John Dyer looked at his notepad. "Hi, Josh," he said. "I was telling Cathy that there are too many people on the patio. The City has rules for a reason." He scanned the crowd. "I'll bet if I did a head count in here, I'd find the same problem. Now I know you don't want anyone to get hurt, but God help you, if there was a fire right now, this bunch would be in a heap of trouble."

Cathy stomped. "This is ridiculous."

Josh rubbed his neck. "Humor me, John. How many citations have you issued like this? Say, in the last year?"

Officer John adjusted his cap. "Just shut 'er down, Josh." He looked miserable. "Please."

Josh clapped Officer John on the arm. "No problem at all. We're nearly finished anyway."

A skeleton crew remained, along with Abby, Cathy, Lisa, and Josh, who sat at the bar grumbling about Mayor Thornton. Abby held her hair off her neck and fanned herself with a campaign pamphlet.

Cathy spoke up. "Why don't you go on home, Abby? Let Josh drive you to the cabin." Cathy pointed to Josh. "She needs to get home."

"I can drive myself."

"And have Officer John stop you for a breathalyzer," Lisa said. "No way. We don't drive when we've been drinking." To which Abby said, "What about you, Lisa?" Lisa shrugged. "Don's coming to pick me up."

That was a perk of marriage. Even if you were mad at your partner, you'd still show up if they needed you. She looked at Josh, wondering what it would be like to have him as her emergency contact. He'd taken his suit jacket off and loosened his tie. The L.C. Confidential blogger had called him eye candy. Abby smiled as she slid off her bar stool. "Take me home, Josh. If I remember right, you promised me a drink."

Chapter Fourteen

On the drive home, the alcohol seemed to kick in even harder. Abby had been too tired to drink. Too hungry. She'd made yet another bad choice.

When she and Josh arrived at her cabin, he turned off the ignition. "I'll help you inside, lightweight," he said. She needed his help. And a little food in her stomach. Maybe a glass or two of water. A few aspirin.

Josh had his arm around her waist as she stood on wobbly legs. He asked for her key. Abby struggled with her purse, but when Josh asked to help, she wouldn't let him rummage through it.

"Where's your extra key?" he asked.

Abby pointed to the river rock that surrounded the hydrangeas closest to the cabin. "There," she said.

"Any idea which rock?"

Abby found the situation hilarious. "The fake one," she said between laughs.

Josh guided Abby to the front steps. Once he'd sat her down, he milled through the stones until he found the hidden key. "Eureka!" he said.

Abby found that even funnier.

Josh opened the door and helped Abby inside. When she kicked off her heels, she said, "You're tall," as if she'd just noticed.

"And you're drunk as a skunk, Abby Rose. I'm fixing you something to eat."

In the kitchen, Abby nearly slid off the bar stool. Josh, his suit coat off and his sleeves rolled up, scooped her up and sat her on the island. He picked up a spatula and aimed it at her. "Stay," he said, which sent her into another fit of laughter.

"Sit," she said when she'd recovered. "Shake."

There was a furrow in Josh's brow. But then he smiled. "You really are a lightweight," he said, speaking of her inability to hold her liquor.

He'd found ground beef and cheddar cheese in the fridge. Hamburger buns in the pantry. A respectable amount of potato chips left in a half-empty bag. When he'd finished cooking, he set two plates on the island. Poured two Cokes. Wiped down the stove.

"Eat," he said, before lifting her onto her feet. Back on the bar stool, she felt a little steadier. The hamburger was delicious, the bun toasted just like she liked. Josh sat beside her, and their being together felt as natural as breathing.

'Thanks," she said, "for everything."

Josh squeezed her shoulder. "Thank you for everything."

Abby dabbed her mouth with her napkin. Outside, Logan's Creek was moonlit and glistening. "Let's get some air when we're finished," she said. She didn't like the idea of Josh leaving.

Josh searched her face. "I'd love to."

Once on the deck, she walked to the railing and looked out over the water. A soft breeze moved the creek in slow ripples, the moon reflecting on its surface.

Josh stood behind her. She could feel him watching, and if she had to guess, he was looking at her and not the water. He put his hands around her waist. He kissed the top of her head. The automatic timer in the hot tub clicked on.

Was being half-drunk a thing? She felt sober, except for the sensations in her body. In her body, she was moving with the creek, swaying, nicely dizzy. Ian popped into her mind. She squeezed her eyes shut. She'd called him a few times. No answer. She'd texted. Nothing. Ian was the city. Josh was home. Home looked pretty good right now.

Abby turned and looked up at Josh. He was as tall as a tree. She heard him groan, give into something. He put his hands on each side of her face and lowered his face to hers. Abby's heart began to race.

At that minute, he pulled away. He squeezed the bridge of his nose. "No, Abby. Not this way. You've had too much to drink. And the last time we kissed my future looked like it was tanking. I wondered then if you'd felt sorry for me. You didn't seem interested in taking the next step, so I stepped back. And we haven't even talked about whether I'm involved with someone. Whether you are."

The sounds of the creek grew louder. The slap of the water on the shore. Occasionally, something broke through the surface of the creek, making a splash. Tree frogs trilled. Leaves rustled, the sound like rain. Abby covered her eyes with her hands. "I didn't pity you."

Josh turned his back. "I'm sorry. You're in no shape to talk about this."

Abby put her hand between Josh's shoulder blades. "Let's go in. Have some coffee. I can do this. The food is helping. The fresh air. I feel nearly normal."

Once inside, they sat on separate ends of the couch. Their coffee cups sat untouched on the coffee table. Abby shifted, turning her body toward his, tucking her bare feet beneath the middle cushion, smoothing her black dress across her thighs. Josh adjusted his body, his arm across the back of the couch.

"What is this between us, Abby?" Josh asked, his voice resonating through the soft night.

Abby grabbed the quilt from the back of the couch. Covered her knees with it. Her grandmother had made it, the one who wasn't all that domestic. The one who might not have married at all if she could have figured out a way to have kids on her own. "I'm not sure," she said.

Josh loosened the band of his watch. When he was finished, he said, "I'm going to ask some questions. You can ask questions. We'll answer honestly, even if the answers hurt. Deal?"

Abby wasn't sure, but she didn't have a better idea.

"I'll go first," Josh said. "Are you seeing anyone?"

Abby shook her head. "No," she said, but then she hesitated. "But I was, before I moved home. That's not quite right. I saw him again when I went to Chicago to sell my apartment. But not since then." Abby felt her face grow hot, the memories of that last night playing like a movie reel.

"Does this person have a name?"

"Ian," she said.

"How long were you together?"

"Three years. A little over three years."

Before Josh could ask another question, Abby said, "My turn. Are you seeing someone?"

"I was. She lives in Fayetteville." Josh took a breath. "An artist. Has her work in a few galleries. But she called it off when I told her I was running for mayor. She lives in a world full of ideals and beauty. Dating a guy who wants to be part of the establishment was something she couldn't get behind."

"How long?"

"Four months," he said.

"Her name?"

"Arbor."

"Was that her real name?"

Josh smiled. "Who knows."

"Did you love her?"

"I could have, but no. Now, back to you. Did you love Ian?"

Abby blew out her breath. "Am I allowed to say it was complicated?"

"Nope," he said.

"All right," Abby said. "We tried to keep it casual. Ian's a photographer, on the road to becoming a famous one. My sights were set on my career."

"That's not an answer."

Abby hesitated. When she answered, she said, "Okay. I loved him."

"It's your turn again," Josh said.

"Did you consider dropping out of the race? To keep Arbor?"

"Absolutely not."

The only sound in the cabin was the hum of the refrigerator when it kicked on. Abby looked at Josh, sitting in her cabin, late at night. He was trying to know her. They should have been talking about Mayor Thornton. How to leverage what had happened that night. Nobody likes a bully, and Thornton was trying to bully Josh. Abby's pulse raced. "We should concentrate on the campaign," she said.

"You didn't ask the next logical question," Josh said. "Is there anybody I'd quit the race for? Someone I'd give anything to have a second chance with."

Abby looked at the quilt, considering what Josh had just said. He moved closer to her. "Is this okay?" he asked, as he pulled her into his arms. "I want to hold you. Like I used to do."

Abby relaxed into him. She put her head on his chest. They stretched out, Josh's feet hanging off the end of her couch. Her grandmother's quilt around them. It was nearly perfect. It was almost right.

As she was drifting off, Abby heard a car on the gravel drive. Headlights arced across the open curtains, across the living room walls. "Is someone here?" she asked.

Josh pulled her closer. "Probably somebody who took a wrong turn."

"I think they stopped."

Josh stroked her hair. "They'd have to stop to turn around. If they don't leave in a minute, I'll go check."

Abby was about to argue, when the car pulled away.

There was a note on the coffee table when Abby woke. A note placed beneath a glass of water. *Best night ever*, the note read. There were two more aspirins on a napkin beside the glass.

Abby chugged the water. Swallowed the aspirin. When she felt better, she drank more water, ate a bagel. Then, she tied on her running shoes and took off. Five miles later, her lungs burned. Her muscles ached. When she thought of Josh, she felt happy. And confused. What was wrong with her?

When she checked her phone, she'd missed four texts from Josh, one from Cathy. Another from the editor of the Logan's Creek Courier. The paper wanted to do an interview with Josh.

Josh wanted to meet for brunch the next day. He'd written:
> *Is it still a campaign expense if all I do is comment on the color of your eyes?*

Abby grinned. Josh was such a flirt. Unfortunately, Abby already had plans. She was going to her parents' Saturday morning.

What's (Really) *Going On?*

TOPIC: Moore than enough trouble at the Tuscan Table

Oh my GOSH, y'all! I have it on good authority that last night's party for mayoral candidate, Josh Moore, at the Tuscan Table was OFF the rails. What do I mean, you ask?

First, the luscious Josh Moore showed up looking like he was walking the Red Carpet. Not too many men can pull off a trim-cut suit. And the women took notice. Josh's sidekick/campaign manager, Abby Carter, lately of Chicago, played interference, but even she couldn't stop the ladies from swarming.

Then, a ruckus broke out near the main bar. It seems that someone had been taking too many shrimp canapes (from other people's plates!). My question is: How many is too many. Those things are TINY.

Also, the cops showed up, shutting down the party for code violations. Seems there were too many people on the patio, or some such nonsense. (Plus, the cheerleaders from the high school—not sure if the school approved their attendance—did a dance number that would have shocked my grandmama, God rest her soul. But that was BEFORE the popo arrived.)

I remember when the most controversial thing in Logan's Creek was that contractor's billboard was over by Walmart that read, *Your Roof Looks Like Hail*. I almost miss those days.

Not really. This campaign is da bomb.

I'd love to hear from Mayor Thornton and Josh Moore. And Abby Carter, of course. She seems like a super-nice person!

Stay tuned to L.C. Confidential. This is turning out to be the ELECTION of the century!

Chapter Fifteen

On Saturday morning, not long after the sun rose, Abby stopped by Mimi's Bakery to pick up the oatmeal cookies her dad loved.

Back in the car, local news was playing on the radio. Someone had been stealing Mayor Thornton's campaign signs. Abby adjusted the sun visor. She was sure Josh would be blamed. It was almost as if someone was out to frame him.

She'd text Josh with the news a little later. No need to wake him if he was still asleep. She imagined him in his bed, shirtless. His hair tousled for once. He really was a beautiful man.

The long, graveled drive to her parents' house curved around a massive oak. Her dad was keen on saving the tree when he'd planned the entry. You couldn't see the house well until you'd passed that landmark.

Abby looked up ahead. Her dad's pickup was parked outside the garage. On Saturdays her dad cleaned the inside. On Fridays, he ran it through the carwash at his dealership. Abby had never seen her dad's car dirty. Beside his truck was another vehicle. Abby couldn't quite make it out. Maybe Dan was visiting.

When she got closer, she identified the Jeep. Black, stickers from several national parks on the back, an antenna that was bent midway. The Jeep was Ian's. Abby slammed on the brakes.

"What in the world," she said aloud. Abby wasn't sure what to do. A day ago, she'd have run inside, ready to see the man she loved. But last night, Josh had held her. Stroked her hair. When he thought she was asleep, he'd whispered, "It's always been you, Abby."

Abby could see herself with Josh. With two kids and a house in town near his parents. On weekends, they'd come to the ranch. Her son and daughter would learn to ride horses here. Would hear the old stories of the Carter family. Would play with Emily and Dan's kids in the hay loft.

But there was another part of her heart that belonged to Ian. And her body knew his in a way she'd never known anyone else. The tilt of his chin meant he was going to kiss her. His eyelids halfway closed when she touched his chest. When he leaned down to hug her, his hair tickled her face. Even the smell of him made her knees weak. It was as if she couldn't help but love him. As if her body and soul were saying *this is it.*

Abby checked her makeup in the car's mirror. She fluffed her hair. She needed to know why he was here, and the best way to do that was to slip inside. To eavesdrop.

She eased in the back, through the door her parents never locked. She'd taken off her running shoes while sitting on the back steps. Her socked feet were quiet on the tile floor. Abby headed to the pantry, where a ceiling vent carried the sounds of the living room. Abby had found the quirk by accident, and she'd used it often. It was how she knew her widowed great aunt had a live-in boyfriend. It was how she'd learned that her parents helped support a disabled woman in their church who'd courageously left an abusive marriage.

She heard her mom first. "More coffee, Ian?" If he was on his second cup, they'd been talking for a bit.

"No thank you, Mrs. Carter. I've had enough coffee to last me a while."

Abby's dad spoke. "Didn't sleep much last night, I'm guessing."

"I didn't sleep at all."

"So, how can we help?" Abby's mom asked.

"I guess I needed to see this place. Logan's Creek. Abby always said this town was like a friend to her."

"That sounds like her," Gabby said.

"She loves you two so much," Ian said. Abby heard a wobble in his voice. "And I care deeply for her. I thought she felt the same."

Abby's dad, Jim, broke in. "Abby keeps her feelings close to the vest, so I'm not sure we can comment. Doesn't tell anybody much, except for the Leading Ladies. They probably know what she had for breakfast."

Abby could feel the air shift in the room. Did her dad think Ian was complaining about her? He'd never put up with that.

"I understand," Ian said. "I'm not really looking for insight into Abby's feelings about me. What I hoped to learn is about you two."

"Whatever for?" Gabby asked.

"It may be because I'm sleep-deprived, but earlier this morning, something came to me. Whenever Abby talked about you, she said that you two had a marriage made in heaven. You didn't fight. You got together, fell in love, and made every day after that better than the one before.

"I think she left Chicago because she thought I was cheating on her." Ian rushed the next words. "I wasn't. Anyway, it seems to me that when we hit a snag, she decided we weren't worth fixing, because we weren't perfect like you."

Abby heard her father laugh. "That's the beauty of sleeping one floor below your kids. They don't hear you fight."

"Now, Jim," Gabby said, but Abby could hear the smile in her voice.

Abby felt as if she was being made fun of. She crossed her arms and nearly knocked over a jar of almonds. The sound was enough to stop the talking in the living room. Abby held her breath. But after a few seconds, the conversation continued.

She could almost see her dad pulling the white handkerchief from his jeans pocket, wiping his eyes. "We almost didn't make it to the altar."

Gabby said, "That's true."

"Gabby found out I'd bought her engagement ring on credit. This was just before the wedding. We'd agreed to no debt; she was always a stickler about the budget. We were already saving for a house. I hadn't lied about the ring, but I hadn't exactly announced I'd gotten it on a payment plan down at Newton's Jewelers."

Gabby chimed in. "It may sound like a small thing, but a lie is a lie. I wasn't going to exchange my good name for a bad one. I gave the ring back."

"There were plenty of fellas ready to step in. I had to win her back. Wasn't easy. We didn't get married until the ring was paid in full," Jim said. "She wore the store receipt stitched on her wedding hanky."

Gabby explained. "It was my something blue, because it was a blue handkerchief, and the whole ordeal had made me *feel* blue."

"Then there was the time you went home to your mother," Jim said. But Gabby stopped him. "Enough," she said. "Ian will think we're a family of hotheads."

Abby *had* believed her mom and dad had the perfect romance. Plus, she'd never heard them argue. Sometimes, Gabby would say, 'We're heading to the barn," just as a conversation between the two was getting heated. Abby hadn't connected the dots. It was likely the barn had heard a different side of the story. Once, when they'd had chickens, even the rooster ran from the barn, scattering along with the hens when her parents walked through the door.

She felt as if she'd been told the Tooth Fairy didn't exist. As if she'd been forced to take off her rose-colored glasses. Of course, her parents fought. Her mother was headstrong, after all. Her dad was quieter, but he still had that veneer that said, *Don't try me.*

When she'd come home from Chicago, Abby had expected her frantic life to calm down. But at home, she'd gotten herself in a mess. First, with Josh. Then she'd found out that dirty politics didn't limit themselves to the big city. She'd gone back to Chicago, and slept with Ian, as if she could do that with no consequences.

Lisa had said it took a few tries to break up; the first time was just rehearsal. But it had only taken her one try with Josh. They were awfully young, after all. Maybe that was why.

Abby eased the pantry door open. She tiptoed to the back door, slipped outside, put on her shoes.

When she got back home, she messaged the Leading Ladies.

Abby:

> *He is in town! What am I supposed to do NOW?*

Cathy:

> *OMG. Wait, who is HE?*

Lisa:

> *It's Ian, right?*

Janie:

> *Are we sure Ian even exists, LOL?*

Cathy:

> *Ian? Get that man to the cabin. Now! YOLO!*

The rest of the day, Abby flinched at every noise she heard outside. She expected Ian to show up. Or Josh. Or both. What a disaster.

Occasionally, she'd get texts from the Leading Ladies. They were mostly gifs of clocks ticking. Or a series of question marks. She'd get back to them when she'd decided what to do.

It was just after seven o'clock, when she heard her parents drive up. As they climbed the steps, she felt her heart in her throat. How was she going to act when they told her about Ian? And should she come clean?

"What a surprise," Abby said as she opened the door.

Gabby was holding a quart of chocolate chip ice cream. "We brought you a treat."

Once inside, they sat at the kitchen island while Abby scooped out ice cream.

Jim waited until the ice cream was served. "We had a visitor today."

Abby held her spoon mid-air. "Oh?" she said.

"Don't you want to know who it was?" Gabby asked.

Abby swallowed. "Of course."

"Your young man, Ian," Jim said.

Abby tried to look surprised. "Ian?"

Jim's spoon clinked against the bowl. "Your photographer friend. From Chicago."

"My goodness," Abby said. She knew she was blushing.

"Seems he has some big feelings for you," Gabby said.

Abby looked at her bowl. "Oh," she said again.

"He had quite a lot to say," Gabby said. "He says there was a misunderstanding between you two, back in Chicago."

Abby waved her hand. "We cleared all that up."

Gabby hadn't touched her ice cream. "Then what's the problem, sweetheart? You know we're not ones to meddle, but now your problem has become ours. Ian came to us for advice. We'd never even met him. I'd say that had to come from desperation."

"I liked him," Jim said. "Stand-up guy. Had a tattoo, but still."

Her dad hated tattoos. Ian must have impressed him. "I don't know where to start; so much has changed. I'd rather not get into it, if you don't mind."

Gabby took Jim's bowl and took it to the sink. "Then fix things with him, one way or another. Because Carters don't—"

"Lead people on," Abby finished. These Carter rules were getting on her last nerve.

Her mother used to say, "A clear conscience yields a good night's sleep." Abby stayed awake into the wee hours, thinking about that line.

Abby hadn't been able to eat breakfast. She'd made coffee, put concealer under her eyes. She dressed in her boyfriend jeans and Vera Wang sky-blue top. Carters weren't procrastinators, she thought as she put on her wedge heels. It was time she faced Ian.

But before she could call him, she heard the doorbell.

She ran her fingers through her curls, bent at the waist and shook her head to get the volume she needed. She opened the door. Ian was leaning against the jamb.

Ian was dressed as usual. White long-sleeved knit shirt. Black cargo pants. Black Doc Martins.

"Ian." She said and folded her arms. She felt as if she needed armor.

"Are you going to ask me in?"

Abby stepped back. "Of course."

It was always hard to be close to Ian. She wanted to touch him, feel the heat of his skin beneath her palms. She resisted. "You look well."

"Got a lot of things off my chest yesterday. Slept like a baby last night. A good night's sleep can work wonders."

Abby stifled a yawn. "Sleep," she said, as if it was a foreign word.

From the deck, the sun glinted off the rippling water. A heron swooped down, finding something worthwhile near the shore. On the road beyond, a truck labored up the hill.

Ian gripped the railing. "This is nice." Pointing toward the boat dock on the other side, and the forest beyond, he said, "All this nature. I see why you love it."

If she'd guessed, she'd say he was regretting not bringing his camera in. He could take a photo of a stream and make it magical. She could only imagine what he could do with pictures of this place. "What do you want?" she asked.

He had slipped on his aviator sunglasses. Birdsong filled the morning. "That's not the question."

It was the second time in less than a week that a man had told her she'd asked the wrong question. It grated against her. Abby's voice hardened. "Then why don't you tell me what the right question is."

Ian grimaced. "Sorry, Abby. I'm not doing this right. Can we sit?"

At the patio table, Ian moved the pot of coral geraniums an inch to the right. Abby brought out coffee. Set out coffee cake. Put out her cloth napkins. Her plates with images of daisies on them. "What do you want?" she asked again. "I've called you. I've texted. And not a word back. Now, you show up at my door. I'm getting a migraine trying to figure out what it is you want from me."

"I should have called. I realize that. But you'd handled our night together like it was a Friends with Benefits situation. After three years." Ian took off his sunglasses. "It wasn't that for me. I thought we'd spend the night together, and things would go more or less back to normal. So that hurt."

Abby moved her plate and put her elbows on the table.

"A real man would have followed you to the ends of the earth. I'm paraphrasing here, but that was the gist of it. You said that. Remember?"

Abby nodded. "Let's finish this inside."

They sat on the couch, the curtains closed. The a/c kicked on, and Abby rubbed her arms.

"So I packed the Jeep and headed out," Ian said. "I imagined showing up at your door. It wasn't hard to find you. The real estate records for this place were already online. I thought you'd jump in my arms."

Abby interrupted. "You didn't come to my door. I would have heard your car door open and close."

Ian laughed a mirthless laugh. "I'd taken the doors off the Jeep."

Abby waited.

"I got to the porch." He pointed toward the front door. "My headlights lit up your living room. Your curtains were wide open. And you were on the couch with someone else, the two of you looking pretty happy."

Abby felt her heart clench. "Ian," she said.

"Was it Josh?"

"Yes."

"And did he stay the night?"

Abby held his gaze. "Yes, but nothing happened."

Ian pointed to the coffee table. For the first time, Abby noticed Josh's watch there. He must have taken it off overnight. Ian said, "Everybody says nothing happened."

"We had broken up, as far as I knew."

Ian hung his head. "That's fair."

"One more time, Ian. What do you want?"

He didn't move toward her. He didn't smile. It was as if he was showing her something important about himself. "I want you."

This was all Abby had ever wanted. Right? Then why wasn't she putting her arms around him?

"But that's not the right question. The question is, do you want me?"

When she didn't immediately answer, he said, "Right." The word was full of disappointment.

Before she could think of what to say, Ian stood to leave. "I'll be in town for the next two weeks. I'm not going to bother you. I have a client up in the Ozarks. He's fixed up an old trout fishing resort. Needs photos for everything. I underbid the job so I could be near you, Abby. I can work my own hours, so if you decide you want to show me the town, let me meet those elusive Leading Ladies, anything like that, I'm yours."

"Are you staying at the Best Western near the Interstate?"

Ian smiled. "Woman, you know I don't stay in chain hotels. I'm at a place called Betsy's B and B." He pointed to a floral needlepoint pillow her mother had made for her that sat on her turquoise couch. "A lot of that kind of thing there. And lots of checkered curtains. Lace." He pulled a face. "See. I'd do anything to be near you."

Those stormy eyes again. Abby loved those eyes. She was about to speak when her phone rang.

After he left, the room was filled with Ian's energy. Abby touched her cheek. It was almost as if he'd touched her there. She dropped onto the nearest chair. Her phone rang again.

"For heaven's sake," she said, as she picked it up.

"This is Rosalynn Medlock, admin for Mayor Thornton."

"Oh. Yes, of course. What can I do for you?"

"Mayor Thornton would like to meet with you. He has a time slot this afternoon at one o'clock," she said, assuming that Abby had all the time in the world to be at his beck and call. Abby bit her thumbnail. She wasn't about to jump just because he was the mayor, but she was interested in what he had to say.

Chapter Sixteen

Abby couldn't ever remember being in the mayor's office. She barely remembered being inside the county courthouse, except for field trips in primary school. And when she had to tag her car for the first time.

It seemed strange that a city office was even there, but nearly a hundred years before, a deal was struck, and the mayor moved in.

The steps to the main entrance to the courthouse were made of limestone from the surrounding hills, which dipped in the center from eons of foot traffic. Two marble columns supported the entryway. The stone came from farther away, in a town now called Marble Falls. It was from there that Arkansas sent one of three stone slabs that were used in the Washington Monument. Abby remembered that from her semester of Arkansas History. It was astounding the facts that remained after so many years.

Inside, the courthouse smelled of old documents and floor wax. The ceilings soared, intricate moldings framed the walls, and the chandeliers shined.

Abby climbed the stairs to the second floor, the heels of her leather boots sounding as she went. Inside was Mrs. Rosalynn Medlock, looking serious in her black turtleneck and slacks.

"Good afternoon, Miss Carter. Have a seat. I'll let the mayor know you're here."

"Thank you."

She returned almost immediately. "You may go in now." She pointed to the mayor's doorway.

Abby followed the gesture and entered Thornton's office.

There he sat behind the largest desk she'd ever seen. Even the pair of leather chairs, placed close by for visitors, seemed small. The desktop, made of mahogany, held at least two dozen photographs of the mayor with his friends and cohorts. Even though the images faced Thornton, Abby could see them from her vantage point. A few showed Thornton with his family, Abby supposed. She'd seen his latest wife around town, so spotting her was easy. The others in the photos could be his adult children, maybe a few grandchildren. A matching bookcase sat across the room. It held even more photos, awards, and golf trophies.

He stood to greet her, holding his hand out to shake hers.

"Ms. Carter," he said, his voice as southern as an Arkansas hoedown. He pointed. "Have a seat. I've been meaning to give you a call, welcome you back to town. I've been so busy; I haven't gotten 'round to it yet."

Abby knew one thing for sure. Had she not been Josh's campaign manager, Thornton wouldn't have cared a lick that she was back in town.

Thornton motioned for her to sit, and did the same. He pushed his chair back and put his ankle across his opposite knee. "I hear tell you have your own little business going. What a big undertaking for a nice young lady like yourself."

Abby could feel herself getting hot under the collar. She had to remind herself she wasn't wearing a blouse that had a collar. He said *nice young lady* like she'd be better off with a hobby, maybe starting an antique button collection. And *little* business? What the actual ...

"I don't have a *little* business, Mayor. I'm the campaign manager for your opponent, as we both know. I'm also a marketing expert. I've won awards for my work. I've been responsible for multi-million-dollar campaigns. I'm incredibly good at what I do."

"I'm quite certain you are, young lady."

Was there innuendo in that remark? Did the mayor waggle his eyebrows? Abby was fuming.

Thornton took off his glasses and scooted up to the desk. His face was bloated, the skin tight on his cheeks. Abby knew he'd been athletic once, played football for the Logan's Creek Cougars, but time, and maybe a little hard living had caught up with him.

"What exactly am I here for, Mayor Thornton?"

Thornton picked up a pen from his desk and held it like a cigarette. "Why, Miss Carter, I'm only welcoming you back to town." He seemed to concentrate. "Although, I do have a word of caution for you."

Abby was done. "Go ahead," she said.

"You and Josh Moore. You used to go together." Thornton made air quotes around the words 'go together.' I've heard the stories. He was a fool to let a pretty little filly like you get away."

"First," Abby said, "that's none of your business. And second, stop talking down to me. I'm not a filly. I'm not a nice young lady. I'm a businesswoman, your rival right now, and if you brought me here to shoot the bull, we can end this talk right now."

"Now, now," Thornton said. A smile played at the corner of his mouth. He was enjoying this, Abby could see. "All right. I forgot to figure in how much living in a big city could change a person, harden them even. Chicago, wasn't it?"

When Abby didn't answer, he said, "Here's the thing. I was hoping to warn you off Josh Moore. He has a way with the ladies, as I'm sure you've noticed. No follow-through, though. That demented woman at the city council meeting? The one with the spreadsheet?"

"Cynthia Burke? Who accused Josh of working against Logan's Creek? What about her?"

"She had an ax to grind. Josh used to court her niece. Her favorite niece. Hear tell Cynthia and the girl had already been wedding dress shopping when Josh found greener pastures, if you know what I mean. The other girls I've seen him with, well, let's just say he didn't meet them at Sunday school. And then there was the unfortunate Penelope—"

Abby cut him off. "Speaking of Cynthia Burke. What's the status of the investigation into Josh? No one's questioned him. No one's asked him to explain why he did legal work for Lone Elm while employed by Logan's Creek."

"Oh now, you know I can't talk about an ongoing investigation." He steepled his fingers. "All I can say is that these things take time."

"But you could clear the whole thing up."

"I don't get your drift."

"You knew what Josh was doing for Lone Elm. You arranged it. You're the one who told him it was his duty to help another town in the county."

Thornton smirked. "My recall is not what it used to be."

Abby rose to leave.

"Fine. I'm not at liberty to disclose details, but I do believe the issue will be resolved in Josh's favor. Not that Josh would do the same for me."

"What do you mean?"

"All my missing campaign signs. Gone in a flash." He snapped his fingers. "All across town, right to the city limits sign. Do you happen to know where your candidate was while this awful crime was happening?"

Abby had a hunch. "Why don't you narrow the timeframe for me?" she asked.

Thornton showed his veneered teeth. "I'd say between 3:47 and 4:00 on Monday morning. Give or take."

"That's quite specific."

Thornton shrugged. "Signs go missing, and folks get riled. Our fine citizens like a fair fight. They certainly don't like a bully."

Abby felt as if she was seeing behind the curtain that was Max Thornton. "The sympathy vote. Of course. You took your own signs, didn't you? Were you also behind the flyers that eviscerated Josh?"

"We have a key to the library, Rosalynn and myself. Print tons over there. Laser printer, best in town. But again, I can't recall. As I said, we print so much."

Abby stood. "I could go out there and tell the whole town what you've told me. I could go to the police."

"Well, now, that wouldn't be advisable. Some of those officers are like family to me. They wouldn't take kindly. They went easy on y'all over that debacle of a party y'all held at the Table. All those people. Acting like the city codes weren't worth the paper they were typed on. And having the public high school participate, the high school funded by tax dollars. That was a mistake of grand proportions. Of course, if I'd been invited, I could have told you that. I could have headed off every problem you manufactured that night."

"I'm leaving," Abby said, but then Thornton clapped his hands. Startled, she stopped and turned back. "I called you here, young lady, to let you know you've gotten yourself into a hornet's nest. You're working for a ne'er-do-well who'd better not win this election." He stabbed his chest with his index finger. "You're working against a man who don't like to lose. You're working against a man who would do near about anything to be mayor for another four years. And finally, if you're behind that rag of a blog that's besmirching my name, you'd better step down." Thornton held his thumb and forefinger so close a paper clip couldn't get through. "I'm this close to bringing that whole mess down."

"Are you threatening me?"

Thornton pulled a comb from his shirt pocket and ran it through his slicked-back hair. "Threat? Absolutely not, Miss Carter. In fact, I'd considered offering you a job with the city. Maybe working up a new tourist campaign to draw in more visitors. That seemed up your alley. But now, I don't know. You're a spirited little thing. Can't hold your tongue." He put the comb back in his pocket. Abby imagined a stain forming there, all that oil.

Abby stepped forward. She put her hands on the desk. "I think you're scared of losing. Bone-deep scared." She remembered a scripture. *What's done in the dark will come to light.* "Mr. Mayor," she said. "You just wait and see."

Thornton guffawed. "Like the goings-on at your secluded cabin? Oh, lamb, men have been seen coming and going like ants to a picnic, if what I'm told is true."

Was he having her followed? Abby was close enough to see the pores on Thornton's face. She felt like slapping him. "Son of a gun," she said. Her hands were in fists.

"I'd love to talk more, but I'm speaking at the Rotary at noon. Integrity in Politics. I wrote the speech four years ago, but it still holds up." He held up his palm, as if to stop Abby from replying. "Before you say anything else. Call me a wolf in sheep's clothing, for example, I'd like you to ask yourself this. Where did the wolf get his clothing? And what did it cost the gullible little sheep?

Back in her car, Abby pulled her phone from her purse. Why hadn't she thought to record Thornton? She started to call Josh, but decided to wait until she'd sorted through what had happened. She hated to admit it, but Thornton had gotten to her. She'd assumed Josh had had relationships—why shouldn't he—but had he really walked out on someone he'd promised to marry? And who was Penelope? And why did the thought of Josh with someone else bother her so much?

Of course, the bigger problem was Thornton's illegal activities. He was more devious than she'd given him credit for. The word *smarmy* came to mind.

Looking in the rearview mirror, she saw a police car crawl by and felt chills run up her spine. Did Thornton really have the police department in his pocket? She drove to the parking lot of the Golden Pheasant restaurant and parked. She had to text the Leading Ladies.

Abby:

Just left a meeting with Thornton. He's worse than I thought.

Cathy:

Did he mansplain the campaign to you?

Abby:

That and a lot more!

Amanda:

Snake in the grass!

Abby:
> *Do you think he's dangerous?*

Amanda:
> *What did he do? Did he threaten you?*

Abby:
> *I'm not sure. It sure felt like he did.*

Cathy:
> *Do you need us to come over? BTW, I don't plan on paying that stupid fine from the city anytime soon. Too many people on the patio, my ass.*

Abby:
> *I'm fine, really. Well, almost fine. LOL. Plus, let me pay, Cathy!*

Amy:
> *You two are getting off topic.*

Janie:
> *If you want me to slash Thornton's tires, just text back, 'The crow flies at midnight.' I'll know what you mean.*

Abby laughed. These women were her posse. She almost asked what the Leading Ladies knew about Josh's past relationships, but it suddenly seemed petty. Why should she care so much? They also knew Ian was in town, and they'd have plenty to say about her fickle nature. Abby put down her phone and started her car.

Abby was on her deck, glass of wine in hand, watching the sun go down, when Amanda called. The wine. The sunset. None of it was enough to settle her mind.

"Just wanted to check on you and see how you were holding up," Amanda said.

"That was the strangest meeting. Old Thornton has a way about him. Part grandpa, part mobster. I was thinking earlier, he was nasty ugly charming."

Amanda laughed. "I might delete the word *charming*. But yeah, that's him to a T. How he's pulled the wool over so many people's eyes is beyond me. Listen, though. He has his minions in town who'll do anything for him, so tread lightly."

"He's losing his mind over the identity of the L.C. Confidential Blogger. And he's going after Josh every way he can."

"Anything illegal?"

"That's the kicker. From what I learned in our meeting today, I think so. But he could be lying to me, wanting me to accuse him of something nefarious. Then he could play the victim in the court of public opinion. He could say Josh is the underhanded one."

"What does Josh say?"

"I haven't told him."

"Why not?"

"I don't know. I almost called him immediately. But I realized I needed the Leading Ladies. Y'all have always been my touchstone. Then, I wanted some time to sort out what I'd heard."

Abby hesitated before she said, "Thornton got under my skin, Amanda, talking about Josh's reputation with women."

Amanda's logic was one of the things Abby depended on. So when she spoke next, Abby tried to soak up every word. "As your friend, I'm going to lay this on the line. We all know Josh is a bit of a tomcat. It's what did you two in, remember? Sure, you two were young, and first love is rarely *the* love. But you tried so hard. And he promised to work on himself. Don't tell me you've forgotten visiting him in Mississippi when he was going to school at Oxford. You found a bottle of Victoria's Secret perfume in his bathroom. And a retainer. Your teeth were perfect, and you'd only wear that perfume that smelled like cotton candy.

"The phone would ring off the wall, but he wouldn't answer it. And then, late that night, a key turned in the lock and that redhead came in. He'd given her a key."

The memory stung all these years later. "In his defense, Amanda, he said he'd thought we were on a break until I showed up at his door."

"Did you think you were on a break?"

"I did not. All I knew was that he'd seemed distracted, and that for the first time since I'd known him, he was making excuses not to see me."

"And you still tried to make it work. Didn't you offer the redhead a Coke?"

Abby could feel the humiliation. "Her name was Simone. She said she'd get it herself. She knew her way around."

"The Leading Ladies came and got you. You were sitting in that pitiful coffee shop with your overnight bag at your feet. I was mad enough to spit nails." Amanda breathed a ragged breath. "It took me years to forgive Josh, and I wasn't the one he hurt. But," she said slowly, "he's proven to be a stand-up guy, by all accounts. If he were otherwise, don't you think the Leading Ladies would have heard about it? If he sees a lot of women, so what? Unless, you're ready to jump back in the deep-end with him."

That was the million-dollar question. To answer it, Abby would have to ask for a lifeline, a clue from her friends. Maybe all the consonants in the first sentence. She had no idea.

Amanda must have felt Abby's hesitation. "Moving on," she said. "Your love life is beside the point. Your first obligation is as Josh's campaign manager. If you have information he needs, it's your job to tell him."

Abby felt her mouth go dry. "I hate it when you're right."

Amanda laughed. "You and every criminal I've ever come up against in court."

After they said goodbye, Abby did try to call Josh. Her call went straight to voicemail, and Abby imagined him in a dimly lit restaurant with a gorgeous blonde, holding hands across the table. She might, she thought, be losing her mind.

For the first time since coming home, Abby felt like she had to get out of town.

Early the next morning, Abby still hadn't heard from Josh. She called again, and this time she left a voicemail. After, she went for a run, and when she returned to the cabin, she dialed Ian's number.

"Are you busy?" she asked when Ian answered.

"Just checking out the downtown area. Did you know there's a shop with a pet rabbit at the register? He'll push your change across the counter like he knows what he's doing."

"That's Albert. And yes, he does know what he's doing. He's something of a town legend."

"What's up with you?"

Abby heard the tremble in her voice. "Your trip to the Ozarks. Want some company?"

Before she could take a breath, Ian said, "I'll pick you up in an hour. Travel light."

Abby almost asked Ian to meet her in town. She still wasn't sure if Thornton was having her cabin watched. But then her resolve set in. No one was going to run her life like that.

Ian brought her a latte made exactly how she liked it. When he handed it to her at her front door, he said, "I remembered." Abby felt her cheeks burn. What else did he remember? If it was half as much as she did, he should be blushing too.

As Ian grabbed her bags from the entryway, then stuffed them into the back of the Jeep, she settled in the passenger seat.

For the first part of the trip, the only sound was the GPS directing Ian to turn or watch for speed traps, but then the two began talking. There was something about the intimacy of a car, something about not having to look into someone's eyes, that helped conversation flow, even if the vehicle was as noisy as Ian's.

The winding roads to Ozark, Missouri covered 172 miles, and the scenery was beautiful. They would arrive in less than three hours, but before that, they'd stop in Branson to eat. She'd decided to introduce him to a small café, The Breakfast Spot, on the shore of Lake Taneycomo. They could sit outside on the deck, watching the boats.

"What is it with you and water?" Ian asked.

"What do you mean?"

"This breakfast place is on the water. Your cabin is on the water. Even your Main Street ends at Logan's Creek. And yet, I've never seen you swim."

Abby thought of her teenage summers. Her wardrobe consisted of bikinis and oversized t-shirts. All the Leading Ladies dressed that way. Those months smelled like coconut sunblock, and cherry snow cones bought at the pool. When they were at the creek, they'd bring ice chests full of soft drinks and sandwiches. Josh showed up often, so did a lot of other boys from town. At night, in bed, she'd been able to feel the lull of the water beneath her. "I swim like a fish," she said now. "It's a thing of wonder to watch."

Ian squeezed her hand. "I have no doubt," he said.

Once at the Breakfast Spot, waiting on their pancakes, Abby said, "Thanks for letting me tag along." She adjusted her sunglasses, picked at her paper napkin. She felt suddenly shy.

"I thought we could get a run in tomorrow morning. Maybe take a boat out. If it were warmer, we'd go for a swim."

"But I didn't bring a suit," Abby said.

Ian flashed that smile. He didn't need to say another word.

Before he could say more, their pancakes arrived. A few boats were on the water. The sun warm on Abby's face. The morning was nearly perfect.

The rock cabin stood in a long row of similar structures. Each had a covered deck with a hot tub, grill, a table and chairs, and chaise lounges.

Ian punched in the code on the lock pad, and they stepped inside. The furniture was leather, the tables made of pine. A fireplace stood in the main room and was made of the same rock as the exterior. A tray filled with pecans, crackers, and candies sat on the kitchen counter. Beside the tray was a picnic basket. Abby opened it. A bottle of wine, a freshly baked cherry pie, and a note that directed them to the refrigerator, where the remainder of their gourmet meal waited.

In the bedroom, a fluffy white robe had been placed across the red and blue plaid bedspread. A box of fishing flies sat on the nightstand. One bed. One bathrobe. Abby hadn't thought this through. Ian, standing behind her, seemed to read her thoughts. "I'll sleep on the couch," he said. He squeezed her shoulders. "If that's what you want."

Abby didn't answer. Instead, she said, "Are you starving, because I'm starving."

An hour later, they sat at the table on the deck. The remainder of their lunch—quiche, chicken salad, lemony potato wedges, and pie— cleared away. The wine was gone, too, making Abby's thoughts soft.

Ian pulled the cover off the hot tub and turned a few switches. The water came to life. "Maybe later?" he asked, and she wondered if he'd remembered she hadn't brought a swimsuit.

He came closer, offering her his hand. "Let's go for a walk," he said.

The woods were beautiful this time of year, the colors beginning to turn. They walked a path lined with pine trees and stepped into a grove of oak and maple. The air smelled of fallen leaves. Cold mornings. Afternoon sun.

They walked farther, all the way to the river, its shore covered in small rocks. Ian picked up a rock and skipped it across the face of the water. Three times.

The wine, the meal, nature, Ian. All those things had turned Abby's worries to curiosity. "Can I ask you something?"

"Anything," Ian said.

"Even if it's about Josh and the campaign?"

Ian skipped another stone. It sunk after one bounce. "Why not."

"His opponent, Mayor Thornton, called me to his office. It happened so quickly I didn't tell Josh." Abby frowned. "That might not be true. Maybe I wanted a chance to see what Thornton was like without having to consider Josh's opinion of him."

"Makes sense. What did you find out?"

"He's a scoundrel." Abby picked up a rock, rubbing it between her thumb and index finger. "But he's not stupid. He set my teeth on edge, if you want to know the truth. I think he could be dangerous."

Ian stepped closer. "Dangerous how?"

"He could be sabotaging Josh's campaign. Making it look like Josh has been stealing Thornton's signs, which is a crime."

"What did Josh say?"

"I've had trouble reaching him."

"What now?"

"I left a message but haven't heard back. I'm a little gun-shy about telling Josh. It could be that Thornton is pulling my chain. That he isn't behind his missing signs, but wants Josh to accuse him so he can play the victim."

"Let's walk a little more," Ian said. And so they walked the shore until they reached the steps that led to the main lodge, which was a massive two-story log cabin.

"I'll bet you can't wait to get out your camera," Abby said, and Ian smiled. "This place is beautiful," he said. There was a trail behind the lodge that led deeper into the woods. Abby tugged her hair into a bun and pulled a clip from her jacket pocket to secure it.

When they reached a spot where a large tree had fallen across the trail, Ian climbed on top of it and took Abby's hand. When she was steady, he said. "I can't get my head around the word dangerous. What aren't you telling me?"

By then, Ian had jumped to the ground on the other side. Abby scooted to the edge, and he helped her down, his hands firm on her waist. "That's just it," she said. "I'm not sure how to articulate it."

A campground was nearby, and smoke from a wood fire curled in the air. Ian put his hands in his pockets. "Trust your gut, Abby."

Abby looked around. The air was crisp. The wood smoke the perfect addition. The trees were gold and green and red. At any other time, she'd revel in the beauty. "Okay then, he was threatening me. It sounds as if he's having me watched. He said some things about wanting to win the election that sounded like he'd do anything to do it."

"You've got to tell the authorities."

"Thornton says the police are under his thumb."

Ian sighed. "Abby Girl," he said.

"I know."

"Do you want my advice?" When Abby said yes, Ian continued. "Let's go back to the cabin. You can get your laptop, because I know you never travel without it. Write down the entire conversation with Thornton, as closely as you can."

"So you can read it?" Abby asked.

"No, so Josh can." Before Abby could say anything else, Ian said, "While you do that, I'll get some shots of the lodge and boat dock. The rest I want to get as the sun comes up tomorrow."

Ian brushed away a purple leaf that had become entangled in Abby's hair. "You always do better when you have a plan, kid." He touched her cheek. "With a list or two."

When Ian returned, it was after six in the evening. Abby had finished her notes, emailed them to Josh, talked to him on the phone, and set up a meeting for the next evening.

"What's that?' Abby asked.

Ian, holding a white, grease-stained paper bag, said, "Billy's Barbeque."

Abby's mouth watered. "Praise the Lord," she said, and laughed.

They sat side by side on the couch, eating ribs and corn on the cob, the restaurant's famous yeast rolls and butter.

"Want to go on the shoot with me tomorrow? It'll be early."

"I can do early," Abby said. "Just don't expect much from my hair." She pointed to her head. "It takes a village to get this under control."

Ian's voice was husky when he said, "I've seen your hair first thing in the morning, and it's glorious."

It wasn't difficult to get up early; Abby had barely slept. Ian was too close, and Abby imagined gently shaking his shoulder, scooting in beside him. It took all her willpower not to do it.

Ian didn't talk while he was shooting, not unless it had to do with the shoot. Abby sat on the shore of the river, watching as he switched lenses and set up his tripod. She watched while he lay on his belly to get the right shot, while he climbed an oak tree for another angle.

A fisherman, bearded and wrinkled, showed up with the dawn. After a short conversation with Ian, the man walked into the water in his waders, his rod and reel lifted. Ian followed, holding his camera above his head. For the next hour, Ian followed the man while he cast his line, and shot photos of the trout he caught. When he was through, Ian came back to shore, sopping wet and happy.

At lunch, Abby had trouble keeping her thoughts off Ian. When she wasn't eating or drinking, she sat on her hands; she was that afraid she might touch him. He'd changed into a flannel shirt and well-worn jeans. When he smiled, two lines showed at the corners of his eyes. Abby looked at his fingers. Was it possible to love a person's hands? She bit down on the inside of her mouth and willed herself to stop.

Ian interrupted her thoughts. "Earth to Abby," he said.

"Sorry."

"Thinking about the campaign?" he asked.

"Sure," she said. "The campaign."

"You're not alone in this," he said. "I mean it. I'm here."

"What exactly does that mean?"

"I'm offering to help. I'll go see Josh with you if you'll let me. Help you two come up with a plan. I can snap a few photos, follow Thornton. Ask a few questions. I might be useful."

"You'd do that?"

"For you? Of course."

Before she could reconsider, Abby texted Josh. She expected him to protest, but he wrote back, Bring Mr. Chicago. I've been wanting to meet him.

It was almost six in the evening when they pulled into Logan's Creek. Abby directed Ian to Josh's office. She smoothed her hair and straightened her wrinkled top. She was about to sit down with the two men that held her heart. Even Thornton's threats didn't scare her that much.

Chapter Seventeen

As Abby and Ian entered Josh's office, her heart fluttered like a million butterflies. She had never been in the same room with Josh and Ian, nor had she ever expected to be. But here she was.

Josh was waiting for them. He was wearing a snug black suit, something that looked like it belonged in *GQ* magazine, not Logan's Creek. "Come in," he said. "Come in." Ian kept his hand at the base of Abby's back until she quickly stepped forward. He'd left a trail of dried mud from his hiking boots in his wake.

Josh led them to the conference room, where bottles of water had been set out. After they sat, Abby said. "I'd like to introduce Ian Reynolds. Ian, this is Josh Moore, our City Attorney."

The men shook hands across the table, holding their grip a beat too long. Could they be challenging each other? Of course, they were. She'd grown up around enough stubborn bulls to know the signs.

Josh and Ian were about as different as salt and pepper. She could see it now. They were both opinionated, strong, liked to exercise. As far as music, goals, ideas, creativity, they were worlds apart.

"Would either of you care for something other than water? I have coffee."

"I'd like a coffee," said Abby as she pulled out her laptop.

"Water's fine," Ian said, scooting his chair closer to Abby.

After Josh brought Abby's coffee, he said, "So, Abby, I've had ample time to go over your email. Thank you for that, by the way. Your recollection is astonishing." He pulled at the cuffs on his white shirt.

"On a scale of one to ten, how bad do you think this is?"

"Six or seven, maybe?"

Ian stepped in. "At least a seven."

Josh's eyes never left Abby. "Do you really think he'd steal his own signs?"

"I have two theories," Abby said. "One, he did. Two, he didn't but wants us to accuse him so he can play the victim."

"The flyers?" Josh asked.

Abby pulled up her notes on her computer. "I'm about 99.9 percent sure he's behind those."

"And you think he was threatening us with all that bluster about wanting to win?"

"Absolutely."

Ian put his arm across the top of Abby's chair. "In my opinion, he sees Abby as the easier target. If he gets to her, he gets to you. That puts her in a lot of danger. Something I'm not comfortable with."

Josh looked at Ian for a few seconds, his expression unreadable. Abby doubted Josh cared a whit what Ian thought.

"One thing I didn't put in the notes is that he offhandedly suggested I might work for him." Abby imitated Thornton's drawl. "A young filly like you. Why if you didn't have such a mouth on you, I could see you doing marketing for the City.'" Abby was mad all over again.

Josh smirked. "That wasn't a real offer, Abby." He lifted his coffee mug that read Boss Man and took a drink.

Before Abby could respond, Ian slammed his fist on the table. "What the hell is that supposed to mean? Thornton would be damn lucky to have her."

Josh stood up, looming over the two of them. "Hey, I'm on her side. Thornton was working an angle, is all I'm saying. No campaign manager, no campaign." He looked down at Ian with fire in his eyes.

"Oh, no need to worry, Josh," Abby said. "Thornton decided real quick that I was too spirited. Couldn't hold my tongue. Which I guess is true."

Both men smiled. Some things were universal truths.

Abby stood and put her hands on her hips. "Sit back down, Josh," she said. Once he was seated, she addressed them both. "Look, you two. I feel the testosterone in the room. Heck, I'm practically swimming in it. So take it down a notch. Just so you know, this isn't a comfortable situation for me, either. But right now, none of our personal feelings matter.

"I know there's more to what's going on with our mayor. We're going to find out what it is. That's a hell of a lot more important than whatever is going on with the three of us. And just so you know, I'm not a prize to be won any more than I'm a little filly with a temper. Got it?"

After a few uncomfortable beats, Ian broke the tension. "Said you couldn't hold your tongue, did he?"

And then Josh laughed. Abby let out her breath.

When the conversation continued, Josh said, "Do you remember the old land surveyor here in town? Daniel Slayer? He'd had the job for years."

She shook her head no.

"Of course, you weren't living here. He knew this land like he knew his mama's cooking. Not too long ago, I did a property search for him in order to finalize a trust. During our meetings, he told me that Thornton made it a point to contact him about any land being foreclosed on, coming up for sale, or being turned over to the bank."

"Why would he do that?" Abby asked.

"Because Thornton has been playing the long game, buying low, selling high. Through his realty company, which, coincidentally, doesn't carry his name. You have to be part of his inner circle for Thornton to confide in you. Daniel was in that circle. With the information on the documents, Thornton knew exactly how low the sellers would go. And his company would offer cash.

"It didn't hurt that the mayor's brother-in-law is the county assessor. So if a property needed to be devalued, guess who could do it?"

Ian rubbed his chin. "The assessor. Now, that's quite an operation."

"And that's when you decided to run for mayor?" Abby asked Josh.

"It was."

Ian tapped the table. "My question is this. Why didn't you go to the authorities?"

"I didn't know who I could trust," Josh said.

"What about the county sheriff?" Abby asked.

Josh seemed spent. "The rivers here run deep, Abby. We just don't know how deep."

Abby closed her computer. "Let's sleep on it. Meet at Chapters tomorrow afternoon at one o'clock? They have that meeting room I'll bet we could use. If anybody asks, we're interviewing our new campaign photographer."

Ian stood. "I'm in. I'll get Abby home and head back to the B and B."

If Abby were clairvoyant, she would have known how much Ian's statement settled Josh. All three of them would be in their own beds. All was well with the world. Before she could stop herself, she tugged Josh's sleeve. "One day soon, you're going to have to tell me who Penelope is. And whether you left Cynthia Burke's niece at the altar."

Josh pulled her to him, wrapping her in a hug. "Your questions are too hard," he said. Abby could feel Ian close by. If she had to guess, she'd say he was seething.

On the way to the cabin, Ian said, "So, Josh." And Abby said, "What about him?"

"Doesn't seem remotely your type."

"Really?"

"Too stiff. Too pressed."

"Pressed?"

"Starched. Ironed. Gelled. Looks more like he belongs in Chicago than I do."

"Good to know," Abby said. She wasn't about to have this conversation.

When they reached the cabin, Ian carried her overnight bag to the porch. "Want me to come inside, make sure everything's okay in there?"

Abby looked at him, at the stubble on his cheeks and the light bouncing off his dark hair. She could drink him in, but she wouldn't. Hadn't that been the deal they'd struck in Josh's office?

"Everything's fine," she said, and Ian answered, "Almost."

He took her in his arms and lifted her onto her tiptoes. She breathed in the scent of him. Laundry dried on a clothesline, wood smoke, pine trees, coffee. Her heart flip-flopped.

Her determination to stay neutral and her need were at war. Abby traced the arch of Ian's eyebrow. She heard him groan. His mouth was on her, hungry. She slid her hands beneath his shirt, touched the muscles at his waist. "No?" she said, sagging against the porch rail. It came out a question. It said, "Convince me otherwise."

But Ian pulled her up by her belt loops, stopping to touch the curve of her jeans where her back pockets were. "See you tomorrow," he said.

All she could do was raise her hand. Her voice had been burned by his fire.

QUESTION: Is this the end of #FITNESSGATE?

Well, folks, I asked for it, and I got it. The Honorable Mayor Maximus Thornton sent a statement to YOURS truly regarding the investigation into City Attorney (AND Thornton's opponent in the mayor's race) HUNKY Josh Moore.

QUICK recap. Josh was called out in a prior city council meeting by citizen Cynthia Burke, who had documents that appeared scandalous. The records showed payments to OUR city attorney from the town of Lone Elm, for legal services involving, but not limited to, the fitness/aquatic center they recently opened. If you'll recall, all my pea-picking little heart has ever wanted is a fitness center like that for our precious town.

While Mr. (DREAMBOAT) Moore has been moving ahead with his mayoral campaign, he must have been feeling pretty low in the hole, as my Great Aunt Gertie used to say. Every day the investigation dragged on was another day voters had reason to doubt whether our City Attorney was on the up-and-up.

Well, Mr. Moore, you can stop worrying.

Read on for Mayor Thornton's Official Statement concerning the results of the investigation:

To the citizens of Logan's Creek,

Let it be known that the investigation into the possible nefarious actions of City Attorney Josh Moore has officially concluded. I brought in a forensic auditor, a detective from the Logan's Creek Police Department, and a panel who listened to witnesses, including Cynthia Burke, who originally tendered the allegations that Moore had committed fraud by receiving payments for legal work from both our city and Lone Elm.

Although many curiosities were discovered during the investigation, none of them reached the threshold of illegality. Since those curiosities did cause me to question the hiring of Mr. Moore, I wish that

I could share them with you.

All I can do is tell you that moving forward, our City Attorney will not be allowed to represent other municipalities, nor will he be able to produce legal work for any entity or person that might be deemed a competitor or enemy of Logan's Creek or its office holders.

I am not allowed to mention the seriousness of the mayoral race in this document, so, suffice it to say, Get out and vote. Integrity matters.

The Honorable Mayor Maximus Thornton

On a personal note, I'm not sure who wrote the mayor's statement, but it sure wasn't Max Thornton. I've heard him speak. He talks more like a good old boy than a Southern lawyer.

The mayor's statement did leave the impression that our Mr. Moore might be underhanded after all. That's ego talking right there. Or maybe it's nerves. Our last L.C. Confidential (unofficial) poll shows Mr. Moore gaining a tiny bit of ground. (Those polled were at the Drip and Shine Carwash, which I HIGHLY recommend.)

One thing I do agree with. Get out and vote!

Chapter Eighteen

Abby's one o'clock meeting was still hours away when she stepped onto the beaten trail beside her cabin that led to the downtown area. She'd grabbed her phone and credit card, maneuvered her curls into a ponytail, and grabbed a bottle of water. She wanted time to herself to think about Thornton.

Could he really be as sinister as he seemed? Could he be even worse? Abby wasn't sure. What she did know was that she was in his sights and it was a terribly uncomfortable place to be.

She passed several people on the sidewalks as they were heading into the shops or the breakfast spots around the square on Main Street. Ms. Vivian's car was parked behind the library. The town librarian probably knew more about Thornton than anyone else. But Ms. Vivian was like a priest; she kept what she'd learned to herself.

Up ahead was Leading Lady Amy's store, Treasures Abound. Abby wiped her brow before she stepped inside. Amy was on a tall ladder changing the light bulbs in the middle of the store. She was in her typical jeans and loud-colored t-shirt with the store's logo. As usual, Amy wore an unbuttoned denim long-sleeved shirt over her t-shirt.

The shelves at Treasures Abound were bright and filled with handmade soaps, lotions, and sprays. There was a white clawfoot bathtub filled with every color of bath sponge. There was a table with necklaces that could hold essential oils. Small bottles of the oil took up half the table. Everywhere Abby looked there was something she wanted. That was the magic of Amy's store.

"Don't you have a maintenance guy?" Abby asked as Amy descended the ladder.

"I only wish. My other half works the fire department more than he wants to admit. I only get him here when it is a dire emergency." She gave Abby that you-know-what-I-mean look. Abby followed her as she took her used light bulbs, wrapped them in newspaper and put them in the trash can beside the checkout counter.

"What's up?" Amy asked.

"I've been working a lot," Abby said.

"Anything else?"

Abby was afraid to talk too freely. Any second, a customer could stop by. "The usual," Abby said. "Seeing the family. Running."

Amy grinned. "And maybe a little canoodling with a certain photographer from Chicago? I hear Ian's in town."

"He is in town. And I want you to meet him." Abby lowered her voice. "But right now, I've got some problem-solving to do. It seems Mayor Thornton is playing hardball."

"What's going on? You know I can keep a secret. I'll even pinkie swear if you want."

Just then the bell above the entry door sounded, and Emily and another woman came into the shop.

"Emily," Abby said. "So nice to see you."

Emily stepped forward. "You missed lunch with Jim and Gabby on Sunday. Is everything okay?"

"Just busy."

Amy stepped in front of the counter. "So busy," she said. "Juggling men and a campaign."

Emily laughed. "Do tell." She seemed to catch herself. "Where are my manners? Do you all know Folly Beckham? She's Ms. Vivian's niece. We do hot yoga together about three times a week."

Folly held out her hand. She was almost as tall as Emily, maybe five ten or so. Her light brown hair was in a messy bun, and she had the greenest eyes Abby had ever seen. Abby shook Folly's hand. "Nice to meet you," and Amy said, "Welcome to my shop."

Abby smoothed her hair. "It must be fun being related to Ms. Vivian."

"It is, mostly because she's the smartest woman I know." As if to make her point, she added, "My aunt's even memorized the Dewey Decimal System."

Amy asked, "Do you talk books a lot?"

"All the time."

Amy straightened a stack of lavender-colored matches. "Does she read anything other than books? Like that spicy blog, L.C. Confidential?"

Before Folly could answer, Abby said, "It drives me crazy that I can't figure out who this anonymous blogger is."

Emily interrupted, "Oh my gosh. Have you seen the latest? Mayor Thornton admitted Josh hadn't done anything wrong when he helped Lone Elm with their legal work."

"Praise the Lord," Abby said, and laughed. "That must have hurt the old son of a gun. It sure took him long enough to make a statement."

"The ego on that man," Emily added.

Folly picked up a bottle of bubble bath and examined the label. "Thornton thinks the sun comes up just to hear him crow," and they all shook their heads. That was Thornton to a T.

Abby looked at her watch. She had enough time to go home, shower, and tame her hair before her meeting. "Gotta run," she said.

"Don't forget," Amy said. "We get to meet Ian soon."

Emily held her mouth just so, as if she was surprised. But Abby knew better. The Carters would have already discussed Ian in length, at that Sunday lunch she'd missed.

It was after twelve-thirty in the afternoon when Abby walked into Chapters. She had thirty minutes to prepare.

It was a perfect day for an Americano. After she got her drink, she walked down the stairs to the meeting room, where she waited for the others to show up.

Ian arrived shortly after one o'clock, sat beside her, and made it hard to concentrate. His easy charm was hard on her.

A few minutes later, Josh and Amanda arrived. Josh took a seat across from Abby, and without even a hello, Amanda set her things down at the other end of the table and opened her laptop.

Abby said, "Amanda, I'd like to introduce you to my friend, Ian Reynolds."

Amanda seemed startled, as she always did when she was interrupted. She walked to Ian, who was now standing. "Hello, Mr. Reynolds. It's nice to finally meet you."

"Please, call me Ian. No formality here."

"Ian it is." Amanda looked at Abby, and gave her a wink.

After everyone had their coffees, Amanda said, "Catch me up."

Abby opened her notebook. "Josh has some information you need to hear."

"Daniel Slayer," Josh said. "Do you remember him? Our former county land surveyor? He left his position a few years ago, moved away. I still do some work for him now and again."

Amanda was taking notes on her laptop. "I remember Daniel." Her expression was unreadable. She might as well have been in court.

"I recently finished a trust for Daniel and his wife. During our last meeting, he told me something interesting. While he was the county land surveyor, Thornton had made a practice of contacting him about foreclosed land and property that had recently been put on the market. Daniel didn't think much of it at first.

"These were random properties; nothing tied them together. But then the rumor mill revved up. A new highway was set to be built on the east edge of Crawford County. It turned out, it wasn't a rumor at all, but officials were trying to keep it quiet. Several years ago, they'd tried to put a highway in the same area, but the affected parties formed a coalition and successfully stopped the project."

"Imminent domain," Amanda said. "The worst kind of news for someone who loves their home."

Josh looked through his notes. "The official word was that nothing was in the works, although, of course, they were in the preliminary stages. Some of those properties were worth very little. For instance, there was a section that was too low to farm, so it had sat fallow for years. A few of the other houses were in disrepair. The K-Mart in that area had closed down, depressing the neighborhood. Still, if the government bought them out, they were set to make more than fair market. No lowballing."

"And Thornton knew this?"

"All we can do is follow the clues. Thornton would have Daniel send him copies of the land he was surveying for the proposed highway."

Abby got up with her coffee and began walking the room. Sometimes she could think better that way. "Thornton's brother-in-law was the county assessor."

"Bertram Riggins?" Amanda asked.

Abby leaned against the wall. "That's him. "Daniel looked at the records, before and after his survey. The property values had tanked."

Ian spoke up. "Does Daniel have the records?"

They all looked at Josh. "No. No, he doesn't. But here's what happened next. The properties Daniel surveyed started selling at bargain basement prices. Daniel couldn't find Thornton's name attached to any of the sales, but he still wondered. Who else would know what Thornton did, and have the money to do something about it?"

Amanda said, "It can't be that hard to find the contracts."

"You'd think," Josh said, "but when I looked at the record database, all I could find were a few LLC ID numbers listed. When I looked up those ID numbers, they all say they were inactive."

Amanda furrowed her brow. "So," she said. "No real proof. Where's Bertram Riggins now?"

"Six feet under," Josh said. "Car accident. In Montana. No other cars involved."

"But your gut tells you there's something to all this. It's not just you wanting to become mayor?"

Josh's face blanched. "Of course not. In fact, this mess is what made me want to run. Logan's Creek deserves better."

Amanda rubbed her temples. "You'll need records showing the undervalued property documents with the county assessor's signature. Then, you'll need the records that show an uptick in price. A before and after." Amanda brushed her long hair over one shoulder.

"There was a fire," Josh said, his forehead in his hands. "Certain records were destroyed, including the documents we need. It was just before Riggins retired. That's why I searched the database instead.

Abby spoke up. "Shouldn't the Highway Department have copies?"

"I thought of that," Josh said, "but I'm Thornton's opposition. If I stir things up and I'm wrong, it makes me look like a conspiracy nut."

Abby had a thought. "What about a Freedom of Information Act Request? An FOIA? Anyone can ask for public records."

"But it can't be us," Josh said, "not this close to an election."

Amanda smiled. "But a media outlet, say L.C. Confidential, could and should ask the hard questions, right?"

Abby could see the plan developing. "Amanda, you have that friend who's an investigator at the State Police Headquarters in Little Rock, right?" Amanda nodded. "See if he's heard any rumblings about Thornton. If we know this much, maybe someone else does too, and maybe that someone has contacted them. Aren't they the ones who'd investigate? Especially since Thornton likes to claim the PD is in his pocket."

Amanda was typing away. "I'll check, but you understand that first I have to contact the Crawford County Sheriff. There's a protocol to follow. But if I had to guess, I'd say the sheriff will push this on up the line."

Abby nodded her head. "Of course." She turned to Josh. "Josh, you need to stay in campaign mode. Shake hands. Kiss babies. Make speeches."

Abby continued. "I can work on L.C. Confidential. They're our best bet for the FOIA. The Logan's Creek Courier might help, but there would be a much greater chance of the story leaking. And we don't need a leak. Not just yet."

Ian said, "What can I do?"

"What you do best," Abby said. "Get your camera out. Watch Thornton. If he's as dirty as we think, he's probably on to another scheme. Even if he isn't, seeing an unidentified man with a camera on his tail, will have him shaking in his boots."

Chapter Nineteen

It had been three days since Abby, Ian, Josh, and Amanda had met, and they were still looking for proof. Abby had messaged L.C. Confidential, asking for a meeting, but the elusive blogger would only communicate by email. Not that Abby was paranoid, but she didn't like leaving a digital trail of her conversations concerning Thornton. So the FIOA request to the Highway Department was still on hold.

Ian had been conspicuous in his tailing of Thornton; he'd spent an entire day showing up wherever the mayor did. At the Flying Penguin, he'd even taken a few photos of Thornton eating a double hot fudge sundae, after a dollop of whipped cream had fallen on his tie. Ian introduced himself as a traveling photographer, on a freelance gig to capture the essence of the American South. Thornton had eyed him suspiciously, which was exactly what Ian wanted him to do. Let the old coot sweat.

Amanda reported back. As she expected, the sheriff declined to investigate Thornton, citing lack of staff. So she called her contact at the State Police. Her friend had been evasive about whether an investigation was underway concerning Mayor Thornton. He'd said, "We've got bigger fish to fry," but something in the way he'd said it caused Amanda to doubt him. She'd told Abby that his response had been too quick, and he hadn't asked one follow-up question.

Josh had been doing his level best at campaigning. He'd even participated in the Logan's Creek Mule Jump contest. Mules could jump fences when they wanted to. Mostly when they were on the hunt for raccoons. Josh had placed sixth, not bad for a novice. Ian had been on hand to snap a photo of him just as Josh fell off the backend of his mule, his feet above his head as he tumbled. Abby didn't want to think about how much Ian had enjoyed the moment.

Now, Abby looked at herself in the mirror above her couch. Her eyes were red. She had bags beneath them that were worse than when she'd partied all night in college. Her hair looked as if it hadn't been washed in a week, even though it had. It also appeared not to have seen a brush for quite some time. She was exhausted from nearly twenty hours of researching the public archives online through the courthouse website.

Sadly, she'd turned up nothing. And election day was closing in.

Abby was glad the Leading Ladies had pushed her into planning a get-together at the cabin. First, to catch up. But most of all they wanted to meet Ian. Thankfully, she'd slept the night before, after she'd broken down and emailed L.C. Confidential. As sparsely as she could, she explained her situation, asking the blogger to request certain records from the Highway Department. Now, the ball was in the blogger's court. With that off her plate, Abby turned to party planning.

She'd order Mexican food, set up a margarita bar, and a karaoke station. She insisted that they come to the cabin for Mexican night. They all loved to pretend they could sing. Several of the ladies had been in choir in junior high and high school, though they'd never been given a solo part. None of them were Lady Gaga but they all thought they could be.

As much as Abby wanted her closest friends to meet Ian, she knew there was a war between Ian and Josh. She could see the fire between them every time they were in the same room. She would, at some point, need to make a choice. But not tonight. For a few seconds she wondered if she was breaking her own rule. She'd told Josh and Ian that any talk of romance was on hold until the election ended. But then she gave herself a break. They all knew Josh. Meeting Ian was giving them a chance to know him.

It would be a casual night. Jeans, a soft t-shirt, and sneakers. Nothing fancy. She didn't have the energy to dress up, and she had told the others the same. There were a few protests—the Leading Ladies loved fashion nearly as much as they loved parties—but they agreed. After all, it was the price they had to pay to meet Ian.

Abby fixed herself a drink to kickstart the evening. Minutes later, Cathy, who'd agreed to pick up the food Abby had ordered from Arkie Markie's House of Mexico, rang the doorbell.

Abby knew Cathy was ready for interrogation about Ian ahead of the others. But Abby decided to wait until they all had arrived so she didn't have to repeat herself. She'd asked Ian to show up about forty-five minutes after the girls did. The Leading Ladies were bound to be early.

Abby's inclinations were right.

After everyone had a margarita in hand, Amanda, the only one who'd already met Ian, said, "High five, girlfriend. I couldn't keep my eyes off Ian."

Abby motioned for the Leading Ladies to follow her to the kitchen, where they filled their plates with chips, queso, enchiladas, and Arkie Markie sauce. The sauce was a weird combination of white flour gravy and jalapenos. Quirky, but it worked.

Once they were sitting at the dining table, Abby said, "Please don't ask Ian questions that will embarrass me. Just so you know, I told him that we're on hold until I get this situation figured out with Thornton and the mayor's race."

"What are you talking about?" asked Janie.

Lisa looked at Janie and rolled her eyes. "Girl, you are woefully behind. Thornton closed down Josh's Meet and Greet at the Tuscan Table. Sent the popo in, the whole nine yards. Cathy has to pay a fine."

Janie set her margarita glass down with a thud. "You go out of town for a couple of weeks and the whole world implodes."

Abby continued, "That's just the beginning." She looked at Amanda.

"But I'm not sure I can tell you much more right now."

"You can't," Amanda said. "I'm speaking as your attorney now. All you have is speculation. But when the time is right, we might need the power of the Leading Ladies behind us, if what we suspect about Thornton is true."

Cathy raised her glass. The others followed. "To the Leading Ladies. Float like a butterfly. Sting like a bee. Nobody messes with me or thee."

After the toast and the laughter, Janie said. "Enough of this cloak and dagger. I want to know about Ian."

"Yes, come on, girl," Amy said. "I've spent weeks wondering if this perfect guy really exists."

"Oh, he exists," Amanda said as she was adding some queso to her plate.

Just then, Abby heard a car drive up. She tugged the pendant on her necklace, smoothed her hair. "Be on your best behavior," she said. Abby looked at Lisa, who was pouring herself another drink. "I mean it."

The doorbell rang and the Ladies squealed. Abby mouthed the word "stop," as she walked to the door and opened it. Ian stood before her, the kind of man who demanded attention, if just for the look of his toned body. For the way his body filled the doorframe.

He was wearing an inky blue long-sleeved Henley that brought out the color of his eyes. His tight jeans coveted the muscles showing in his thighs, as did Abby if she was being honest. Ian had a two-day beard, and smelled of shampoo. Abby's knees felt weak.

As they walked into the kitchen, Abby said "Ladies, I'd like you to meet Ian Reynolds. I think I've told you about his photography."

They all were standing, waiting to shake his hand.

The slanting light from the window danced across Ian's dark hair. "I hope you don't all expect me to remember your names, at least for a little while. I'm usually pretty good, but five all at once is difficult." He held his hand out to Amanda. "Hi, Amanda," he said. As if to explain to the others, he said, "We're in the trenches together. Like the Hardy Boys."

"In this group? I'd say we're like Nancy Drew," Amanda said, and Ian said, "touché."

The girls all but melted as they got him a chair, a margarita, and some chips and dip. You'd have thought he was a prince.

Lisa led Ian to the table and brought him a plate. "I hope you're hungry," she said.

Janie sat across from Ian, moving aside a half-eaten enchilada. "You're a little bit too good-looking," she said. "My daddy warned me against good-looking men. Said they didn't have to try at all. Just had to, you know, be gorgeous."

Ian didn't miss a beat. "I'm in a room full of beautiful women." He pointed to a container of Arkie Markie's gravy. "I feel about as attractive as whatever this is."

Lisa was leaning on the table, her voice husky. "See, that's the thing. That gravy might not look so good, but it tastes divine. That was Janie's daddy's whole point."

Abby's face was burning, so when Amanda yelled, "Karaoke time," Abby clapped her hands. "Yes," she said, "karaoke." She glanced at Ian. Even though he hadn't eaten much, he looked as relieved as she felt.

When Abby and Ian sang "Shallow," she felt Lady Gaga with her. Ian was her Bradley Cooper. She hoped for a better ending than theirs. Abby held the microphone between, getting her body as close to his as she could.

Later, she'd blame what happened next on the alcohol, the party, even the music. But after the song ended, she shooed the Leading Ladies away and held tight to Ian's arm when he tried to join them.

Abby woke in the middle of the night. Her body felt as if it weighed nothing, but her head, that was a horse of a different color. When she reached for the extra pillow to cover her eyes, it wouldn't move. Ian raised his head from it. "Want me to leave?" he asked.

Abby looked under her covers. Not a stitch of clothes on. Her body held almost no tension, meaning whatever the two of them had done had worked miracles. "It's just that we made a deal." She was holding her hands over her eyes.

Ian reached over and kissed her cheek. "Not to dwell on the details, Abby Girl, but you seduced me."

When Abby's alarm went off at seven o'clock, she hit snooze. She looked around. Ian was gone. And then her phone rang.

"I got a call back from my friend at the State Police Department." Amanda said.

Abby sat up. "Do tell."

"He's still not admitting to an investigation, but he did hint at one."

"What do you mean?"

"He gave me a what-if scenario. As in, what if an underhanded person, i.e. our "subject," was pulling in money that couldn't be traced back to him. That person would likely upgrade their lifestyle. Take exotic vacations. Make significant changes."

Abby thought. "But our subject is driving a decades' old car."

Amanda said, "Have you seen our subject smile? All new veneers. Plus, divorced last year. New model this year."

"Much younger?"

"From the looks of her, yes."

Abby stretched. "Vacations?"

"I have no idea. It's not like he's on social media."

"What do we do now?"

"Let the State Police follow the money. And hope they're fast."

Abby lowered her voice, although she couldn't say why. "I'm still determined to find out who L.C. Confidential is. I have the strongest feeling that our blogger is the key to all this."

"Great," Amanda said, "but pull L.C. Confidential off the FOIA search with the Highway Department. I have a feeling they don't want any additional attention on their 'hypothetical' case."

"Will do," Abby said.

"I gotta go," Amanda said. "My real job is calling."

Chapter Twenty

Abby climbed the steps to her parents' house. Three pumpkins sat beside the front door, a wreath of corn husks hung on the door, tied with a purple ribbon. She'd come for lunch, and a hug from her mom if she was being honest.

In the kitchen, the table was already set. "I hope you still like taco soup," Gabby said, turning from the stove.

"I don't like anybody's but yours, Mom. Everybody else adds sweet corn."

Gabby winked. "They weren't raised right, honey."

"Is Dad coming?"

"He had some business down at the lot. He's missing a cashier's check from Mr. Dobson. He bought an F-150 and used the check as a down payment."

Abby reached for the Tostitos, near the stove. "Is Dad worried?"

"Not really." Gabby wiped her hands on a tea towel. "He misplaces things now and then, but he always finds them."

When the two women sat at the kitchen table, Gabby said, "I heard Ian is still in town."

Abby took a bite of the soup, stalling. "He is," she finally said.

"And you two have had a serious talk?"

"We have."

Gabby sprinkled cheddar cheese on her soup. "That's all I need to know." The smell of the taco soup filled the kitchen: oregano and chili powder. Corn chips. "How's the campaign going?"

As much as Abby wanted to tell her mother, she couldn't say much. They'd worry, and her dad would move onto her front porch—with his shotgun. So Abby said, "It could go either way."

"If your dad and I need to knock on doors, let us know. Josh is like family to us."

Abby spooned out sour cream, dropping it in her bowl. It would thrill her mom to have Josh as her son-in-law, and Abby knew his sights were set higher than mayor. He could be a state senator one day. Maybe the governor.

Abby changed the subject. "Remember the state highway that went in near the old K-Mart?" Gabby shook her head yes.

"Do you remember any scuttlebutt? Did the landowners who had to give up their property ever protest?

Gabby frowned when she concentrated, and two lines formed between her eyebrows. "I don't remember anything like that. But in the months before the demolition of those houses, the bank deposited quite a few checks from folks in that area. All the checks were from the same LLC, although I can't recall the name." Gabby raised an eyebrow. "Does any of this have to do with the campaign?"

"I'm not sure," Abby said.

"I could look up the name of the LLC."

Abby didn't want to appear eager. She shrugged. "If you have a chance, that would be great."

It was getting dark when Abby finished scheduling social media posts for Josh's campaign. How many iterations of 'more' could she find before it was all over? Josh Moore-Innovation was getting noticed. *Give Me Moore* was a nearly viral sensation. She'd almost taken that slogan down. It could be interpreted in a few too many ways. Even L.C. Confidential had commented Yes! Yes! Yes!

It was enough to make Abby blush. She cleared her mind before picking up the phone. "I wanted to make certain we were on track," she said, when Josh answered. "I have you down to speak at the Rotary, the Kiwanis, and the Chamber this week." Abby looked at her calendar. "And the Catholic church, and the Presbyterian church next week."

Josh's voice was smooth. "Good evening to you, too, Ms. Campaign Manager. Yep, I have the same. You know I have a calendar, right?"

He was teasing her. "You'd better have your calendar synced with mine, Mr. I-Want-Moore. You've been known to be late on occasion."

Abby liked the way you could know someone was smiling without seeing them. Like now, when Josh said, "I was late for one date with you, Ms. Carter. And that was when I stopped to buy you a box of Fruit Roll-Ups. You'd been complaining that your mom was out. I think you said, 'I will absolutely die without them.'"

Abby laughed. Sometimes she still felt that way about Fruit Roll-Ups.

Abby grabbed her earbuds and phone, and hit the trail leading downtown. As she turned the corner at Fifth and Main, memories rushed back of her high school years. Even then the buildings on the square seemed ancient. Not far from the square, the two-hundred-year-old oak trees stood on the courthouse lawn, a fiery orange from this vantage point. A parade of maples stood close by, their leaves as red as cherries. She was close enough now to hear them flutter in the breeze coming off of Logan's Creek, a few hundred yards away.

Abby had been two years old when the worst tornado in Logan's Creek's history tore through the town, toppling cars as easily as toys. Destroying entire neighborhoods. Abby's parents had told her about the President's visit, the days of mourning for the three people lost, and how the National Guard came in to serve meals and help clean up the damage. Since then, every school and nearly every home had a storm shelter. You didn't have to tell Logan's Creek twice. Threats could come out of nowhere, and they could devastate your life.

Just as Abby returned to the present, she saw Emily walking out of Amy's store. "I didn't expect to see you this afternoon, Emily. Come give me a hug, if you don't mind me being all sweaty."

Emily hugged her and then pulled Abby aside. "I was hoping I'd see you. Something's been bothering me. Would you mind if we spoke in your car?"

Once they reached Abby's car, Emily said, "Actually, could we go to your place? I'd feel better talking there."

What if Emily and Dan were having marital problems? They'd married young. Never spent much time outside their little town. "Is it Dan?" Abby asked.

"No, nothing like that. Although, if you could get him to quit leaving his towels on the bathroom floor, that would be great."

"I'm not a magician," Abby said, remembering what sharing a bathroom with her brother had been like.

Abby offered Emily sweet iced tea, a drink she knew she couldn't resist. Unlike most people, the calories didn't bother Emily. She stayed as lean as a willow branch.

After they sat at the patio table on the deck, Abby said, "Okay, Emily, spill."

Emily cleared her throat. "Do you remember when I introduced you to Folly, Ms. Vivian's niece?"

"Of course."

"Do you remember what she said?"

"Not specifically."

Emily squirmed in her seat. "We were talking about Mayor Thornton. She said, 'Thornton thinks the sun comes up just to hear him crow.'"

Abby wasn't getting it.

Emily said, "Think, sister. Who does that sound like?"

Abby mouthed the words to herself. Suddenly, a light went off, and then a thousand bells. "Oh my gosh, Emily, that sounds like L.C. Confidential."

"Bingo," Emily said.

"And you're sure?"

"I confronted Folly as soon as I figured it out."

"But why didn't you want to tell me this in my car?"

"Because there's more."

Every time Abby heard the word 'more,' she thought of Josh. "Not about Josh," she said.

"Everything I'm telling you has to stay between us. I haven't breathed a word of this, not even to Dan, which makes me feel icky, by the way. Can you do that? Keep this a secret?"

"I can," Abby said. She felt like she was smack-dab in the middle of a spy movie.

"Good," Emily said. "Here's the thing. Folly's come across evidence that could implicate Thornton in a fraudulent land deal. A major land deal with ties to the government."

Abby's heart pounded. Could this be the thing that took down Thornton? Still, she had questions, such as, could Folly be working for the opposition? "Folly claims to be a journalist," Abby flared, "the Fourth Estate and all that. So shouldn't she be exposing what she's learned?"

"Folly's in over her head, Abby. She's scared."

"And you trust that she's on the up-and-up?"

"I do."

Abby then recalled her interactions with the mayor. She shivered. "I can see where she'd hesitate. Folly may be a journalist of some sort, but she's still so young."

"Plus, she doesn't have an organization behind her. She's the sole entity behind the blog." Emily took a sip of tea. "Folly needs your advice. I told her you'd done crisis communications for some of your clients in Chicago. Taught them how to spin a bad choice into a learning lesson. She thinks you could help her make sense of what she's found, and protect her reputation."

"She hasn't broken the law, has she?"

Emily adjusted her sunglasses. "She may have 'borrowed' the evidence she has without permission."

"Do you mean stolen?"

"Tomatoes, tamahtoes," Emily said. "Anyway, you also need her. Folly can help bring down Thornton. That couldn't possibly be bad for Josh's campaign."

Abby folded her paper napkin around the base of the glass holding her sparkling water. She was stalling. How in the world could she not help Folly? Finally, she said, "Bring her over tonight after dinner, say nine o'clock. Park behind the cabin, and come through the back door. I'm afraid Thornton's minions are watching me, but if you two hurry in, no one should be able to see you." Abby felt tension in her shoulders. What in the world was happening to her peaceful little town?

Abby itched to tell Josh, but she'd made a promise. She could hear her dad saying, "Carters don't break confidences." So instead of calling Josh, she straightened her living room, made another pot of coffee, and paced the floor. Nine o'clock seemed as if it would never arrive.

But it did, and as the clock chimed on the mantle, Abby heard the familiar crunch of tires on her gravel drive. Someone had arrived.

She reached the back door just as Emily and Folly stepped out of Emily's Bronco. Abby waved them in, holding up her cell phone with its flashlight shining.

"Come in," Abby said, and the three women walked to the living room.

"Thanks, sis," Emily said. "You remember Folly."

"Of course. Folly, welcome. Have a seat anywhere."

Folly took a seat on the sofa. Emily sat beside her. After Abby pulled her chair closer, she said, "You do a great job on L.C. Confidential."

Folly smiled, and Emily touched her arm. "That means a lot coming from you, Abby."

"I'm curious. Why L.C. Confidential? You could have blogged about anything."

Folly shrugged. "I've always wanted to be a journalist. My parents didn't approve. They had examples of how the industry was shrinking. Our local paper in Kansas had been bought out by a national conglomerate. The news was generic, lackluster. When a girl from our town won Miss America, they didn't even cover it. And they had horror stories about TV reporters. Low pay. Stalkers. Being sent out in hurricanes and tornadoes and wildfires to report on the weather.

"The one thing that held my mismatched parents together was their mutual dislike of me studying journalism. After I graduated, Mom and Dad broke up. They wanted me to be a nurse or a physical therapist. People would always get sick. Or fall. They'd need medical help. When I stayed the course, they got so mad. Would've folded me up like Sunday laundry if they'd had the chance. Plus, they were right. I couldn't find a steady writing job to save me. So Aunt Vivian took me in. Nobody believes in the power of words more than she does."

Abby smiled despite herself at Folly. *Folded up like Sunday laundry.* That was what made the blog sparkle. She'd deliberately started with Folly's background. She needed to know if she was a serious person, or someone who brought drama everywhere she went. Her next question was critical. "Why do you write as if you're a bit older than you are? Why does it seem as if you've lived in Logan's Creek all your life?"

Headlights swept across the living room windows. Someone might have made a wrong turn, or someone might be spying. Abby stood up, cracked open the drapes to see, but the car was already turned around, headed the other way.

Sitting back down, she said, "It's nothing. Lost drivers love to turn around in my driveway."

Folly continued. "I wanted to be accepted, trusted as a good source. I wanted to blend in. I also wanted to give 'news' a makeover. Make it fun, but also serious.

"Plus, by the time I started the blog, I'd overheard enough gossip at the library to fill a book. And not a thin one, either."

Abby couldn't help herself. "The stuff you write about Josh Moore being handsome. Is that hyperbole or not?"

Folly leveled her eyes at Abby. "He could eat crackers in my bed anytime."

Abby refused to look away, and then Emily said, "I feel like we're getting off track," and the moment passed.

"Right, right," Abby said, rearranging herself on the cushioned chair. "You have evidence?" she asked Folly.

"One night, about a month ago, I couldn't sleep. Aunt Vivian goes to bed fairly early, and I needed to work on my blog. I do a lot of my writing at the library after hours, so no one can trace my location or find out who I am. The library uses a VPN, a virtual private network that encrypts your IP address. No address, no way to be found. It's to keep patrons' information confidential. That's actually where the confidential part of L.C. Confidential came from.

"Anyway, when I arrived, there were ten cardboard banker's boxes—I think that's what you call them—right beside the circulation desk. Each was marked with the name Dunham. I couldn't resist opening them.

"A lot of people donate family histories to the library's genealogical collection. I've helped Aunt Vivian get them in order before, so that she can catalog them and get them into the system."

Abby scooted to the edge of her seat. "What did you find?"

"The usual. Birth announcements, newspaper clippings, graduation programs, wedding invitations. But at the bottom of the first box, was an envelope that had a red wax seal." Folly's green eyes were nearly sparkling. "It was begging to be opened.

"I almost took it to Aunt Vivian. I imagined waking her up, having her unseal the letter, and maybe finding a million-dollar donation to the library. But I couldn't wait. I opened it while sitting on the library floor."

"Dunham," Abby said. "Why is that name familiar?"

Emily took over. "Let me," she said to Folly. "Harold Dunham was one of the wealthiest men in the county. He owned two or three businesses here, including the stock auction out on the old highway. You'd see him and Max Thornton together all the time. I can't believe you don't remember, Abby. He must have bought a car from your dad at some point. He did all the business he could in Logan's Creek.

"About two years before his death, the gossip around town was that the two men had fallen out. No one knew why. But they quit being seen together, and the golf tournament Thornton and Harold co-sponsored fell by the wayside.

"The next thing I remember is hearing that Harold had cancer. In his lungs, I believe. He was rich enough to buy the best treatment, but it wasn't enough. He died at home; his wife had already passed. The only comfort he had was his money that paid for the staff who took care of him. He left his favorite nurse his Cadillac.

"But get this. Thornton showed up at the funeral. Bawling like he'd lost his best friend, which I guess he had, but not through death. Harold had given up on Max two years before."

Folly pulled a letter from her purse and passed it to Abby. "This will explain everything," she said. Abby read it twice. When she put the letter on the coffee table, Folly said, "What should I do?"

"Have you told Ms. Vivian?"

Folly shook her head no.

"Then don't tell her now." Abby bit her lip, hesitating. "You could publish it."

Folly hugged herself. "I hate to say it, but even with all my bravado on the blog, I'm not brave enough. My grandmother was Thornton's first wife. His starter wife. They were married less than a month. She said his heart was nothing but a thumping chicken's gizzard, meanest man she ever knew. She left with only the clothes on her back, and she was happy to do it. Grandmama Alice was afraid of him till the day she died."

Emily said, "I thought his first wife was Nettie Calloway. She was the mother of his children."

"Everyone did," Folly said. "When grandmama married Thornton, he was selling insurance door to door in Kansas. She never stepped foot in Arkansas."

"What about now?" Abby said. "Has Thornton threatened you?"

"Not directly. I had a reader tell me I couldn't find my own butt with both hands in my back pockets. And then the reader remarked, Watch your back. That was after I'd written a rather scathing article about Thornton. But, as far as I know, no one knows who L.C. Confidential is."

"Did you start the blog to bring Thornton down?" Abby asked. Folly concentrated. "Not really. Of course, I dreamed of telling him off. But I didn't plan to do that on the blog. I understand my obligation to my readers, and I know personal grudges have no place in journalism. I always thought of myself as Switzerland when I sat down to write. Totally impartial. At least about the facts. I didn't mind painting a colorful picture."

Abby nodded. "You're going to have to trust me, Folly. I want to take this letter to an attorney I know. She has a contact at the State Police headquarters in Little Rock. I think he'd be interested. No need to worry the Logan's Creek P.D."

"Maximus Thornton is lower than a snake's belly," Folly said, after she'd agreed to let Abby take the lead.

"So much lower," Emily said.

"He'd have to reach up to find rock bottom," Abby said. Abby's phone pinged. Her mom had sent a text:

> *The name of the LLC involved in the highway land deals is HERO. Strange name if you ask me.*

Chapter Twenty-One

Sometimes Abby imagined she could make Ian contact her just by thinking about him. She'd been remembering a date they'd had early on, the one where he'd told her about a dog named Bubbles Bigelow that he'd had as a boy. And just like that, her phone rang.

"Ian," she said, and he said, "Abby."

The line was quiet for a second, and then Ian said, "I'm checking in."

Abby snapped back into campaign mode.

"Did you find something?"

"I'm not sure. Thornton spends a lot of time talking to his buddies at Lucy's Diner on the Square. He has a wife that looks like she could be his daughter, and I'm being generous. Granddaughter is more like it."

"The upgrade wife. The new model," Abby said. "Not that I imagine his ex-wife minds. Can you imagine waking up to that every morning?"

"I cannot," Ian said. His voice was light. "Also, there's a lot of traffic at the courthouse after hours. I can't say the men coming in and out are there to see the mayor, but his office light is the only one on."

"You have photos of them?"

"The problem is that it is getting dark earlier, and the men are using the back entrance, so the street lights aren't illuminating them." Ian paused. "I do have a telephoto lens back at the B and B. I'll see if I can get a better likeness.

"What about on your end? Any progress with the blogger?"

Abby exhaled. She hated lying. "Some," she said.

"Do you have a good feeling about it?"

"I do."

"We'll get there, Abby Girl. We're too good together not to."

Loneliness spread across Abby's body. "We are," she said. "Aren't we?"

Ian must have been in Chapters. Abby heard the whoosh of the coffee grinder. The chatter of customers. His voice dropped lower. "Come see me at Betsy's Bed and Breakfast. I'm in room three, or as Betsy likes to call it, 'the rosebud room.' You can forget the campaign for the afternoon."

She really could. In Ian's arms, she nearly forgot her own name. Abby imagined the room. Wallpaper with red roses, probably. Lace curtains. A four-poster bed. Her body tingled. "We had a deal," she said, weakly. If he tried any harder, she'd not be able to resist.

"You're maddening," Ian said. But his voice was soft. Even that sentence sounded like seduction.

Abby's heels clicked as she stepped across the tiled floor in the prosecuting attorney's office. She'd come on the spur of the moment, as much to take her mind off Ian as to see Amanda. When she reached reception, she asked if her friend had time to see her. "Fifteen minutes," Abby said. "All I need is fifteen minutes."

Amanda's assistant buzzed Abby in. When she reached Amanda's office, her friend, sitting at her desk, asked, "What's wrong?"

"I have to tell you something."

"Go on," Amanda said with a look only an attorney could give.

"First, I need discretion."

Amanda said, "You know I can't promise you anything until I know what's going on."

Another lawyer answer, Abby thought. She'd forgotten how tough Amanda could be when she was working. "Here's the deal. Emily figured out who the blogger is."

Before Abby could say more, Amanda asked, "How did Emily get involved in this?"

"That's not the point."

"Fine," Amanda said. "Skip to the part where you tell me who the blogger is."

"Hold on. First, you need to assure me you won't share her name."

"As long as she hasn't committed a crime."

"A crime? I don't think so." Abby felt her face grow hot.

Amanda's phone rang. She ignored it.

Abby slowed down, telling Amanda the story from the start. When she was finished, she handed over the letter.

> August 11, 2022
>
> To Whom It May Concern,
>
> My name is Harold Dunham. I am a lifelong resident of Logan's Creek. I love my home and the people of my town. I'm writing this letter with very little time left—I have a fatal case of lung cancer. I know this is my last chance to unburden my heart.
>
> Throughout my life, I learned to tolerate what others considered intolerable. The person whose behavior this most applies to is someone I once considered my closest friend. Our families had farms next to each other. We grew up alongside each other. We played together as young children, double-dated in high school. The only time we were apart for any significant time was when he moved to Kansas for a year or two. Later, we each married and raised our children together while operating adjoining farms.
>
> His name is Maximus Thornton, the current mayor of Logan's Creek. I knew Max had a bad streak, a meanness that could cut like a dagger. But because I loved him as a friend, I chose to overlook this character flaw.
>
> Over time, I became aware of the dishonest and unruly things he was doing to the people of our town. Because he was my friend, I chose not to do anything. But as my time comes closer, I have to hope someone can do what I did not. He needs to be stopped.
>
> There are misdeeds that I won't address here. A predilection to cheat. An inability to see his own flaws. A passiveness about the hardships of others.

What I will address is what is easiest to prove:

Max Thornton formed a realty company that did not carry his name. (This allowed him to operate incognito.) The entity was formed under the name HERO, LLC. The office is/was? in Lone Elm and is/was? managed by a lady I do not know. The company mail is sent there, and then forwarded to Thornton's post office box in Logan's Creek. I have firsthand knowledge of this.

This also:

I sat on a parcel of property that had been in my family for generations. I was not going to sell this parcel; then I heard a rumor that the State was bringing the new highway through the eastern part of the county. It would run through the middle of my property. I was one of many in this position. When I spoke to Thornton about this information, he assured me it was without merit.

Soon after I'd heard the rumor, however, the land in that area was surveyed by the county. Daniel Slayer was the county land surveyor at the time.

Once Slayer's office completed the survey, he submitted it to the county assessor, Bertram Riggins (now deceased). Riggins worked in conjunction with Thornton to undervalue all the property in question. Why would Riggins do this? It might help to know that Riggins was the brother-in-law of Thornton.

At first, many of the landowners were ambivalent about the assessments. As long as they weren't planning to sell, the lower values mean lower property taxes. But then the announcement came. The State was indeed shopping for land in our general vicinity, and because of imminent domain, we would be given fair market value, and not a penny more. Remember though, nothing official had been decided.

Then a stranger thing happened. A company called HERO, LLC mailed out letters to myself and many of my neighbors. They wanted the land as well, and they were willing to give us ten percent more than the assessed value.

Ten percent was better than nothing, and so we all agreed to sell. We did sign an NDA, meaning we weren't allowed to discuss what we'd gotten for the land. We grumbled among ourselves, but said nothing to those on the outside.

The State drug its feet, as the State will do. But when they did buy a year later, all the property was owned by Thornton's company. As you may have already guessed, the property had undergone a new assessment, raising the value of the combined parcels to well over a million dollars.

> The official county documents will show the signatures of the county assessor on the undervalued parcels of land. You should be able to find them in the courthouse archives. They are public record.
>
> After I'd figured all this out, I confronted Thornton. All my life, I had assumed that even though he treated others badly, he would never treat me that way. Weren't we more like brothers? But in the argument we had, he called me the most vile names. I remember his being appalled by my naïve nature. He never would have stood for his land being undervalued. I also remember him calling me a dry-land turtle, a man without imagination, for going along with the crowd. "You just rolled over and took it," he said.
>
> Now that I'm closer to my eternal life, I want justice for the others Thornton cheated. I could have given my land away and been fine, but he cheated others out of their homes and livelihoods. I also want Thornton to know that everyone who rolls over isn't a chump. Usually, they're the better sort, unable to imagine the kind of immorality it takes to cheat your neighbor.
>
> Son of Logan's Creek,
> Harold Dunham

Amanda leaned back in her leather chair, staring at Abby. "Well?"

"We have a criminal leading our town."

"Not for long, if I have anything to say about it," Abby said.

"If we can find the documents Harold Dunham referenced, we've got Thornton by the... well... you know."

Abby wiped her brow like she'd been paddling a boat for miles. "It's good news, though, right? And the proof fell in our laps."

Amanda grinned. "My little optimist. I remember being like that. Of course, that was before I lost a few legal battles to the dark side."

"What do we do now?"

Amanda held up the letter. "Leave this with me. Tell your blogger friend not to fret. And get back to worrying about your crowded love life. Can anyone say first world problems? *Which hunk do I chose?* Now, get out of here."

As Abby left Amanda's office, she heard footsteps. Mayor Thornton was several steps behind her. She turned around.

"I see that you've been visiting your little friend, the Prosecuting Attorney. I hope everything is all right, little lady." He frowned. "No one's taken any of Josh's campaign signs, I hope."

Abby wouldn't play his ridiculous game. Thornton was worried, and she wanted him to stay that way. "We were discussing the complexities of small-town life. How difficult it is to keep secrets. One way or another, they always come out." Without waiting for a reply, she turned on her heel and marched away.

When she reached the door to the stairwell, Thornton called out, "Be careful on the stairs, Ms. Carter. With heels like those, you could fall and break your neck."

Abby yanked the door open and hurried inside. She couldn't let Thornton see the fear on her face. As she climbed carefully down the steps, she thought about Folly's grandmother. What had he done to her in the month she'd been married to him? She stopped to make sure she heard no other footsteps in the isolated spot.

Her phone didn't work in the stairwell, another peculiarity of the old courthouse. When she reached her car, she called Amanda.

"Keep notes about your encounters with him. Detailed notes. Be aware of your surroundings, Abby."

"Anything else?"

"Have you thought about going back to your parents' for a while? Until the election is over?"

"I couldn't do that. Dad would go ballistic if he thought anyone was threatening me. Plus, I could be getting them into the middle of something they're not equipped to handle. I couldn't do that."

"What about Ian? Pull him from surveillance. Put him on security."

Abby hadn't played damsel in distress since she was in elementary school. And that was in a play. Plus, Ian made her want things she'd be embarrassed to admit out loud. "Couldn't the Leading Ladies ride shotgun with me for a while?"

"Just call him," Amanda said. "Call the man."

Before she could make the call, Josh rang Abby. He'd added Ian to the call, a sign the two were at least working together.

"We have news," Josh said. "I ran into Ian at Chapters, and he showed me the photos he has. We're at my office now. You're on speaker phone."

"Good to know," Abby said.

Josh continued. "I couldn't make out anyone's face, but I do recognize one of the cars parked close to the courthouse's rear entrance."

"Who is it?" Abby asked.

"Our very own chief of police, Furman Hanna."

"Not his official car?" Abby asked.

"No, his Malibu. I had a friend run the tags. It's him," Josh said.

Ian spoke. "It's not illegal, but it doesn't look good. All that fraternizing. Josh and I got to talking. He swears there were plainclothes officers at today's Rotary Club luncheon."

"There were three of them," Josh said. "Standing in the back. Windbreakers. Dead giveaway. They wear those to cover their weapons. While I was shaking hands, I caught sight of one of their holsters. They were locked and loaded, Abby."

Abby stopped while Gus Abernathy made his slow move across Main Street. "Do you think they're detectives with the State Police?"

"They certainly aren't local," Josh said.

"Something's up," Ian said. "I feel it in the air."

Abby decided that now was as good a time as any. "Speaking of that. I got another veiled threat from the mayor today. One of those I-hope-nothing-bad-happens-to-you threats. I was meeting with Amanda, and after he approached me in the hall."

"That bastard," Ian said.

"This is getting ridiculous," Josh said. "I want to win, but not if it means you get hurt. Maybe I should finish the campaign without you."

Abby could hear the sacrifice in Josh's voice. He needed her, that much she knew. Because of that, he might think her plan was a good one. "I have a better idea," she said. "What if Ian kept a closer eye on me?"

"I could do that," Ian said, a little too quickly, and then Josh said, "Like a bodyguard? Seriously, Abby? What about me? I could protect you as easily as Ian. And I know everyone in this town, so I wouldn't be wasting my time worrying about our local characters that might look dangerous to the untrained eye. Wait a minute," Josh said. "Is this about you wanting some alone time with Mr. Chicago?"

Abby could imagine Josh and Ian, the two in Josh's conference room. The phone sitting between them. They'd be standing on either side of the table, hands in fists on the table, leaning forward.

"Hey!" Ian said, his voice booming across the line. "I thought we'd agreed to work together to keep Abby safe. Or was that bullshit on your part? Because if I thought you'd be better at this, I wouldn't hesitate. But then, my ego isn't nearly as fragile as yours."

Abby could hear the two men breathing. "Besides," Ian said, "shouldn't you be concentrating on winning the mayor's race?"

The silence that followed was suffocating. When Josh finally spoke, he said, "Just so you know, Ian. I could have my pick of women, and I'm not saying that lightly. But I've been concentrating on this race, and I've been biding my time, hoping for another chance with Abby. But if I wasn't... just let me say, I could have my pick of women."

It was as if the two had forgotten Abby was on the line. When Ian spoke next, he said, "I'll make sure nothing happens to Abby."

Josh said "Fine," the way a teenager says fine when they've lost a battle with their parents.

Ian's voice shifted, the lilt of it teasing. "You are a fine-looking man, Josh Moore. It must have been quite the sacrifice to take yourself off the market."

Before Josh could answer, Abby said, "Enough, you two. So we have a plan?"

Josh sounded surprised to hear Abby's voice. "Abby," he said, as if she'd caught him wiping his mouth with his sleeve. "Yes, we have a plan. I need to get my head back in the game if I want to beat Thornton. And no offense, Abby, but you can be quite the distraction."

"Duly noted," Abby said. She felt as if the three of them had made their way across a wide field, a prize bull chasing them. They were okay for now, but the good Lord help them if they had to cross that pasture again.

Whats (Really) Going On?

QUESTION: What, exactly, does anonymous mean?

This is going to be a quick one, folks. While researching a story WE journalists call "developing," I was also watching KCRW, to keep up with the goings-on in the county. What I saw and heard made my blood BOIL.

Why, you might ask?

A reporter—the older guy who looks like he's wearing a hair hat—was covering the building permit that was recently issued to Devil's Cupcakes in Lone Elm. Well, there had been plenty of controversy over the new business, namely the name.

KCRW talked to the City, and got MOSs, for a broader viewpoint. (MOS stands for man on the street, for those of you not in the know. And YES, I agree. It should be POS, for person on the street.)

The reporter—you're not going to believe this—showed video of a woman with her face pixelated, BECAUSE, you know, she was speaking anonymously. And then he said, I KID you not, "Tammy Welby is speaking anonymously about the bakery she says is satanic."

My lord, KCRW. Do better.

Not to worry, Tammy. I reached out to Devil's Cupcakes. The building permit got it wrong. The business is called Devil's FOOD Cupcakes.

Chapter Twenty-Two

Josh rang the video doorbell Ian had installed the day before, just as Abby stepped from her bedroom. She glanced at the new security app on her cell phone, saw Josh waiting, and hurried down the stairs. Her entire property was now a secret agent zone, with cameras that sent real-time alerts to her phone, and Ian's phone, if so much as a bumble bee flew onto her porch. The Leading Ladies were taking turns spending the night, so she was rarely alone. She and Ian texted on the hour from eight in the morning until eight at night, and Ian alerted her when he was on a shoot at the fishing lodge in the Ozarks. On those days, she worked at Chapters. Being around people she knew seemed like the best idea.

When she unlocked her front door, then unlatched the screen door, Josh said. "Reporting for duty, Captain." He was carrying a covered casserole dish. He lifted it with both hands, which were protected by red pot holders. "Mom," he said. "Chicken Noodle Casserole."

Abby waved him in. "With Ritz Cracker topping?"

"The same."

"Have I told you how much I love your mother?"

"You have, indeed."

Josh followed Abby to the kitchen, where she had two place settings ready on the island. "Sit," she said, and dished out the casserole, along with a cranberry-pecan salad she'd prepared earlier.

While they ate, they talked about the campaign. "What do you think of our chances?" Josh asked.

Abby looked at the ceiling and blew out a breath. "Right now? Honestly, I'm not sure. That's why this town hall meeting is so important."

"Any idea what kind of questions I'll have to answer?"

"It depends on the audience. Your supporters are younger. Have kids in sports and after-school activities, so their time is precious. It's set for six o'clock, which gives the advantage to Thornton. His followers skew older. Many of them are retired. Six o'clock is after supper for them, but not so late they won't show up. I'm generalizing, but their concerns are more about keeping the status quo, making sure taxes don't rise. They're not the ones calling for innovation or new ideas."

Josh's fork was halfway to his mouth. "How do we compensate? A lot of what I want to do will hopefully drive new business here, and I think we should be looking at solar power, at least in city buildings."

"We do what we're doing today. We practice, knowing the news media will show up. We need succinct answers, conviction, that charisma you're known for. If your ideas are visionary, the media is more likely to pay attention. And think ten- to fifteen-second soundbites. KCRW will likely break up their reporter's story that way, although they'll use more than one quote. For print and online, they'll be looking for a few strong sentences sprinkled throughout their articles. They rarely let you have an entire paragraph on your own."

Josh leaned back in his chair. He cupped the back of his head with his interlaced fingers. "Think of it as opening and closing statements in a trial. And then break that down into smaller bites."

"Exactly."

"What if one of Thornton's cronies asks me something personal, or outrageous?"

"Ah," Abby said. "That's the beauty of the town hall meeting. You don't answer those questions. Instead, you answer the questions you wished they'd asked." When Josh looked unconvinced, Abby said, "Try me."

Josh leaned forward, moving aside his empty plate in the process—no one could make a chicken noodle casserole like his mom. "I hear you've got two men on a string, Ms. Carter. Would you say that's a sign of instability, or are you one of those uninhibited city women my mother warned me about?"

Abby eyed Josh. Was the question as lighthearted as he was pretending? She moved her plate to the side and folded her hands on the table. "That's a great question, Mr. Moore. As I'm sure you're aware, leading an active life is a priority for me, which is why I plan to establish two additional city parks, one of which will be dedicated to senior citizens. Those are all the rage in Europe, with equipment specifically designed for older adults that allows for safe exercise to improve both strength and balance. And that aquatic fitness center Mayor Thornton was unable to make happen? On day one, I'll have a committee named to work on that project."

Josh laughed. "Abby Carter, my spin doctor."

"You know it," Abby said. The lush light of early afternoon filled the kitchen. It was one of the things Abby loved most about the cabin. Light danced, it skittered across the fireplace, lay in pools on the hardwood floor. She remembered lying beside Josh on the living room sofa, her body molded to his, her head on his chest. She had heard his heart beat. Loudly.

"Let's go for a run," he said, and she said, "Now?"

"If we don't, I'm going to kiss you," Josh said, his dark eyes serious.

Abby slipped into her running clothes before they started. She was no match for Josh's long legs, so after a bit, she dropped back.

They stopped in the clearing that had a bench made out of split logs that had been smoothed by time. When she sat beside him, she noticed his foot tapping. She put a hand on his knee.

Josh took her hand and kissed it. "Josh," she said. "Please."

She was asking him to save her from herself, a very unfeminist thing to do. She didn't want to admit how lonely she was, how desperately she wanted to be touched, kissed, held.

Josh pulled her onto his lap. He nuzzled her neck, ran his hands across her body. The boy Josh hadn't had much willpower, but adult Josh seemed to want to take his time. When he touched the skin below her sports bra, she knew she would make him stop. She would tell him any second now.

Ms. Vivian had been chosen as the moderator for the town hall meeting, which was at the old Jenny Lind Theatre downtown. She stood at a podium adjusting the microphone. This evening, she wore a rust-colored cardigan over a pale-yellow silk blouse. Her black hair was loose, and she had on tangerine blush that Abby could see from the second row. After the candidates gave their opening remarks, Ms. Vivian said, "As a lifelong citizen of Logan's Creek, it is my honor to moderate tonight's debate between the current mayor, Maximus Thornton, and Mr. Joshua Moore, our City Attorney, who's opposing him. As your town librarian, I want to tell you that there are numerous books in our collection that deal with governments of other countries and how they compare to ours. There are books that tell of the dark history of mankind, or as my niece Folly would say, personkind." A few laughs erupt. "I've learned so much from those books, and every election season, I'm reminded of the words in our Constitution, 'In order to form a more perfect union.' That's what I think of as I vote. What would make our country, our state, our town more perfect?

"As we hear from these two esteemed gentlemen, we will learn what motivates them to serve, and what plans they have for our future. Please be respectful of their time and ours. We are not here to fight or to be frivolous. Rather, we are here exercising one of democracy's greatest privileges: the right to ask questions of our leaders and potential leaders, without fear of retaliation or insult.

"Now for some housekeeping. Audience members will have one minute to address either candidate. We have four volunteers with microphones, and we'll bring them to you after I recognize you. Please be polite, and just as in the library, absolutely no cursing or gum chewing."

The audience, many of whom grew up under Ms. Vivian's influence, chuckled. Someone called out, "Should we use our inside voices?" Abby relaxed. What was the worst that could happen?

A woman in a ruffled plaid top was the first to be recognized. After the microphone squealed for a second, the woman spoke. "This is for both candidates," she said, looking at her notes. "I belong to the Red Robin Bird Watching Society." She looked up, and her glasses slipped down her nose. "We meet every other Thursday at the Senior Center, then head out from there to birdwatch. "In the last year, we have noticed a sharp decline in the number of American Goldfinches we've been seeing. Blue Jays are still abundant, little troublemakers. But the goldfinches." The woman trailed off, then shook her head. "We're worried about our precious goldfinches."

Ms. Vivian interrupted. "Is there a question you'd like to ask?"

She pointed at Josh and Thornton, each standing at a lectern on either side of Ms. Vivian. "Yes ma'am. I want to know what these two plan to do about it. It's the cats that are responsible. In New Zealand, cats have destroyed certain species. The Kiwi, I think? Anyway, I have a neighbor who used to live outside Auckland. She said that cats were required to wear bells when they went outside. At least then, the birds got a warning that danger was nearby."

Thornton spoke first. "My dear," he said, "are you suggesting we make it a law that kitty cats must wear tinkerbells?" He rolled his eyes. Someone in the crowd meowed.

The woman jutted out her chin. "I am."

Thornton chuckled. "I hunt quail, and ducks, and turkey, and I'm not about to wear a bell." A few of his old cronies, sitting in his line of sight, clapped.

The woman tapped her temple. "Well, Einstein, you should. You should give those poor creatures some kind of a chance." A group of women in purple hats, seated to Abby's right, guffawed.

Josh spoke up. "It must be awful for you," he said to the woman. "Do you mind repeating your name?"

"Edith Simmons."

"Edith," Josh said. "I raised a mourning dove that had fallen from its nest when I was a boy. When it was old enough to fly away, it nearly broke my heart. I swear, that bird came back now and then. It would swoop down and sit on my shoulder.

"You're not asking to harm any cats. We know how much people love their pets. A collar and a bell aren't too much to ask. We could even have a fundraiser to get started."

Edith was nearly in tears. "For Whom the Bell Tolls," she said. "We could call the fundraiser that."

Abby caught Josh's eye. He was smiling. Abby looked around. Three buff, windbreaker-wearing men stood against the back wall, their arms folded. Buzz cuts, khaki pants, running shoes. It looked as if they were wearing transitional glasses, the kind that turn to sunglasses when it's bright. The glasses didn't appear as light as they should be now that they were indoors.

When Abby turned back around, one of Thornton's buddies stood up. "Hamp Nettles," the man said. He was seventy if he was a day. Round belly. Pinky ring. Cowboy hat. "This here is for Mr. Moore." Vivian said, "Go on."

"We got the new senior center because of Max." He paused. "I'm sorry, because of Mayor Thornton. We got that new shooting range down in the hollow. Got a new Sonic near the bridge. What I'm saying is that Mayor Thornton can get things done. Now, boy, you still look wet behind the ears. What in the heck fire fuzzy do you know about wheeling and dealing?" Hamp looked around at the audience, pulled a toothpick from his pocket and stuck it between his teeth. Several people clapped.

Josh stepped from behind the podium and came to the edge of the stage. Looking down at Hamp, he said, "All those things are good, aren't they, Hamp? Especially when it's Happy Hour at Sonic. You can't beat a Route 44 lime slush.

"As I recall, the Chamber met with the future owners of the Sonic near the bridge. Took them on a tour of the town. Even scouted out a few locations where they might build. The City Council got involved. I know this because I was in that meeting. They sweetened the deal.

The mayor was instrumental in that he signed the declaration making their grand opening Sonic Day."

Ms. Vivian held up her hand when Thornton started to object. "The question was asked of Mr. Moore," she said.

"The shooting range? That was likely all Mayor Thornton. He does love to shoot. The new senior center is a thing of beauty, but again, it came about through the combined efforts of the City, community groups, and even a grant from Active Arkansas. I know, because I wrote that grant.

"As for wheeling and dealing, I'd say a mayor needs to do more than that. A mayor needs to bring the community together. The mayor needs to understand the needs of all the citizens, and listen to all of them. A town needs to serve all ages of its citizenry."

Hamp scowled at Josh. "So you're saying you can't wheel and deal?"

Before Josh could answer, Ms. Vivian stepped in. "That's enough, Hamp Nettles," she said, and the man bowed his head and walked back to his seat.

Thornton spoke. "I did so bring the Sonic to town," he said. "Everybody knows."

The next speaker was a bombshell blonde with an accent like Dolly Parton. "This question is for Mr. Moore," she said. "How can a single man concentrate on the office of mayor? From what I've heard, you got a big old social life, with ladies tromping in and out of your house at all hours." She leaned forward, showing her cleavage. "Won't that make it hard to govern?"

Josh, to his credit, looked the woman straight in the eye. "Your name?" he asked.

"Dawn Vallaquette," she purred.

"Dawn," Josh said, his eyes bright. "My love life is not nearly as exciting as you make it seem. But on the subject of young adults in Logan's Creek, I will say that I believe we should have more to offer. The fitness center has already been discussed, but we need to bring more events to town. When musicians perform in Tulsa and Fayetteville, they could easily come to this theater between those visits. We could get some big names here. Not to mention traveling Broadway productions." Josh held out his arm. "Who wouldn't want to perform here, in this turn-of-the-century wonder." He pointed to the red velvet curtains on either side of the stage. "They come to Arkansas, but never here. We should fix that."

Thornton took some easy questions. What did he think was his biggest accomplishment? (The senior center.) What did he think of the motorcycle rally planned for the spring of next year? (He was riding himself.) How hard was it to run the city? (Not hard at all if you're as qualified as he is.)

The next questions were for Josh. A man in a sweatshirt that read, *If you think I'm sexy, you should see my tractor*, scanned the crowd while he waited for the microphone. "Demus Blake," he said. "Our mayoral elections are usually on the dull side. If something risky happens, it's usually someone upchucking after eating too much pie at the campaign's pie supper. Or someone carrying a candidate's sign gets too close to the polls on election day." Demus shook his head. "But man, Josh, you changed all that."

Abby saw a look of recognition flash across Josh's face. Before he could speak, Ms. Vivian said, "Question, please."

Demus nodded at Ms. Vivian. "What's different about this election?" he rubbed his chin. "Mayor Thornton's stolen campaign signs. Accusations that you worked against us with Lone Elm, and got a pocketful of money to do it. Some anonymous blogger who seems to be more of a Josh Moore evangelist than a reporter. L.C. Confidential, my rear end. Plus, that fancy campaign manager that ain't even from here. How does any of that reflect the values of Logan's Creek?"

Josh gripped the edge of the podium. "Demus Blake," he said. "It's been a minute, hasn't it?"

Demus shook his head yes.

"I'm eager to talk about the differences in this campaign. Yes, Mayor Thornton's signs were stolen. No, I didn't steal them. In fact, I welcome a visit from the police department, although they've not seen any reason to visit me. In fact, the whole issue seems to have been mysteriously dropped.

"Also, an investigation into the work I did, with the blessing of Mayor Thornton, proved I did nothing more than help our neighbor. I have no idea who L.C. Confidential is, but if you recall, the blogger has raked me over the coals, even digging up a traffic ticket from years ago.

"What makes this campaign different is the crossroads we find ourselves staring down. Do we want to continue with the same old, same old, or do we want to create a brighter future for our hometown? I have plans, Demus, many of which you'd benefit from, like having the school cafeterias use local produce. You grow enough potatoes to feed an army. But some of those go to waste. They shouldn't.

"I want to expand the walkability of downtown. And bring our food partners together to take meals to our senior citizens. Your mom and dad are still living on their own. And while I'm sure you take excellent care of them, a hot meal every day would ease your mind. Any excess crop you have could be sold at a discounted price to make that happen."

Demus was shuffling from foot to foot. Josh took advantage of his discomfort. "Now I have a question for you."

Demus raised his chin, and Josh asked, "How's Penelope doing?"

By the looks of things, Demus didn't like the sound of Penelope's name in Josh's mouth. "Better than ever," he said. "Farm life suits her. And if she's told me once, she's told me a million times, 'Josh Moore don't hold a candle to you.'"

"I was never good enough for her," Josh said, and Demus's bottom lip quivered. "I appreciate your admitting that," he said.

A sprinkling of laughter fell across the audience.

So far, Josh was killing it. And while she hadn't learned a lot about his former girlfriend Penelope, at least she knew she'd landed on her feet.

Earlier, when Abby had tied Josh's tie, she'd said, "You're ready for this," and he'd said, "I'm so nervous I can't even tie my tie." But Abby wondered whether that was true. Up close to him on her tiptoes—he was bending down—with her hands slipping the tie around his neck, she felt that old tug, the one that pulled her back to another time, before Josh had broken her heart. Now, Abby shook her head, making herself pay attention.

The Leading Ladies had shown up together tonight. Josh's parents were here, as were Abby's family. Folly was around, although Abby hadn't seen her. Ian was in the crowd somewhere, snapping photos. Abby glanced at her phone, checking the security feed of the cabin, making sure nothing untoward was happening. Just then, Cathy stood and was recognized by Ms. Vivian.

"I'm Cathy Foster, owner of the Tuscan Table." The other Leading Ladies cheered until Ms. Vivian called them down. "It's no secret that I'm voting for Josh Moore. Because of that, one of his parties was held at my restaurant."

Ms. Vivian spoke up. "Cathy, I hope you have a question. So far, you've only endorsed your restaurant and Mr. Moore."

Cathy smiled. "I'm getting there, Ms. Vivian. So, at this party, Officer John Dyer showed up to issue a citation. I'd been fined for having too many people on the patio."

Ms. Vivian drummed her fingers on the podium.

"First," Cathy continued, "how did Officer John know how many people were on my patio? And what did Mayor Thornton have to do with all this?"

"This question seems to be for you, Mayor Thornton," Ms. Vivian said.

"Why, Mrs. Foster, I had absolutely nothing to do with the fine. I do not control the police department, nor do I issue citations." Cathy opened her mouth to speak, when Thornton continued. "I suppose Officer John heard all that awful noise, all those people whooping and hollering. You were serving booze, weren't you? Makes for a rowdy crowd."

When Cathy said, "So?" Thornton huffed, "And children were there?" Thornton waved his hand. "No need to answer. Children were there, including some of our schoolchildren. And Ms. Carter, your bosom buddy and Mr. Moore's campaign manager, was loaded up to the gills."

Abby rubbed her temples.

Cathy bowed up. "Abby was... fine. And there was nothing illegal going on."

Thornton jumped at this. "Illegal? Dadburn. Illegal? I didn't say that, but now that you mention it, maybe there was. You young people and your loosey-goosey morals. And all to get your buddy elected mayor. What favors did he offer you, Ms. Foster, if he beats me?"

One of Thornton's buddies yelled, "Ain't gonna happen, Max. Not on our watch."

Ms. Vivian seemed to rise above her heels. Suddenly, her shoulders were visible behind the podium. "Enough," she said. "We're not here to brawl. And Cathy, this sounds more like a grievance than a question. I suggest you deal with this another time."

Amy popped up from her seat. At barely five feet tall, she was the smallest Leading Lady, and she was also the quietest, at least until tonight. She waved her dainty hand, and Ms. Vivian, said, "Yes, Amy?"

"Amy Ann Rogers Lynch, here," she said after she'd taken the microphone from Cathy. Her brown eyes were as big as a hoot owl's when she said, "Um, my question is for Mayor Thornton."

Thornton scanned the crowd. It was likely that Amy was a little hard to see. Cathy yelled, "Over here, Mayor. Right beside me."

Ms. Vivian hung her head.

"What do you want to know, Miss Rogers Lynch?" Thornton asked.

Amy gripped the microphone. "I want to know why you never paid my granddaddy for the chainsaw you bought from him, back in the 1980s." She used air quotes around the word *bought*.

Thornton turned to Ms. Vivian, as if to say, Get these people under control.

"That's enough, Amy," Ms. Vivian said. "We're not here to air our personal grievances."

Abby expected Amy to fold, but instead, she said, "It's not personal." She considered. "Well, it is personal, but it also goes to character. If the mayor won't pay his debts, what does that tell you?'

The chatter in the room escalated. Abby reached across Cathy and took Amy's microphone.

Ms. Vivian looked like an ad for BC Powder headache remedy. "Abby," Ms. Vivian said, "I'll let you speak, but as a citizen, not as Mr. Moore's campaign manager. And no more of this petty business. We're here to educate the electorate, not put the candidates on trial."

"Of course," Abby said. She took a breath. "I want to take a second to talk about unity. The thing I love about Logan's Creek, the thing I missed most about it in Chicago, was the friendships we have here." She pointed to the Leading Ladies. "Friends you collect in childhood that follow you through your life."

The Leading Ladies beamed at her.

"One day soon this election will be over; early voting starts on Monday, as you know. In ten days after that, one of these two men will be our mayor. Some of us will be disappointed with the outcome, but what will remain is friendship.

"I know Josh has those lifelong friendships, because I'm one of them. And I know Mayor Thornton does too." Abby flashed a smile. "We've heard from his cheering section tonight." Hamp Nettles tipped his cowboy hat.

"The mayor has hunting buddies, business pals, golf partners."

"Abby," Ms. Vivian warned. "You're rambling. Is there a question?"

"I'm almost finished," Abby said, and Ms. Vivian looked exasperated. "I think about those friends, and I remember a story I heard not too long ago, about the bond our mayor had with his neighbor Harold Dunham. The story of Mr. Dunham's funeral, where the mayor wept like an infant. Now that's a friendship."

Ms. Vivian interrupted, "I'm losing patience," she said.

"To sum it up," Abby said, "all this combativeness tonight will soon be over. What matters most is how we treat other people. We need to be kind, to our families, our friends, our acquaintances. We need to be honest in our business dealings. We need to treat our neighbors with care, and we need to be good citizens.

"I'm thrilled to be back in Logan's Creek with all of you. And like Ms.

Vivian, I'm overjoyed to be part of this exercise in democracy."

The audience cheered. The reporter from KCRW inched her way to Abby. Josh looked puzzled. But it was Thornton Abby cared about. His face had gone ashen. He looked as mad as a wet hen. At that moment, Abby spotted Folly. She was shaking her head at Abby, a world of disappointment showing in the way she hugged her body. She seemed to be asking Abby what the heck she had unleashed. Abby turned her attention to the reporter.

Abby noticed a pair of headlights behind her on the way home. When she got near the final turn to the cabin, the dark-colored car zoomed around her, flashing its lights. She wanted to believe it was an annoyed driver, but the incident left her shaky.

QUESTION: Are there heroes among us?

Something happened at last night's town hall meeting (Mayor Max Thornton vs. Mr. Josh Moore) that went unnoticed by most of the crowd. I'm not at liberty to say what it was, but let me tell you, watching that act of bravery sent me to my prayer closet. Someone I barely know put their neck on the line to show that secrets, like a yard dog's favorite bone, will never stay buried.

I was so overcome I couldn't even tell you what #eyecandy Josh Moore was wearing.

So I got home, and I got down on my knees. I don't profess to be the best Christian, but I'm trying. And part of that trying involves making myself be braver.

You see, not so long ago, I came across some shocking information concerning someone you'd know in a heartbeat, if I dared to speak that name. But instead of telling y'all what I knew, I kept it to myself. I was worried I'd get in trouble. Or worse. Yep, the intel I found was that scary.

I'd been calling myself a journalist (even if nobody else did), but when push came to shove, I hoisted that bit of news onto someone else's broader shoulders. A real journalist would have done the right thing. Would have reported the evidence and let the chips fall where they may.

I'm ashamed. But not so ashamed that I can reveal what I know just yet. I have my reasons—other than cowardice—and I'm asking you to wait just a little while longer.

I know, I know, I sound like one of those vague Facebook posts. "Asking for prayers, can't say why." "Don't ask me what happened, just know that I need you in my corner." "Life sucks right now, send thoughts and prayers."

My grandmama once knew a man that she said was so crooked, he could swallow nails and spit out corkscrews. Did she tell anyone? Warn anyone? Well, she told me, but not until I was nearly grown, and she only let loose of the information because it was a cautionary tale.

She was afraid, you see. Like, really afraid. He'd hurt her, and she'd walked away with her tail between her legs. Walked away with nothing. Looked over her shoulder for the rest of her life.

Some folks talk about generational trauma. I understand what that is. All that Grandmama went through with that silver-tongued devil seeped its way into my mama and then made its way to me. I wasn't a naturally brave person.

I want to do better.

To the person who did speak up last night, let me say, you are my hero. And to the person my person called out, tread lightly. Because secrets, like a yard dog's favorite bone, won't stay buried forever.

Chapter Twenty-Three

Abby sat at the biggest table at Chapters. Surrounding her were nine volunteers from the junior college in Lone Elm, all of them sipping the sweetest drink the coffee shop had to offer. "The question is simple. If the mayoral election were today, who would you vote for?"

The political science majors jotted notes. One of the guys who sported an impressive beard for a nineteen-year-old asked, "Should we get names?"

"No names," Abby said.

"Can we ask about global warming?" asked a serious looking girl who was chewing her pencil.

"No questions other than the mayoral vote," Abby said. "Make a checkmark for each affirmative answer, under the appropriate candidate's name. That's all we need today." She glanced at her watch. "We'll meet back here at three. And thank you," Abby said. "This will be a great help to Mr. Moore's campaign."

The pollsters scattered. Equal trios headed to the gas pumps at Walmart, the Light O' Day Laundromat, and the parking lot of the Dollar Store.

Abby was monitoring the team at the Laundromat when she got a notification on her phone. There was a new blog post on L.C. Confidential. She sat in the curved plastic chair and started to read.

She was staring straight ahead, her mouth open, when one of her pollsters walked up. "Are you okay, Ms. Carter?" the girl with bright blue hair asked.

Abby startled. "I have an errand to run."

"You're sure you're all right?" the girl asked, and Abby tried to smile.

Abby raced from the parking lot, squealing her tires as she went. When she arrived at Ms. Vivian's house, she bolted up the steps. Knocking on the door felt like trying to take down a castle wall.

When Folly answered, she asked, "What's wrong?"

Before Abby answered, she was pushed by Folly and motioned for her to shut the door. "What's wrong? Are you kidding me? Today's blog post? Does that ring a bell?"

Folly looked as nervous as a cat. "My aunt could have been here."

In Abby's heightened state, she'd forgotten herself. If she was being watched, she didn't need to be seen anywhere near the L.C. Confidential blogger. Much less Ms. Vivian. But her temper was still flaming.

"That's true," Abby said, willing her breath to slow. "But you know who else could show up here? Anyone who figures out you're the blogger. Including Thornton."

"I told you, there's no digital trail leading to me."

"Let's sit, Folly."

A beige floral couch, with purple irises on the fabric, sat in the living room. On the opposite wall, on either side of the fireplace, were two bright purple Queen Anne armchairs. The coffee table was made from a stack of old dictionaries, the kind that were so big they needed their own stand. A heavy piece of round glass sat on top. The room looked just like Ms. Vivian.

Folly must have seen her assessing the room. "Her bedroom is painted lilac. The ruffled bedspread has violets scattered across it. That woman loves her some purple."

"Folly," Abby said, reaching across the expanse of the sofa to squeeze the blogger's hand. "You were careful not to release Mr. Dunham's letter, due to the consequences that could follow. Why in Heaven's name would you publish something incendiary regarding Thornton? You know he reads L.C. Confidential."

Folly's hands were balled into fists. "I get so mad," she said. "My grandmama. Harold Dunham."

"And we're working on that. It's not just you. You could compromise Ms. Vivian's livelihood. You're not an employee, yet you have twenty-four-hour access to the library. You were able to take property that belongs to the library without her knowledge. That could land her in serious trouble.

"Then there's me. You might be flying under the radar, but Thornton has his sights set on me. After my little performance at the town hall, he could reasonably assume I'm the blogger."

Folly dropped Abby's hand and shrank into the couch cushions. "What do I do? Take the post down?"

"It's too late for that."

"Reveal myself?"

"Absolutely not."

"Then what?"

"Keep blogging, but ease up on the innuendo. As we speak, Mr. Dunham's letter is in the hands of the State Police. Trust them to do what's right.

"Another thing, it's time I told two more people about you and the letter. Ian, who's in town working with the campaign. And Josh, who needs to be aware of this development."

Folly chewed her thumbnail. "Will Josh think less of me?"

"What would your grandmother say about that question? Needing to win the favor of someone else instead of believing in who you are?"

"She'd say, 'A wink is the same as a nod to a blind horse.'"

"I don't understand that at all," Abby said, and Folly answered, "Girls as pretty as you seldom do."

Abby was about to respond when she saw a text message from Ian. It was time for their two o'clock check in.

The polling numbers hadn't been great. Six percent of those polled didn't know who Josh Moore was. One percent didn't realize Thornton was mayor. Excluding those residents, the numbers showed sixty-seven percent favoring Thornton. That news, plus the topic of Folly and Harold Dunham loomed large as Abby turned off the main road and headed for her cabin.

She decided talking to Josh and Ian could wait until she'd had a shower and a glass of wine. She'd just dried off and put on her fluffiest robe when she heard sirens.

Abby sailed down the stairs, ran to the living room window and pulled the curtains open. Her phone rang, and Ian said, "Police are headed your way. I'm not far behind. Stay inside until I get there."

Whatever was coming couldn't be good. Abby texted Amanda, and her friend messaged back. "Call me, and put me on speaker. Make sure I can hear everything."

After the officer pulled up to the cabin, he took his time getting out of the police car. He was a small man, slender except for a pot belly, like a snake that had swallowed a baseball. He wore a cowboy hat with his uniform. Aviator sunglasses.

Ian roared up behind him in his Jeep and swung out of the front seat. Abby slipped on her sneakers and stepped onto the porch.

"What's the problem, officer?" Ian said, squaring off against the smaller man.

"That's Chief Furman Hanna, to you." The chief had a little rat face. His mouth was small, and a halfhearted mustache framed his top lip. He took off his sunglasses, showing two close-set brown eyes. His nose was sharp enough to cut string.

Abby could imagine him being called Vermin (rhymes with Furman) in school, bullied every day of his life. She almost felt sorry for him.

He sized Ian up. "Are you Abby Rose Carter?" He waited. "No? Then I ain't got a darn thing to say to you."

"I'm her bodyguard," Ian said as Furman widened his stance.

"You don't say." He waggled his mustache. "Bodyguard? What are you protecting her from?"

Abby came down the steps, clutching the neck of her robe with one hand. "The mayor," she said.

"The mayor, you say? Why, I got first-hand knowledge that he done offered you a job with the City. That don't sound a bit threatening."

"I'd call it a bribe," Abby said.

"If you was so scared, why didn't you come tell me? I've knowed your daddy and them since before you was born."

"I was afraid you'd think my complaint was politically motivated." She wasn't about to tell him they'd spotted him meeting with Thornton after hours.

Furman scratched the side of his face. "Well, is it?"

Ian stepped closer to Abby. "What do you want here?" Ian asked. "Is Abby in any legal trouble?"

Furman rocked back on his heels. "Nah, nothing like that. I'm following a lead about that libelous blog, L.C. Confidential. Trying to sort out who in the heck is writing that mess. I'm here more or less as a courtesy." He pointed at Abby, who'd tightened the belt on her robe. "All you need to do is hand over your computer. I'll take it down to the station, have a look-see. If it turns out it's clean, everything's hunky dory."

Abby was holding her phone flat in the palm of her hand. "I have my attorney, Amanda Hernandez, on speaker. I think she has something to say."

Amanda's voice was steady. "Furman, I don't know who's giving you your orders, but you're out of line. You're violating so many of Ms. Carter's rights, I can hardly keep up."

Furman was scowling. "Now hold your horses," he said.

"You're going to get in your car and head back to the station. If you have any further interest in speaking to Ms. Carter, you'll go through me. Is that clear?"

Furman's face fell. "Are you mad at me, Amanda?" The word *are* came out *err*.

"I am," Amanda said. "For one thing, blowing your siren was a bridge too far, not to mention harassing my client. But we'll talk this over next week. I'll give you a call."

Furman put his sunglasses back on. He muttered, "A man can't even do his dang job no more."

After he'd driven away, Abby had a short conversation with Amanda. Then she turned to Ian. "How did you get here so quickly?"

He lifted an eyebrow. "I stay close," he said, and Abby asked, "Even at night?"

Ian was noncommittal. "The Jeep's not that bad."

"You know I have one of the Leading Ladies here every night."

"And if someone needed a good tongue lashing, they could be deadly," Ian said. He was starting to talk like he was from Logan's Creek.

"Cathy brings her shotgun."

"Of course she does."

Abby climbed the steps, her knees shaky. Ian had that effect on her, plus, she was aware she had nothing on under the robe. "Come inside for a minute," she said, her thoughts the least little bit impure. It felt as if #behave was in bold print just above her head. Like a warning.

Chapter Twenty-Four

Cathy carried a shopping list as long as her arm. "I'm heading to the farmers' market." She looked at her watch. "I should be back by eight. Help yourself to coffee."

Abby had asked to use the Tuscan Table for her morning meeting with Josh and Ian. She wasn't exactly paranoid, but she did worry that her cabin might be compromised. Josh's office felt too, well, his.

Now, sitting in the back room, a coffee service on the linen tablecloth, she began. "It's been an interesting few days," she said.

Josh wore a cranberry-colored cashmere sweater and starched black jeans. "We're in the home stretch now. How do you think we're doing?"

"Relatively well," Abby said. She didn't want to talk about the poll just yet.

Ian sat across from Josh, wearing a plaid flannel shirt and old jeans that were frayed at the pockets and hem. "We must be doing something right. Thornton sent his lap dog to visit Abby."

"What do you mean?"

Abby stepped in. "Furman showed up at the cabin." Before she could say more, Ian interjected. "Sirens blaring."

Josh's dark eyes seemed even darker. "And I'm just hearing about this?"

"It was late yesterday afternoon. I knew we'd be meeting today." Abby took a sip of Cathy's perfect coffee. "He wanted to check my computer. See if I was L.C. Confidential. I didn't let him."

Josh leaned his elbows on the table. "I suppose you were there."

Ian tapped his chest. "Bodyguard," he said.

For a few seconds, the two men eyed each other, and then Josh said, "Damn it, Abby, I'm a lawyer. The City Attorney. Why didn't you call me?"

The question took her aback. Why didn't she? Amanda knew about the letter. That was one thing. That, and she trusted her with her life. Abby improvised. "I was already on the phone with Amanda. She advised me not to hang up."

All true. She'd sort out the rest of his question later.

Josh pulled his lips into a tight line. Ian leaned back in his chair. Abby said, "There's more."

She explained about Folly, the letter from Harold Dunham, and Amanda's intervention that landed the letter in the hands of State Police.

Ian was the first to speak. "That was what you meant when you spoke about friendship at the town hall. You talked about Harold Dunham. You were poking at Thornton."

Josh exhaled. "Harold Dunham. That proves the story Daniel Slayer told me. You had this information in your hand, and you let it go?"

The table was quiet. Finally, Josh said, "Why didn't Folly publish it?"

"She was afraid. Thornton terrorized her grandmother when her grandmother was a very young woman. Folly's frightened of him."

Josh stood, pushed his hands into his pockets. As he paced, he said, "Folly's a journalist. Doesn't she have an obligation to publish?"

Abby said, "Folly's a spontaneous twenty-two-year-old who's in over her head."

"I could persuade her," Josh said, the wheels of his brain turning so fast Abby could almost see them.

At the same time, she and Ian said, "No."

Josh looked like the kid left out of a game of tug-of-war. "Then what?"

Abby spoke carefully. "I conducted an unofficial poll. Who would you vote for if the vote were today? I could have picked the wrong locations. The poll could be totally skewed. But still."

"Just tell me," Josh said, his voice full of apprehension.

"You're polling at thirty-three percent."

Josh slapped his forehead. "You're kidding." When Abby didn't answer, he said, "Early voting starts Monday."

Abby said, "Which gives us four days to raise your numbers."

"Impossible," Josh said.

Ian had been writing on a piece of paper. "Not necessarily." He looked at Abby. "Remember that gnome party you did in the park? Promoting travel to Iceland, Land of the Gnomes?"

The lights went on. "I planned that in less than a week. It was one of the best marketing stunts I ever pulled off."

Josh sat back down. "You want a gnome party. Are you kidding?"

"No," Abby said. "I want a rally in the park that's more fun than a gnome party. Live music. Food. Soft drinks. Hot chocolate. A bounce-around. An energetic speech from you. Campaign merch.

"We'll hand out tickets for the food and drink. The Leading Ladies will help, I'm sure of it."

Ian was scrolling on his phone. "According to the city website, the park is open to political events. You call this number"—he held out his phone—"and tell them you want to use the pavilion. That's it."

Abby said, "Saturday night. We'll call it *Give Me Moore*. Until then, you shake every hand you can. Folly can help us promote the rally. I think I can get you on the radio. That morning show they have is hard to fill."

"You really think this can work?" Josh asked, and Ian said, "Trust her."

Chapter Twenty-Five

There was multi-tasking, and then there was running around in a frenzy. Abby was somewhere between the two when her phone rang. Without looking at the number, she answered. Her former assistant, Joy, said, "Please hold for Mr. Cromby."

Abby sputtered out a laugh. "You can't be serious."

Joy lowered her voice, "You'll want to take this."

When Cromby came on the line, he said, "How's life treating you?"

"Life's a peach," she said. Although right now, she wasn't really sure. She was working on the budget for Josh's rally. The numbers looked bleak.

"Glad to hear it." Cromby stalled, and Abby let the uncomfortable silence play out. When Cromby spoke again, he said, "I need some help on the Acton campaign."

The Acton company made custom RVs. In their initial round of marketing ideas, Abby had come up with the slogan, "Acton RV stands for Royal Vacation. Travel like Royalty with Acton RV." The image was of a young woman, a martini in one hand, a glittery paper crown on her head. She was sitting at the dinette table, dressed in a peacock-blue evening gown. Coming up the RV steps was a butler, towel over his arm, offering the woman a chocolate biscuit cake on a silver platter, which happened to be Queen Elizabeth's favorite dessert.

The client had loved it.

"I don't work for you anymore," Abby said, deadpan.

"John Willis can't handle it. Has no idea how to expand the campaign."

"Excuse me if I'm not surprised."

"He's been demoted."

"No more executive washroom for him," Abby said, not even trying to hide her sarcasm. "No more Shark cologne."

"I need you back."

"That's not happening."

"I'll give you a raise. Give you Willis's title."

"It's too late, Mr. Cromby. I have a job."

"Joy told me about the mayoral campaign. That's small potatoes for someone like you."

"And that's such an elitist thing to say."

Cromby regrouped. "This isn't going how I planned. I made a mistake, Abby. I never should have let you go. Now, I'd like to fix that."

Abby looked at the list she'd been working on. She had the live music scheduled for Josh's rally. She had the Bounce-around and corn hole games. She had popcorn and cotton candy. Even hot chocolate. But she was struggling to afford burgers or hot dogs. "I have an idea," she said. "Windy Dogs is still your client, right?"

"That's right."

"Could you get a few thousand of their hot dogs to Logan's Creek by Saturday?"

Cromby didn't hesitate. "I could do that."

"I need them for a party I'm throwing."

"Consider it done."

"And another thing," Abby said. "Tear up that non-compete I signed."

When he spoke next, Cromby sounded like he was sharing a secret. "It was never worth the paper it was written on anyway," he said. "Consider it gone."

"Fine," Abby said, more relieved than she was willing to admit. "Then here's what I'll do. After the election, I'll finish the Acton campaign, but from here in Arkansas. We need to hit hard on the fact that the

RV backs itself into a campsite. We need to talk about the self-leveling system that allows campers to push a button and be more or less set up. Luxury in the Land of Plenty. That kind of thing."

"I don't even know what that means."

"That's because you didn't grow up camping. We tent camped until I was ten, then my dad bought a small RV. I know it all, including what to do at the dump station."

Cromby's voice was shaky. "I don't want to know."

"But that's it, Mr. Cromby. I'm not coming back."

The Leading Ladies coordinated their schedules. Some would help set up. Cathy would bring her famous sugar cookies. Amy made small bottles of organic hand sanitizer and labeled them with Josh's logo. Amanda would hand out food tickets. Lisa was in charge of decorating the pavilion. Janie put together an automatic call to a phone list she'd created for Logan's Creek. Everyone would get an invitation to the party.

A semi-truck pulled up to the pavilion at three on Saturday afternoon. Once the freight doors opened, six hot dog stands were rolled out. Windy dogs not only sent the food, they sent a van load of their workers to serve it. The carts were wrapped with Josh's image, along with the slogan, *Give Me Moore*.

To offset the introduction of out-of-state food, Abby had hired the local Neat Eats to furnish soft-baked pretzels, chicken sliders, and Walking Tacos, which were individual bags of corn chips topped with taco fixings. Her budget covered the food, but barely.

KLOG radio showed up to broadcast live from the rally. Josh had made quite the impression on their morning show. And Ain't That a Lick, a surprisingly upbeat country duo, brought their own portable stage.

Just before the first guests arrived, Abby gathered the Leading Ladies, Josh, and Ian. She passed around the miniature bottles of Shark cologne. "This," she said, "is the smell of victory." She wrinkled her nose. "I stole these from Cromby's executive washroom with no idea what I was going to do with it."

Amanda said, "Don't admit to criminal activity in front of me," and Josh patted her on the back. "Ease up, Mandy," he said. "We're sharks tonight, not lawyers." To which, the rest of the group laughed. "What do you mean? Lawyers *are* sharks," Cathy said, and then quickly added, "JK."

Abby was still on a high from Cromby's call. His apology was as satisfying as she'd dreamed it would be. Admittedly, John Willis should have been fired, but Abby didn't really want to take away his livelihood. She dabbed the cologne on her wrist, and she felt unstoppable.

Josh's speech was short but inspiring. Sometimes Abby thought anything he said was enhanced by his good looks. You could get lost in those dark eyes, in the dimples, the muscles, the tallness. Abby fanned herself. Plus, he'd gotten his point across. A vote for Josh is a vote for progress, unity, and maybe a few more parties in the park.

Ian was taking photos, and Janie was helping post them to social media. The hot dogs were a huge hit, and nearly all the kids had taken a turn in the Bounce-around. A fierce competition was taking place at the corn hole arena. A young girl in pink overalls was beating everyone who challenged her. Her freckled face was a beacon of joy.

Abby was working her way to Josh, when she saw Folly next to him. Folly was wearing her hair up. Tight leggings, a nubby V-neck sweater, over-the-knee leather boots. Her lips were shiny and caught the light. Josh was smiling down at her. Abby turned the other way. What was that feeling? More than jealousy, Abby supposed. But not quite heartbreak.

Timothy and Kennedy rushed to her side. "Auntie Abby," Timothy said. "I just had the best hot dog of my life." Kennedy had a unicorn painted on her cheek. "Look at this," she said. Abby ruffled the girl's hair. "I wish you two were voting age."

Dan stood behind them. "Don't go wishing their lives away, sister. They're growing too fast as it is." Abby saw the flash of Ian's camera. He'd captured the moment for her.

Ain't That a Lick was singing "Crazy," by Patsy Cline, when Abby heard the ruckus. Thornton's Lincoln pulled into the parking lot at the shopping center across from the park. When he got out of the passenger's side, he was stumbling. Behind him was his wife, Sugar Dudley, wearing high heels, high hair, and a tight jacket zipped to the neck.

Thornton crossed the street, with Sugar not far behind. When they got close, Abby heard Sugar say, "Don't do it, Max." She didn't put much emotion behind it.

"These are my people," Thornton yelled as he parted the crowd. "This should be my damn party."

It was evident that Thornton's party had started hours before. Sugar, who didn't look as young as Abby had suspected—just well preserved—stayed a couple of steps behind.

Thornton staggered to the stage, pushing the lead singer, Levi Gill, to the side. The band stopped playing. "Listen here," Thornton said. "I got something to say."

Josh headed toward the stage, but Abby reached him first. "Let him have his say," she said.

The crowd grew quiet. "Y'all shouldn't be falling for this phony," he said, his oily hair falling across his forehead. "Mr. Dimples. Mr. Ladies' Man." He rubbed his thumb across his forehead. "He's no good, I tell you. Might even be a crook."

Cathy, now beside Abby, called out, "Projecting much?"

Thornton was swaying, and then his voice broke. "I used to sing like a dang angel," he said, and sang a few bars of "Mamas Don't Let Your Babies Grow Up to Be Cowboys." He wasn't bad. But as he moved the microphone with both hands, the cord tripped him up, and he fell to his knees.

Josh moved to stop the spectacle, but Abby said, "Wait." She hadn't seen Chief Furman Hanna at the rally, but now, there he was, ushered by Amanda. The DJ from KLOG had stepped out of the station's van, and he was doing a play-by-play of the action for his Saturday night audience.

Amanda stopped at the foot of the stage and let Furman climb the steps alone. He grabbed Thornton by the scruff of the neck, and the bigger man scrambled to get his legs under him.

"What the hell do you think you're doing, Furman?" Thornton said, the microphone picking up his slurred voice.

"My dang job," Furman said as he pulled handcuffs from his belt.

"Now see here," Thornton said. That's when Levi and the band stepped in to help the chief.

The last thing Abby heard Thornton say was to his wife. "Sugar, honey, call Titus to meet me at the station."

Titus Choate was the meanest attorney in Crawford County. Sugar said, "Sure, baby," just as she unbuttoned her jacket. She slipped it off, showing one of Josh's campaign shirts. Give Me Moore was emblazoned across her considerable chest. Somehow, she'd found time to bedazzle the words.

Ian had caught it all. Folly had shown up beside him. "Send me those and I'll get it on the blog," she said. She likely wanted a scoop, but then the DJ from KLOG announced on air, "The mayor of Logan's Creek has just been arrested for drunk and disorderly, at, get this, his opponent's rally."

The crowd let out a whoop. Sugar Dudley sashayed to her husband's car and drove slowly away.

It wasn't until later that Abby learned Folly had contacted Sugar earlier in the day. Told her the awful story about Thornton and her grandma. Seems Sugar was already souring on Thornton, who'd paid for her chest expansion, but was tight with the rest of his money. When Folly told the story, she raised her hands like a surrender. "But that's all I did, the rest of the night was orchestrated by Sugar Dudley."

Josh hopped onto the stage, grabbed the microphone, and said, "Early voting starts Monday, folks. As you can see, we're having one heck of a race." Furnam flicked on his lights and siren just then, and

Josh waited for the sound to fade away. "I'm imperfect myself, so I'm not going to comment on our mayor, who seems to be having issues only a professional should address."

Taffy Preston, who'd gone to school with Abby and Josh, wolf-whistled. "You are so perfect, Josh, honey." Her longtime boyfriend, also a classmate, said, "That's enough."

But then Josh said, "Anyone want to hear another song?" and the duo started playing "Lord, It's Hard to be Humble," by Mac Davis. Taffy bounded the stage, took Josh's hand, and started to dance.

Abby wondered if the Shark cologne had gone to Josh's head.

Whats (Really) L.C. Going On?

QUESTION: The mayor's race is hotter than Satan's toenails.

(For my visually impaired readers, the photo accompanying today's blog is of a disheveled Mayor Thornton in handcuffs, being led to a Logan's Creek police car by Chief Furman Hanna, at a Josh Moore for Mayor Rally this past weekend. The woman in the background, wearing a Give Me Moore campaign shirt, is none other than Mayor Thornton's wife, Sugar Dudley. #truthisstrangerthanfiction) Photo: Ian Reynolds

This is one story that won't end with "A fun time was had by all." On Saturday night, Mayor Thornton, who appeared to be knee-walking drunk, showed up at Josh Moore's rally at the city park. Oh. My. Word. It was like watching a little ant carry off an entire bucket of Kentucky Fried Chicken.

Thornton made his way to the stage where Ain't That a Lick was playing, took the microphone, sang a couple of lines from a Willy Nelson song, stumbled, and fell. Chief Hanna climbed up on stage and arrested him for drunk and disorderly.

The last image the crowd saw of our mayor, and yes sir, there were kids around, was of him bawling his eyes out while being placed inside a police car, in HANDCUFFS.

On Sunday, the Logan's Creek Courier conducted an online poll (more anecdotal than scientific, but still) that showed the mayor tied with Josh Moore. I, for one, couldn't believe it. Do we really want Mr. Drunk and Disorderly as a role model for our children?

Well, this campaign certainly has been a doozy. From an investigation into stolen campaign signs (Thornton's), which stopped as quickly as it started, to aspersions about Josh Moore's legal work. My favorite question, though, was about whether Mr. Moore endorses the Arkansas Razorbacks. So not Logan's Creek. Who do we think we are? L.A.? New York City? Nashville?

Up until now, I've kept my choice for mayor to myself. No more. L.C. Confidential happily endorses Mr. Josh Moore. He has a vision for Logan's Creek. He has integrity. Values. He has dark eyes that look like midnight. Oh wait, that last part just makes him dreamy. LOL

As you know, early voting started at seven this morning and continues until election day on November 5. Do your part to make Logan's Creek the best it can be. And as my grandmama always said, "The head hog ain't worried about nobody but hisself, especially when he's at a full trough." Don't make the mistake of voting for the Head Hog. And as always #WPS

Chapter Twenty-Six

When Abby arrived at the Tuscan Table for Josh's watch party, her arms were full of party horns and noisemakers that she prayed they'd need. She had barely stopped all day, but she did make sure she had time to get ready. Her navy-blue jersey wrap dress clung to her curves, and her red suede, wedge, open-toe shoes showed her painted toenails.

Josh met her at the back entrance, which opened into the storage room, and held the door for her. "Let me help," he said.

"It sounds like a crowd in there," Abby said while handing over the biggest boxes. "I thought I was early."

"Technically, you are. But most of the volunteers and a dozen or so major donors showed up thirty minutes ago." Josh walked to a table near the giant cans of pureed tomatoes and set the boxes down. "I think everybody is ready for the party to start," he said as he took the remaining boxes from Abby.

Josh had always been good at scanning her body in the least obvious way possible. In high school she'd called him out on it, and he'd said, 'I can't look straight at you. That would be like staring at the sun.' Tonight, he didn't bother hiding anything. Taking her hands in his and pulling her close, he said, "No matter which way this goes tonight, I'll always be glad we did this together."

Josh's hands were warm, his dark eyes intense. He was wearing pants that hugged his thighs like two lovers saying goodbye. Abby touched his smooth face, like a friend would, she thought, but really, who was she kidding?

Cathy bounded into the room. "Girlfriend," she said when she saw Abby, then she stopped in her tracks. She pulled at one of her pigtails, seeming to come to grips with the scene in front of her. "Um, I'm just getting a few more cans of mixed nuts." She waved her hands. "You two ignore me."

After Cathy backed out of the room, Josh smiled down at Abby. "Seems we've been caught." And Abby said, "Nonsense. Let's get you out of here." She pushed him toward the dining room door. "Go charm somebody else."

Abby stayed behind for a minute, trying to get her breath to return to normal.

The polls closed at seven thirty. It was eight o'clock before the first numbers trickled in. Reporters were stationed at the courthouse down the street, in the biggest courtroom. Mr. Ebby, from the Election Commission, came in periodically and wrote the new totals on a giant chalkboard. Ian had volunteered to be their stringer tonight, and when he texted Abby with the update, her hands shook while she read the message.

Josh hovered beside her. The first votes counted showed Josh leading, but only by a one percent margin. Josh's shoulders fell. "What the hell?" he said. "Thornton probably still has the stink of the jail cell on him, and he's tying with me?"

"Tying isn't the right word," Abby said. "He's behind. And if you're going to get this rattled when you're *ahead*, you're going have a nervous breakdown before the night is over."

Josh shoved his hands in his pocket. "Just my luck he didn't get arrested for fraud. That's the real crime, and that would have done it. But no, he was only drunk and disorderly. Maybe that helped him, bought him a few sympathy votes. Made him seem vulnerable, relatable."

"I can tell you that the ladies from the Baptist church aren't feeling relatable. Sister Bonnie's daughter found a bottle of rum after her mom passed away, stuck way back in the broom closet. It had a note wrapped around it that read, 'I only used this for making my famous Caribbean Coconut Cake. It was really my Caribbean Coconut Rum Cake, may the Lord forgive me.' The daughter said there was only the teensiest bit left in the bottle." Abby lowered her voice. "And as for the fraud charges, those could come any day."

Josh's face relaxed. "Folly says the majority of the L.C. Confidential followers wouldn't touch Thornton with a ten-foot pole." Abby wondered how often the two of them talked.

"So chin up, Josh. Get back to your people. Announce that you're ahead. Because you are."

The party erupted when Josh took the stage. His parents joined him, bookending their son. When he finished the speech, a woman wearing a white mini-dress and gold knee-high boots, shimmied while calling out, "Marry me, Josh Moore."

Abby caught Cathy's eye as if to say, "I thought we'd agreed on a no-alcohol night." Well, except for the celebratory champagne she hoped they'd be opening. But Cathy only threw up her hands. Then Cathy motioned for Abby to follow her to the kitchen.

There, the Leading Ladies stood around a prep station, each holding up a glass of wine.

"What is this?" Abby asked.

"Are you kidding me?" said Amy. "It's your birthday, you dodo head."

A chorus of 'happy birthday' rang out. Cathy handed Abby a glass of wine. "Let's toast. Quick. Before you get pulled away from us."

"Love you, girl," Janie said.

Lisa leaned in close, "You're the only woman I know who could forget her birthday because she's too busy sorting out her men."

Abby's face burned. "Ian and I are, well, I'm not sure what we are. And Josh and I are just friends," she said, but then Cathy said, "Cat's out of the bag, darling. What I saw in the supply room was more than friendship."

Amanda swooped in for the save, "Let's toast our sister." She raised her glass. "Happy birthday, Abby. May all our problems be as tall, dark, and handsome as yours."

Once in the dining room, Abby checked her phone. She had dozens of texts, social media alerts, and missed calls from Ian and her family. She checked her email. There were birthday wishes and gift cards from Sephora and Chapters. There was even an alert that a package was waiting for her at home, sent from Chicago. Abby suspected Mr. Cromby had sent along another bribe to get her to come back.

As the night wore on, new numbers were reported as soon as they were available. Since there were multiple races, it took some time for Ian to work his way to the board to see how Josh was doing, although he'd told Abby he'd gotten good at elbowing his way through the crowd of reporters.

Abby made the rounds, greeting supporters, thanking volunteers, making sure the platters of toasted ravioli, and spaghetti cups, one of Cathy's creations, were being devoured. They were. She spotted Josh on the patio, huddled with three former classmates, all of whom played football for Logan's Creek.

For a second, she was back in high school, cheering the Cougars on. Cathy had brought back a routine from her mother's era, an old cheer that went: "Two bits, four bits, six bits a dollar, all for Logan's Creek stand up and holler!" Only when they did it, they had a significantly higher percentage of hip movement and high kicks.

If Abby joined them right now, she'd feel about sixteen. She might even take Josh's arm and wrap it around her shoulder, the way she'd done back then. Abby shook her head to clear it. All that mattered was the election. She should tell that to her stupid heart.

Before she could take another step, Officer John Dyer appeared at her side. Abby said, "No sir. Not again. You're not shutting us down a second time." John tipped his cap. "I'm an invited guest," he said. "Cathy told me to come after I tore up her citation."

At five after nine, Ian called. "You're not going to believe this. Josh and Thornton are tied at forty-nine percent of the current vote." Abby was holding her finger in her free ear, and she walked outside, trying to lessen the background noise. "Shouldn't that be fifty percent? One of them has to reach more than fifty percent or there's an automatic runoff."

"It should be fifty percent, but get this. There's also two percent of the vote going to a write-in candidate."

Abby pinched the bridge of her nose. "Elvis," she said.

"The King himself." Ian paused. "You can't make this stuff up."

"There's an Elvis fan club that's been around forever. At Christmastime, they decorate their houses in blue lights, and blare "Blue Christmas" from speakers they sit on their front porches. They each have blue suede shoes. And of course, they write in Elvis every election. I should have remembered. Gotten Josh to go to one of their meetings."

"Tell Loverboy to hang in there," Ian said. "And turn the TV on when you get back inside." Before Abby could ask why, Ian hung up.

KCRW News appeared on the big screen that had been brought in for the party. Abby ran to the controls and turned up the volume. The main anchor, Louie LeRoy, who looked as if he'd been pulled from a deep sleep, shuffled his notes. "We're breaking in with breaking news." He shook his head as he read the redundant use of 'breaking.' "New producer," he said, shifting the blame for the amateurish writing. Louie, growing visibly perturbed, growled, "Cut to the video, for heaven's sake." He cleared his throat, touched the IFB in his ear, where the voice of his producer must have been. "Fine," he said. "Cut to the *KCRW exclusive* video."

The screen filled with an impressive perp walk. Two State Police officers were holding up a slumping Mayor Thornton as they led him to their car.

Abby looked around the room for Amanda, who was on her phone, waving her arm. She spotted Josh, mouth agape. Folly, who stood nearby, looked as if she'd been handed a present.

Louie read from the prompter. "Logan's Creek mayor, Max Thornton, is arrested tonight. Thornton, who is in a dead heat with his opponent, Josh Moore, is taken into custody by State Police, while at his watch party at a private club." The writing, again, didn't seem to please Louie, and he ripped his glasses off and tossed his script. "Just play the soundbite," he boomed.

The next bit of video showed a close-up of a fuming Thornton. "You'll be damn sorry you did this," he yelled at the officers cuffing him. "I know more important people than the two of you have forgotten in your sorry little lives. People who could eat you for lunch if they wanted to. I promise you, I'll have your ever-loving jobs for this."

The studio camera zoomed in on Louie. "Look," he said, "I don't need a script to tell you what's going on. As you can see in our exclusive KCRW video, Mayor Thornton is now in the custody of State Police. There has reportedly been an ongoing investigation into certain business dealings conducted by the mayor. At issue are several real estate purchases made by Thornton's company, HERO, LLC. How he obtained the property is of special interest, since sources tell me he may have used his political influence to make money off the transactions. No word yet on charges."

The video continued to roll. There was a tight shot of the police car driving away, no lights, no siren. It was as if they were cruising on a Saturday night, not in any particular hurry to get anywhere. Then, the video panned out to show additional cars.

"In this video provided to us by our loyal viewer, a Mr.—" Louie pulled a Post-it Note from the anchor desk. "Mr. Ian Reynolds. You can see that there are three police cars in total, one in front of Thornton, and one behind."

Louie leaned forward on his elbows. "Now, folks, I've been doing this job for thirty-two years, and let me tell you, when the State boys show up three cars deep, you've got trouble. We have a reporter headed to State Police Headquarters to learn more. There will be a full report at ten."

The station's breaking news graphic swooshed across the screen, and Louie was gone.

Amanda hurried to Abby. "Seventeen felony counts, Abby. Seventeen.

I just got confirmation from my guy at headquarters."

Josh stood by his parents, with Folly still at his side. The room buzzed with chatter. Abby reached Josh, pulled him aside, and said, "Get ready for the reporters, Josh. I'd expect them to show up any minute. There needs to be no joy in your voice when you talk to them. Say something like, 'This is an alarming night for the citizens of Logan's Creek, but we will pull through it together, etcetera, etcetera.' Wait for the final vote tally to celebrate a victory tonight. We're in the home stretch, but we're not there yet."

Folly tapped the video icon on her phone and held it up so that she and Josh were shown side by side on the small screen. "Me first," she said, and tossed her perfect hair across her pale shoulder. "What are your thoughts as you contemplate Mayor Thornton's second arrest in less than two weeks? And how in the heck are you holding it together on a night when the votes are so close?" As Josh, looking reasonably somber, began to talk, Abby felt her phone buzz.

Ian said, "He did it. Josh got more than fifty-one percent of the votes. He's your new mayor." Abby held the phone over her head. "We won!" she said, and Folly wrapped herself around Josh.

Abby put the phone to her ear. "How did you do it, Ian. How did you know about the arrest?"

Ian's voice was velvet. "Well, I didn't know what to get you for your birthday, you see, so I'd been chatting with these undercover guys that are all over the courthouse, and I said I thought you'd like a video of Thornton—something with action and drama—and things got crazy pretty quick. Turns out an iPhone works as well as a news camera in a pinch."

"Ian," Abby said, and Ian answered, "Abby." And then he added, "Happy Birthday."

Chapter Twenty-Seven

Abby arrived home after two in the morning. Out of habit, she scanned the latest video from her security system, although the threat she'd feared was now wearing striped clothing and going by a number instead of a name. At least that's how Abby liked to think of Thornton.

She'd forgotten to leave on her porch light, so her phone's flashlight led the way. The glow illuminated a cardboard box, as big as a suitcase, beside her front door. It was her package from Chicago. Cromby's bribe.

Abby unlocked the door, flipped on the porch light, dropped her purse on the entry table, and returned to grab the box. It was large but not very heavy, and she carried it to the island in her kitchen.

The thing people don't talk about is that the euphoria of winning a campaign can be immediately followed by a let-down. By a "what's next?" feeling. Abby had that in spades.

Now, she sat heavily on her sofa, the sharp beginning of a headache behind her left eye. She looked at the clock on the mantle. It was a new day, and she was no longer thirty. Somehow, she'd let thirty-one in the door with barely a hello. She remembered Amanda's toast. "May all our problems be as tall, dark, and handsome as yours."

Abby had the feeling that she'd overplayed her hand. Waited too long to decide between her tall-dark-and-handsomes. The two men vying for her attention had reasons to move on. Ian would go back to Chicago. And Josh? He'd be mayor. And she'd be? Abby stretched out on the sofa. She'd probably be alone.

When she'd left the city, her anger had fueled her. She'd show Cromby and the rest of those Mad Men what she was made of, and they'd be sorry they let her go. But her fury at Ian had really been devastation. The way he'd held her, loved her, the way her body fit with his. When she'd seen him at the airport, the regal Esme on his arm, something deeper than her heart broke. Her entire being screamed at her to run.

Abby looked around. At least she'd run home. This cabin, her family a few minutes away, the Leading Ladies, it made whatever happened next okay. But did it really?

Abby woke with a crick in her neck, a mouth as dry as the Sahara, and a headache in full bloom. It was dawn, the sun splashing its first light across the water of Logan's Creek. Abby walked to the kitchen, downed a glass of tap water, then climbed the stairs to her bedroom, where she slept for the next thirteen hours.

When she awoke, it was dark, and she could hear voices downstairs. Probably the Leading Ladies, she thought, checking on her. They knew where the key was hidden. She reached for her phone on the bedside table, and then realized it was downstairs, still in her purse. Abby raised up on her elbows; her headache nearly gone. Only a fuzzy feeling remained.

But those voices didn't belong to her friends; they were men's voices. Abby strained to hear. Ian's deeper voice and Josh's smooth one, a lawyer's voice. She heard her kitchen drawers close. Then the refrigerator squeaked open. Then the pantry door slapped shut.

"She's not been eating enough," Ian said. "Or apparently sleeping."

"Have you seen Folly eat?" Josh laughed. "She eats like a farm hand."

"Abby likes my omelets," Ian said. "When she comes downstairs, I'll see if she wants one."

"We got too many groceries," Josh said. "A case of Fruit Roll-Ups?"

"She'll plow through those," Ian said. "Trust me."

"She loves Dr Pepper," Josh said. "We should have bought that instead of this kombucha business."

"Josh," Ian said, "when was the last time you saw Abby drink Dr Pepper?"

Abby made her way to the top of the stairs, and sat. She was in the blue dress from the night before, but sometime in the night, she'd fished her bra off through one of the sleeves. She touched her hair. It felt as if a thousand birds' nests had found a home on her head.

The men sounded relaxed, cordial even. Somehow, they'd become friends, or friend-adjacent.

"For your information, Mr. Chicago, she drank Dr Pepper all the time in high school," Josh said.

"Dude," Ian said, "that was a lifetime ago."

"Not everything changes," Josh said, and Abby imagined him with his bottom lip sticking out. "She still looks at me with those sultry eyes."

A cabinet door banged shut. "Those are just her eyes, Josh. First thing I noticed about her."

"In high school, she wore these wedge heels," Josh said. "Most all the girls did. And short, bohemian dresses that were made of soft cotton. Every red-blooded guy in school had his eye on her."

Ian spoke. "On our first project together, Abby had this look that spread across her face, curiosity and wonder. She seemed about six years old—she hadn't straightened her hair that day—and these corkscrew curls framed her face.

"When she worries, she talks non-stop. She'll say, 'This is the last time I'm going to mention this,' but of course it's not. And that temper. Whew. I've been scorched by that a few times myself. The best, though, is when she comes up with a new idea. It takes over her whole body. She waves her hands. Tucks her hair behind her ears. She smiles from somewhere deep inside. You just know something great is about to happen."

"I always hoped she'd come back here," Josh said.

"And I never thought she would."

"What do we do, Ian? Now that the election is over?"

Abby's feet were on the second stair from the top. She lifted her toes toward the ceiling and leaned forward. After a few beats, Josh said, "She'd make a great mayor's wife."

Ian didn't hesitate. "Abby's great just the way she is."

"Do you want to marry her?" Josh asked. "Not that I'd let you."

Ian's voice dropped slightly, something Abby noticed happened when he was irritated. "It's funny that you think you have any control over Abby. Or that anyone does, for that matter. But go ahead, dream big, Loverboy. See where it gets you."

Abby heard the sound of a cabinet door opening, and then the sound of her heavy cast iron skillet noisily placed on the stovetop.

Josh spoke next. "Are you staying for the victory party?"

"I am."

"Then it's back to Chicago, right?"

"I'm not sure."

"What do you mean you're not sure?"

"Cromby was my biggest client in Chicago. I'd already signed a contract for three more shoots when Abby left. After that, I let him know what I thought. I haven't taken another job from him since."

What's (Really) **Going On?**

QUESTION: Am I the thorn in Thornton's flesh?

Last night, I was the first journalist to interview (hottie!) Mayor-Elect Josh Moore. (I Want Moore was a campaign slogan I could get behind—or underneath, ha!—if you know what I mean.). *Click on the video link for the entire recording.* I had planned to focus on that story today. I mean, come on! The incumbent mayor arrested at his watch party at the Bendy Bear Critter Club. Most of you saw the breaking news on KCRW, shot by one of my newest buddies, Ian Reynolds, (also dreamy, by the way) who has been in town helping with the Moore campaign. And NO there was no funny business. Ian just happened to be in the right place at the right time.

I asked Ian why there weren't more videos, given that Mayor Thornton was taken away in cuffs from his watch party. Mr. Reynolds said, and I quote. "They were all in a conga line, shaking what the good Lord gave them, with Thornton in the lead. Nobody had time to grab their phone." Okay, full disclosure, Ian might NOT have said "shaking what the good Lord gave them." But he should have.

Then I realized that the Thornton story is everywhere. (Just try NOT to find it on social media!) Plus, awhile back, I promised to one day share a story that has been heavy on my heart for years. (Remember that vague post that left you wondering what in the heck was going on with yours truly?)

That day has arrived.

Here we go. If I could have put the handcuffs on Max Thornton myself, I would have. What he did to my family had nothing to do with the (OKAY, fine, ALLEGED) dirty land deals that locked him up in the slammer.

He was a young man when he met my Grandmama Alice, and she was even younger. This was in Kansas, when Thornton was brand new to the area. My grandmama was a trusting soul, as innocent as a lamb, but our incarcerated mayor already knew how the cow ate the cabbage. Grandmama was also a beauty, and Thornton wanted her.

There are no wedding pictures, no pictures at all of the two of them. I only learned of Thornton when I got to be dating age. Grandmama sat me down at her table with her cautionary tale. She was silver-haired by then, a widow woman, still beautiful. And she said to me, she said, 'Baby girl, not all men are willful sinners, but plenty of them are." Then she told me about marrying Max Thornton, the meanest man she'd ever met. A man who put on the dog in public, and kicked the dog at home. She wouldn't tell me specifics, but she shuddered enough while telling her story, that I got the drift.

She wanted an annulment—they'd only been married a month—but of course, the two of them had "been together" already, so her daddy got a lawyer and they paid Thornton to sign the divorce papers and leave town. "I never trusted another man with my whole heart after that," she said, "not even your grandpapa."

My grandpapa spent most of his adult life trying to convince my grandmama otherwise, and it was a hard row to hoe.

There are scars that are hidden by dresses and face powder, and scars hidden deep in the soul. My grandmama had the second kind.

When I came to live in Logan's Creek, I got my first look at Thornton. His voice was like the devil's doorbell, and that stupid wave he gave, with his two gnarled fingers, set my teeth on edge. I saw right through him.

I didn't start L.C. Confidential to call him out, but I didn't mind when he started showing his behind. It gave me good reason to show y'all what he was really like. Not just a slick-haired politician, but the kind of man who treats evil like a parlor game.

I'm not surprised he's sitting in the county jail today, and I won't be surprised when he's in a prison uniform. A man who could take a sweet woman like my grandmama, and butcher her opinion of all men, wouldn't blink twice about taking away someone's house and land, maybe even their livelihood if their land was a farm.

To Grandmama I say, I told the story that should have been heard years ago. To Thornton, should he read this in jail, I repeat what my grandmama told me, "That man is going to hell in a handbasket, and when he does, the devil better hire him some good bodyguards." To my followers I promise, I'll be back directly. But first, I have a Josh Moore victory party to get ready for.

Chapter Twenty-Eight

The package from Chicago wasn't from Cromby. Ian had contacted Abby's favorite boutique and ordered the softest leather jacket she'd ever seen. Her name was embroidered on the lining, near the collar, in yellow script: Abby Rose Carter. She planned to keep it forever.

Abby slipped on the jacket, and it caught the bracelet Josh had given her to celebrate their victory. WINNER was engraved on the solid gold bangle.

The victory party was held on Main Street. Cathy had pulled strings with the downtown commission to block off an entire section of the street. Instead of Cathy catering, Abby had brought in several food trucks. She wanted Cathy to enjoy a party for once.

The Leading Ladies insisted they go to the photo booth together, and that's how their picture ended up on L.C. Confidential. They each had props. Abby held opera glasses to her eyes. Lisa wore a faux mink shrug. Amanda held a #winning sign, and Janie and Amy sported oversize hairbows. Cathy, of course, donned a chef's hat. Just as the photo was taken, Cathy had whispered in Abby's ear. "Your mom sent me her recipe for cinnamon rolls."

That's why Abby's mouth was shaped like an O in the photo. Abby and Cathy had begged Gabby for the recipe since high school, when they were trying to win a Home Ec. Baking Extravaganza. When Cathy opened the Tuscan Table, they'd asked again. But Gabby's response had always been, "Carters don't give away family recipes."

It felt as if all of Logan's Creek had turned over a new leaf.

On the way out, Abby saw her Realtor, Dawn Collins. She was wearing an "I Want Moore" t-shirt, stretched tight across her bosom, a pink coat over that, and she was holding an ice cream cone aloft like the torch on the Statue of Liberty.

The street was decorated for Christmas, with flickering white lights, and street lamps wrapped like candy canes. A singing tree, not yet activated, and tall as a four-story building, sat near the train depot. Beside the tree, The Elvis Fan Club sang "Blue Christmas" to the passersby, even though it was still November. Gus Abernathy was speaking to Ms. Vivian, and by the looks of things, the discussion had something to do with the nearby traffic light.

Abby knew that Folly had confessed to Ms. Vivian that she'd taken Harold Dunham's letter and given it to the police. Ms. Vivian was still mad about it, and Folly no longer had twenty-four seven access to the library.

Abby walked down the street, the heels of her leather boots sounding on the pavement. She wore a long-sleeved white t-shirt under her leather jacket, and old jeans. She was scanning the crowd, looking for the man she loved.

The local band, Three Amigos Plus One, played in one of the small parks along the street. Abby listened. They were playing seventies hits. She stood on tiptoes, trying to see farther. Sure enough, she spotted her parents dancing, her dad's hand around her mom's waist. Her mom's hand on his shoulder.

The band sang John Denver's "Take Me Home Country Roads," while the two people who had given her life looked at each other like teenagers in love.

Amanda's friend from the State Police was getting her a funnel cake from one of the food trucks. Out of his uniform, dressed in dark cargo pants and a brown sweater, he looked like the lead contestant on one of those dating shows.

Josh was supposed to give his speech in fifteen minutes, and Abby strained to find him in the crowd. Then, Dan and Emily came up behind her, and Timothy and Kennedy jumped up and down, the way only kids who'd been given clouds of cotton candy can.

"Winner winner, chicken dinner," Dan said. The sentence seemed to be directed at her. He stood behind her, holding her in a headlock, and rubbing her head with the knuckles of his closed fist. She amended her opinion that everyone had turned over a new leaf.

She was about to move on, when Chief Furman Hanna came her way. Holding out his hand, he said, "Dance with me, Abby. Let me tell you how awful sorry I am."

The band could play a lot of songs, but "Stairway to Heaven" wasn't one of them, and they sang it haltingly. Abby, in her heeled boots, was nearly as tall as Furman, and the two did the best they could. To his credit, he held her at a gentlemanly distance, and only stepped on her toes twice.

When the song ended, he asked, "Are we friends yet?" The word *are* came out as *err* again. Abby said of course they were.

This was enough. A town she loved, her family, the Leading Ladies, her cabin on the creek. Even Chapters seemed like the personification of a friend. It was enough, but it wasn't everything.

Abby made her way toward the stage where Josh was about to speak. It was decked out in red, white, and blue banners. Old-fashioned hay bales were stacked near the rear, audio equipment on top. Josh waved at her from his spot beside the stage, but with the crowd, she couldn't get close enough to speak.

Josh climbed the steps and tapped the microphone three times. "Hello, Logan's Creek," he called out, and the crowd cheered. "I'm here tonight because of all of you. Because you had faith in me. I won't forget that." He pointed to his left. "My mom and dad are here." The crowd clapped. Josh pointed to the crowd. "And somewhere out there is Abby Carter, the world's best campaign manager." The crowd clapped, if not quite as enthusiastically.

Abby noticed that the first row was filled with pretty women. Their hair was shiny, and their jeans were painted on. One of them was wearing about half a blouse, by Abby's calculations. The knockout yelled, "I think I'm gonna faint, Joshie."

Joshie? Really? The man was her mayor.

Before Abby could see how Josh reacted, she felt a hand on her shoulder. She turned to find Ian. He wore a patterned scarf roped around his neck. She didn't know another man who could pull off a scarf.

The band began singing a James Taylor song she knew, "Don't Let Me Be Lonely Tonight." The song is about a man wanting a woman so badly that she could treat him wrong, lie to his face, do anything at all as long as she'd stay for the night. Not a healthy relationship, but still, Abby understood the gist of it.

Ian took her in his arms. They were barely dancing, mostly they were merely moving together. You couldn't have gotten a sheet of paper between them. Abby closed her eyes, put her head on his chest. Her hands were clasped behind his neck, her fingers tangled in his thick hair. And his hands were in the back pockets of her jeans. The ones he liked the best.

"Here we are," she said. And he said, "Here we are. In a small town somewhere," and she smiled, remembering.

That was how they'd started. Two people so attracted to one another, they couldn't have resisted for all the money in the world. Abby, for one, hadn't wanted to.

The song grew into a bubble that contained only them. In the beginning, he'd spent so much time mapping her body, he'd forgotten the simple facts of her life, like the name of the town she was from.

Now, he had her valleys and curves memorized. "Don't you have a cabin in the woods, Abby Girl?"

She breathed him in. "I most certainly do."

"And a rickety bed with the squeaky box springs?"

Abby kissed the spot that covered his heart. "I can't imagine how you'd know that."

"Lucky guess," he said, his voice carrying the hint of a tremble.

Abby led him through the crowd, saying goodbye to her family, the

Leading Ladies. Past Josh who had Folly on one side and the fainting devotee on the other. She waved and thought, Good luck to 'em.

They were in front of the Tuscan Table, when Abby heard the crowd. "Woo. Pig. Sooie." Josh must have been making good on his promise to Call the Hogs, must have had his hands in the air, his fingers wiggling. The Arkansas Razorbacks, the great unifier.

Once in Ian's Jeep, they drove past the courthouse, outlined in Christmas lights, and the club where Max Thornton had held his final watch party. The club was dark.

When they reached the cabin, they slipped out of the Jeep. Ian kissed Abby at the door, and then in the entryway, and then all the way up the stairs. On the landing, he lifted her up, carrying her to her room, where he kicked open the bedroom door with his foot.

Abby still didn't know his body as well as she might. Lucky for her, she was also a cartographer; making her own map even now. She kissed the spot on his neck where she imagined the headwaters of a mighty river. She kissed his closed eyelids, which hid the deep pools of his sea-blue pupils.

"Open the window," she whispered, and Ian walked to the window with Abby in his arms, set her down, and raised the glass. Outside, Logan's Creek was full, a result of recent rains, and water lapped against the shore, under a moon nearly covered by clouds.

Abby lay on the bed, and the breeze off the water stirred the curtains, chilling the room that would be warm soon enough.

Abby Rose Carter breathed in the creek. She had always craved the water. The rush of it, the shallow places and the deep, even the dangerous places where the water roared. The trick, though, was not to get in over her head. She concentrated, trying to remember that as the man she loved slipped out of his clothes.

– The End –

for now

Gabby's Cinnamon Rolls

Hot Rolls Recipe:

Pour 2 cups hot water or scalded milk over:
- ¾ cup shortening
- ½ cup sugar*
- 3 teaspoon salt

Cool to lukewarm, then add
- 2 cakes of yeast dissolved in
- ¼ cup lukewarm water
- 2 well beaten eggs

Add about 7 or 8 cups sifted flour
To make easily handled dough
Knead on floured board until dough springs back to touch
Place in greased bowl.
Let rise, punch and make into rolls.
Let rise again to double in size.
Bake 450 degrees for 10-15 minutes

Cinnamon Rolls Family Secret Recipe:

Start with Hot Rolls recipe —
   *¾ cup sugar when making Cinnamon Rolls instead of the called for ½ cup for Hot Rolls

After rising in bowl, take about ¼ of dough;
Roll out on board
Brush with melted butter
Sprinkle with cinnamon and sugar mixture (a 50/50 mixture)
Then lightly sprinkle with sugar again.
Roll dough up and slice about 1 ½ inch slices in order to make the cinnamon rolls.
Put in baking pan and let rise again.
Bake 450 degrees about 15 minutes until browned

Fix glaze with powdered sugar, little butter, little milk and vanilla. Mix well, then pour over slightly warm cinnamon rolls.

ACKNOWLEDGEMENTS

Thank you to everyone who had a role in making
this story come to life. It took a village.

Appreciation goes to all who have been mentors in my
life, helping me accomplish those things I never thought I
could. There are many of you.

One of those is Marla Cantrell, my friend and editor.
Without her, this book wouldn't have happened. She talked
me into a writer's workshop several years ago;
the rest is history.

To the small town where I grew up, I thank you for being a
place where you can still walk along Main Street and feel
safe. Where people know each other's names and
who their people are.

I am forever thankful to my family, friends, and my Leading
Ladies. Mostly I am grateful to the love of my life, my
husband Alan. He has always supported
my dreams, walking beside me as
we achieved them together.

PRAISE FROM EARLY READERS OF *A SMALL TOWN SOMEWHERE*

Deborah Spencer Foliart's debut novel, *A Small Town Somewhere*, captures the quirkiness of a quaint southern town where a loyal, strong-willed group of ladies push Abby Carter to take charge of her chaotic life. The author's humor and poetic talent shine through as she navigates Abby's crowded love life. Which scrumptious man will Abby choose? Deborah also introduces us to the extended Carter clan, who live by the homespun family wisdom handed down through generations. Well, at least they try! Things get even more interesting when twisted small-town politics come into play, and a not-so-nice mayor throws his weight around. This book kept me guessing until the last page!

— *Linda O'Brien*

"Family dynamics, sister friends, love heartstrings, and dastardly politicians — Foliart's first novel, *A Small Town Somewhere*, has it all! A witty and delightful read that reminds us all of our hometown values in Any Town, USA."

— *Lisa Huckelbury Fort*

"*A Small Town Somewhere* was witty and endearing. I could see the characters so clearly that I think it could easily be a movie. A great read!"

— *Jan Carr*

"I loved this book and can't wait for the sequel. The suspense continued throughout with the mystery surrounding a crooked politician, and a spicy love story that kept you guessing who will get the girl! Everyone will love *A Small Town Somewhere*, the story of the small town and those who live there."

—*Diane Brown*

About the Author
DEBORAH SPENCER FOLIART

Author photo by Malachi Davis

What happens when a writer buys a bookstore? For Deborah Spencer Foliart it meant being surrounded by books that gave her the inspiration for a novel she'd been thinking about for a long time. She has since sold the bookstore/coffee shop, giving her the time to finally write the story that's been brewing for far too long.

She'd already written dozens of business and visitors guides, a ton of marketing copy for Arkansas newspapers, and had hosted leadership seminars that drew in thousands. While she found writing non-fiction satisfying, nothing compared to creating a story filled with characters that took on a life of their own.

Deborah spends much of her time traveling and taking stunning photographs with her husband Alan. Often, they take their cat along for the ride. When she's home in Arkansas, she's usually visiting her family, trying to figure out her mom's famous cinnamon roll recipe, and meeting with her longtime girlfriends, the Leading Ladies.

CONNECT ONLINE

www.DeborahSpencerFoliart.com

DeborahSpencerFoliart

DeborahSpencerFoliart

Milton Keynes UK
Ingram Content Group UK Ltd.
UKHW040305181024
449757UK00005B/342